PAUL CLÉMENT

PROVINCE OF THE DEAD

A GLIMMER AT DUSK

Translated from the French by Jennifer Nance.

To you, *Maman*, for your lifelong support.

CONTENTS

CHAPTER 1
BLOODY HARVEST

The heat was grueling that day. I was enjoying the shade from the tree that graced my house's yard as I sipped a nice, cold beer. Its smoothness quenched my throat, so parched from the dryness of the air. The sensation was most pleasant. Yet, one thing delighted me even more.

About a hundred yards away, several dozen drivers were stuck in an endless traffic jam while the sun's rays fiercely assaulted the hoods of their cars. Seeing all those idiots unable to move like that amused me to no end. It wouldn't be long, though, before I learned that the misfortune of some doesn't always result in the happiness of others.

It had been several years at this point since they'd built that road right down the middle of my fields, dividing my land into two sections of several acres each. Every day, hundreds of people used it. Early in the morning to get to work and late in the evening to return home after an exhausting day on the job. And every day, they patiently waited for long periods of time in endless lines of vehicles.

When the prefecture's good, loyal envoys were extracting my signature by way of blackmail, leaving me no other choice but to fill out their damn paperwork, they had convinced me that the road would make the traffic flow smoothly and that I would thus be contributing to the community's well-being. The work hadn't even started, and I was already sorry I hadn't done my good deed right in those incompetents' faces.

I finally got used to the presence of this strip of asphalt disfiguring my estate. The traffic was continuous, and the peacefulness of my fields had long since disappeared. But how could it have bothered me? When the first cars jammed up, and all their horns started honking, I'd already been working for over an hour, and when the last one faded in the distance, I was still slaving away.

It was different that day. My ankle was killing me, and I had decided to give myself a well-deserved rest. So, I had taken a seat at the base of the hundred-year-old oak tree whose branches covered the front of my home, almost tickling the shutters of the upstairs bedrooms with the tips of its leaves. I liked the coolness of its shade, sprinkled with spots of light from a few small gaps in the foliage.

Ever since I'd been alone, I'd gotten into the habit of hanging out there, once the work was done, to have a beer or two and sometimes a lot more. In fact, this was my first time sitting there while the sun was still so high in the sky.

It was the only tree on my large property. Everything else was just wheat fields and fallow land, with my house standing in the middle of it all. The ears of wheat were beginning to take on a gold hue, and very soon, the first tourists would be stopping on the roadside to photograph this little house drowned in a golden field jostled by the winds: a precious souvenir of their vacation in Provence.

The line of vehicles was particularly long and the honking of horns much louder than usual. It must have been almost ten minutes since the cars had moved forward, and the drivers were starting to get impatient. The road was a good couple of feet higher than the level of my fields. There were no trees or bushes growing on the slope that linked the asphalt to the first wheat plants, so I could easily see the motorists' dripping faces.

One of them, exasperated by so much waiting, even got out of his vehicle and was fanning himself with a magazine. His face was a dazzling red that would have made winter sports enthusiasts paradoxically green with envy.

This scene was amusing me greatly, and I took a perverse pleasure in seeing so many of these turkeys literally roasting in their cars. The minutes ticked away; the line stood still, without a single car passing from the other direction.

"Another one of those morons," I thought out loud.

The road provided access to a freeway ramp a few miles away, and the junction was well-known in the area to be particularly dangerous. The regional press regularly granted itself the powers of Death and publicly displayed the demises of young and old alike who ended up crashing and burning in the middle of the intersection.

Often, these accidents even made the front page, and they had a way of brightening up my days. As I worked, I would think about the idiots who got themselves killed by accelerating in vain, under the pretext of trying to gain a few extra miserable minutes at home. All they got was a one-way ticket to the cemetery. Compassion was not my strong suit.

Speaking of imbeciles, a Mercedes, which had been stuck for a long time, was now taking the opposite lane in the wrong direction in the hope of passing its companions in misfortune a little further on. It took off and soon disappeared.

With the average driver not being much smarter than his peers, others decided to do the same thing, and very quickly, the line split in two – all for nothing. After just a couple of minutes, the two columns of vehicles were just as immobile, and it was now impossible for any of them to turn around. The exasperation was intensifying, and the spectacle was becoming more and more interesting.

Almost all the drivers had gotten out of the sweltering enclosures of their cars. Some had sat down on the shady side of their vehicles, others had gathered to chat and complain, and the angrier ones were bellowing into their phones. Mr. Tomato had returned to his car and was holding his head in his hands. He appeared to be asleep.

Seeing that they were trapped, some of the motorists gave in to hysteria and seemed ready to get into a fistfight. The tension was mounting between the most fervent of them, and I was taking bets in my head when the first scream rang out. A woman's scream, piercing and frightening. It was barely perceptible, as the noise from the car radios and arguments was so loud; the engines themselves had been turned off a long time ago.

Nevertheless, everyone looked into the distance. Some of the drivers seemed worried, and others were already making assumptions about what had just happened. I figured it was nothing more than some woman who had flipped out: nothing out of the ordinary. But when more screams rang out, even closer, doubt overcame me. The radios fell silent, and almost all of the motorists returned to their seats. The reckless few who preferred to stay outside gathered between the two lines of cars, in the middle of the road.

The air was suddenly filled with the sound of motorcycle engines rolling up the road from the opposite direction. At first, only the mechanical rumblings of their machinery were heard, but very quickly the first bikes appeared, slipping as best they could between the vehicles. They were speeding ahead and nearly falling off with each swerve. The motorists who had remained outside their cars ran to take refuge on the side of the road so as not to be mowed down by the frenzy of bikers. The flood of motorcycles was impressive, as if all the workers who had ridden to their jobs in the morning and found themselves stuck in this traffic jam had decided to turn around at the same time, moved by a bestial survival instinct. They reminded me of those animals we saw on TV leaping all over the place whenever they aired footage of the fires that so often ravaged the region.

For his part, Mr. Tomato seemed to have come out of his torpor. Large drops of sweat were streaming down his face, and the muscles in his neck were tightening strangely. Oblivious to the motorized wave surrounding his car, he whipped open his door and extricated himself from the fiery hell of its frame. The collision was brutal.

Mr. Tomato was thrown about fifteen feet, his face riddled with glass from the window that had exploded upon impact. He was no longer moving, and a pool of blood was starting to form under his body. The biker's head had hit the car door violently and was hanging limply at an unnatural angle. The scene was horrible, and the two men were almost certainly killed instantly.

Those who had taken refuge on the roadside rushed to come to their aid. Meanwhile, the last bikes, blocked end-to-end between the two lines of vehicles, were thrown to the ground by their owners as they ran off. The tension was palpable as two small groups formed around the two victims. One woman, visibly at the end of her rope, threw her phone down on the asphalt and bellowed:

"They're telling me that all the lines are busy, there's nothing we can do!"

"Same for me," confirmed another driver. "Impossible to reach the firefighters or the police."

"Why didn't those asshole bikers stop? What got into them?" asked a young woman who was having trouble hiding her anger. "How can you just abandon two people like that? Shit!"

"They're dead," sighed a man who had just examined the two bodies and removed the biker's helmet. "There's nothing more we can do, so let's try to calm down."

From my cool little nook, which a normal man would have left long ago, I had the perfect angle to see the body of the biker hanging from what was left of Mr. Tomato's car door. My beer was almost finished, and the more this story progressed, the more I told myself that I deserved a second one. But the last sip almost killed me. When Mr. Tomato's seriously bashed-in head emerged from behind the vehicle that had been hiding his body until then, I just about choked.

At first, I was stunned that a man could get back up after such a crash and with injuries like that, but I realized far too quickly that Mr. Tomato was already long gone. The face of the man who had declared his death crumpled as he saw Mr. Tomato standing in front of him as if nothing had happened.

My apprehension grew when I heard a new series of screams, even closer now. At that moment, the world as I knew it was already gone.

No sooner had the screaming stopped echoing than Mr. Tomato lunged at the man and tried to pry his jugular off with his teeth. Of the ten or so people who had tried to tend to the wounded, only two attempted to intervene. Mr. Tomato's victim whimpered as the former sank his teeth deeply into his flesh. The man was hitting him with all his strength, but it started to wane as his blood flowed freely. His two rescuers finally managed to tear Mr. Tomato off him, but it was already too late: he was dying with a heinous gurgling noise as he collapsed to the ground.

Mr. Tomato was out of control, and it was not long before he gained the upper hand over his attackers. Panic was at a fever pitch, and screams were heard from all around. Engines were being restarted, and everyone was trying desperately to push the other vehicles in order to turn around; the maneuver was doomed to fail since there were so many of them. Driven by madness and fear, the first motorists left the road in an attempt to pass through the fields. Some, due to lack of speed, ended up stupidly blocked by the small canal, about twenty inches wide, that bordered the road below the embankment it was built on. Others, generally those with the bigger cars, managed to overcome the obstacle and were now hurling themselves through my fields in an anarchic ballet. They shot straight ahead then suddenly changed direction, mowing down my wheat and destroying hours of work in their hysteria.

I was gaping as I watched this disaster, unable to understand how it could have come to this in a matter of minutes.

The pleasant taste and freshness of my beer had been replaced by a strange sensation. With my mouth feeling mushy, I stood up, sending my chair flying across the dirt and knocking over my glass, which rolled slowly across the table before smashing on the ground. I didn't give a crap, as there were more serious things happening: a large portion of the motorists were now heading towards my home.

I ran as fast as my ankle would allow and rushed into the house. I immediately shut the door behind me, locked all the bolts, and allowed myself three seconds to think and to catch my breath, which was already failing me. I couldn't have all these people in my house; it was out of the question that they come in here. I had no idea what was happening, and the doubt that was overwhelming me made me unable to act with clear-sightedness. Only one certainty stood out: if anyone were going to survive this madness, it would be me.

My isolation and my profession had always pushed me to worry about no one but myself, and calling for outside help seemed idiotic to me. I decided to try to call the police anyway, but when I picked up the receiver, its grave, ominous silence convinced me to do whatever it took to save my own skin.

Only a few seconds had passed since I'd gotten inside the house, and already the first fugitives were pouring into the yard, shouting to be let in. Had they seen me from the road? Did they know I was there? No matter. I hurled myself at the roller shutter control switch. Since I had been burglarized several years before, I'd had them installed on the ground floor to protect the house during my short nights. It had cost me a fortune and a few hours of my time having to put up with the presence of those half-wit builders, but at least I no longer had to close the old wooden blinds every night. Their creaking used to annoy me so much. As the roller shutters began their descent in more than perfect silence, the yelling in the courtyard grew louder, and the fifteen or so people who had just gotten there wasted no time in hammering on my door. Unable to see what was going on outside, I ran upstairs. I needed to know what was going on if I wanted to organize my defense and prevent these strangers from setting foot inside my precious home.

I rushed into the bathroom, where one of the windows, the smallest one, opened out just above the front door. It was way too high for me to see anything without stepping on top of the toilet. So, I climbed up on it and slipped my head out the window. What I saw almost made me scream. Madness had given way to the apocalypse, and my fields looked like they had been razed by a raging army. Cars were piling up in all directions, some of them overturned on the side of the road. Before my eyes, in a shower of sparks, one of them struck the utility pole that held up the cables leading to my house from the road. The wires were torn off by the violent collision and fell softly into the ears of wheat. Luckily, no fire started, but my electricity went out.

Some people were fleeing across the fields or running on the road, away from the carnage that lay in front of me, but the majority continued to flock towards my home, the last ray of hope for many. But the worst thing was the men and women who were chasing the fugitives. Like Mr. Tomato, they seemed to have only one goal: to kill and feast on the flesh of their victims. Mr. Tomato was up front, and his murderous insanity had not ceased since his first attack. He grabbed by the hair a young woman who was trying to flee. His movement was incredibly swift and extremely violent, so quick that he tore a handful of hair from the scalp of his victim, who collapsed in a cry of fear and pain. He wasted no time before biting her face, immobilizing her under his full weight. She wouldn't give in and tried to push him away, in vain. Mr. Tomato was already chewing on a piece of her cheek. She sank one of her fingers into the eye of her attacker who, with complete indifference, tightened his grip even more. The young woman quickly ceased her fighting when the monster, abandoning his prey's soft cheeks, devoured her neck. This scene was being repeated everywhere, nonstop, and the number of predators seemed to be getting bigger and bigger.

When I saw Mr. Tomato's first victim chasing a teenager, I knew I would soon be dealing with a massive problem. The flesh of his neck was hanging indelicately, and almost all his blood had left his body, leaving a large pool on the road, over forty yards away. How could he still be moving? This man was most certainly dead, and yet he was wandering through the middle of my fields, ready to pounce on the frightened motorists. Was it contagious, this madness that even death could not stop?

Confirming my suspicions, the young woman Mr. Tomato had lost interest in rose and ran towards the crowd that had gathered outside my door, too. There must have been at least twenty of them charging or dragging themselves towards that flock of defenseless sheep. About thirty people were now trying to get in, but fortunately, my door was holding up well. One man had grabbed a log from the pile of wood stacked up along the front of the house and was frantically attacking one of the roller shutters. Each strike left an ominous mark on the shutter, and there was little doubt it would soon break. I didn't even have to take action: the first madmen were already reaching the group.

A man had been thrown to the ground by one of them, who was trying to bite him. He gripped her neck to keep her from getting close, but he was starting to grow weak. The distance between life and death was small, and no help was being offered.

Frightened and cornered, the other fugitives just stared at him as more and more enemies approached. Finally reacting, they ended up grabbing pieces of wood and trying to defend themselves. The man with the log set the example by rushing at an opponent and hitting him hard in the face. A horrible cracking noise accompanied this motion, and a large part of the madman's face was torn off. His nose, crushed by the blow, was nothing more than a bloody lump, and his cheek was covered with unevenly deep gouges. Blood was flowing freely from his wounds, but it didn't bother him. Off balance from his attack, the man with the log couldn't stop his adversary from clasping his arm in a deadly grip. Blows rained down on the creature, but he never let go, and it was not long before his victim was bitten in turn.

While the men and women who were beneath my lookout post had outnumbered their attackers thus far, they soon found them-selves dominated by forty or so monsters. It was now clear that getting bitten meant joining the ranks of that army of darkness. Within a mere two minutes, this pocket of resistance was almost done for, unable to defend itself with simple pieces of wood. Still, a few maniacs were lying on the ground, their skulls transformed into a disgusting mush of bone, blood, and brains. The sight was repug-nant.

I thought the crazies would leave once their macabre mission was accomplished, but now they were staring at the front of the house, their eyes riveted just a few feet from the window through which I was witnessing the gruesome scene. But I wasn't the one they were staring at so avidly: a man had managed to climb up the side of the house, clinging to the old stones. He had almost reached an opening on the second floor. I ran to the next room, opened the window wide, and held out my hand to him. When he grabbed it, I hoisted him up a few inches before throwing him down into the bear pit. His "motherfucker" didn't have time to cross the threshold of his lips before a rain of arms fell on him and tore him to pieces. And it was then, the last survivor having fallen, that they started to take an interest in me.

Almost simultaneously, they turned their heads in my direction, their glassy, demonic eyes assessing me with an insatiable appetite. I closed the window and dropped to the floor. The back of my neck was resting on the window frame, and I could feel the beating of my heart in the exact spot where the wood touched my skin. I felt like it was going to explode in one final palpitation, leaving me lifeless on the parquet floor in this guest room that I used to appreciate so much when my family still visited me. I had done some really bad things in my life, but killing a man was a big first.

I tried to convince myself that it wasn't my fault, that the force of events had pushed me to do it. After all, my teeth weren't covered in the stranger's blood; only the monsters who were pacing in the yard and trying to get inside had savored that sordid liqueur. Now was definitely not the time for remorse. By grabbing his hand, though, I had unjustly offered him the luxury of hope. He wasn't just a face bellowing for me to come to his aid like the others; he was the man hanging from the front of my house who, not hesitating to grasp my hand, had placed all his trust in me. I could still feel the imprint of his fingers on my skin, the firm, strong grip that I had released. I was disgusted with myself, but I knew I'd made the right choice. It would have been impossible for me to deal with a situation like this with a stranger in my home whom I could not have relied on. He was better off dead; it saved him from having to know the extent of the madness that was, without my knowing it yet, affecting the entire world.

Aware of the importance of acting quickly and barricading the house, I then tried to calm myself down and to contain the urge to vomit that was becoming more and more present in my throat. Downstairs, the madmen were scratching at the shutters and hurling their bodies violently against the door and the walls in the hopes of finally being able to dedicate themselves to their goal of death by scattering my remains throughout my home.

I pulled my back away from the wall and, on all fours, tried to fix my gaze on a specific spot on the floor. My eyes flew from one point to another, unable to stop and preventing me from having clear thoughts. The adrenaline rush that had allowed me to act up to that point was now pinning me to the ground.

Breathless, I spotted a wooden knot on the floor, right next to the thumb of my left hand, and started staring at it. At the slightest scraping sound coming from the floor below, my gaze slipped away – and the clarity of my thoughts with it. I had to pull myself together and fast. I cleared my mind, creating a bipolar world around me: the knot and me. I imagined myself isolated in a universe where the only thing that really mattered was this knot in the wood. I concentrated on this strange irregularity in the middle of the oak slats of the floor and gradually succeeded in calming my mind by taking an interest in the knot's contours, curves, and colors. Little by little, I regained my composure, and my heartbeat slowed down. I stayed there for a few minutes, not blinking, and my eyes began to sting and to cloud over with a thin layer of tears. I had regained my senses, and I was ready to do something.

Very quickly, I came to the conclusion that it would be impossible for me to secure the ground floor; the shutters would give way soon, and I wouldn't be able to block all the exits in time. I had no choice but to hide out upstairs and barricade the only staircase that led up there. It would be easy. But first, I had to hurry downstairs to grab anything that would be of use to me. I ran to the bathroom, put the plug in the tub drain, and turned on the water.

I then rushed over to the stairs. The steps creaked ominously, and my ankle pain came back with an extreme intensity. I had almost forgotten about it. But time was running out.

When I reached the entryway, the crazies redoubled their efforts against the house's meager protections, as if they sensed my presence. Some of the roller shutters were already letting larger and larger rays of sunlight pass through into the dark interior. I sped into the kitchen, which was as neat and clean as usual, and opened the drawers to grab the biggest knives I owned. I then tackled the adjacent storage room. I flipped the light switch repeatedly, cursing the darkness of the small room, before remembering that the power had been cut. The bulb was hanging naked from the end of its socket, without even a fixture to dress it, and refused to light up.

I had never bothered to organize this pantry, and I used it to store all kinds of things, from food to backup home improvement supplies. Groping, I went for the essentials and filled a large bag that was lying there with all the foodstuffs that I could easily keep upstairs for a few days: canned goods, pasta, jars of pâté. That done, I gathered a box of nails and a hammer, then plunged a little deeper into the storeroom in search of my cherished gas camping stove, the one that had saved me more than once when heavy snowfalls had left me without power during the wintertime. I couldn't find it. I rummaged through the pile of objects cluttering the back of the small room, moved the old ironing board, which let out a cloud of dust, and unceremoniously pushed aside boxes filled with trinkets I no longer had any use for, until I saw it.

There it was. My father's old gun. I had taken it when he died: his favorite hunting rifle. An object of death that I had no interest in, but a weapon so important to my father that I had kept it all that time, in the back of the closet, cloaked in grey dust. I grabbed it by the barrel and pulled until the butt emerged from the mess that had been hiding it. As I brought it towards me, I knocked over one of the plastic bags that was caught on it. Two cartridges fell out. They rolled and got lost between two other, full bags. I leaned the rifle against the closet door and concentrated on finding them before slipping them into my pocket. As I was bending over to pick them up, I saw my gas stove. Perfect. I gathered my booty and somehow dragged it all to the foot of the stairs.

The bag was cumbersome, heavy with the reserves it contained. I had enough to last a good week while waiting for someone to come and deal with the monsters, who were tirelessly continuing their assault. With no shoulder strap, the rifle complicated things, and it was hard for me to hold both the weapon and the stove with one hand.

After climbing the first few steps to carry everything upstairs, I realized that I had forgotten to get my lighter. I rushed back towards the kitchen to retrieve it, leaving all my stuff behind, but I stopped abruptly on the way. The little window above the back door of the house revealed a dramatic sight: a woman and her little girl, with two madmen on their heels. With an enormous ruckus, a gigantic camper van appeared in view. It crossed my fields at full throttle. And without slowing down, it crashed into the two monsters before separating the child from her mother.

The vehicle continued its crazed course, carrying with it the woman's body, which was lying across its hood, her face bloodied and her body contorted in an unthinkable position. In a last burst of love and maternal instinct, the mother had been smart enough to let go of her daughter's hand a few tenths of a second before the impact. That had most certainly saved the child's life. But not for long: the little girl, who must have been no more than seven or eight years old, was sprawled out full length on the ground, her knees bleeding, an expression of horror on her face, unable to see the threat that was rapidly approaching her.

CHAPTER 2
TEARS FROM THE WARDROBE

"Son of a bitch!" I exclaimed.

Within seconds, I had made up my mind. I retrieved the rifle, turned the key in the lock, and rushed outside, trying my best to slide the two cartridges into the magazine. The last time I had handled such a weapon was almost forty years ago, when my father took me hunting. That day was dreadful for me, and I had retained a deep aversion to that barbaric activity. But I would have to live with it if I wanted to save my own skin as well as this poor kid's.

I did not understand what was driving me to rush out headfirst like this and risk my life for a child I did not know. A few minutes earlier, without batting an eyelid, I was sacrificing a whole group of innocent people and sending a poor, unfortunate man to burn in the flames of hell. Now I was playing the hero.

In any case, I couldn't retreat at this point. My decision had been made, and my life currently depended on this shotgun. If it were to jam or misfire, that would be the end of me.

Several monsters, attracted by the racket, were moving towards the girl; some were running, and others were dragging themselves with exasperating slowness. I had to reach the child before the fastest ones, at all costs. I was going as quickly as my ankle let me.

One of the crazies was already dangerously close to the little girl, staring at her with his opaque eyes that were filled with a ferocious appetite. With the rifle loaded, I raised the barrel towards my target and fired. As I was unable to stabilize the weapon and had not anticipated the recoil, my shot missed the creature by far. Without any training, how could I have hit a moving target, more than fifteen feet away, while running?

My target took no interest in me and continued advancing on the little girl. If I wanted to hit the bull's eye, I had no choice but to get between it and the girl and shoot it head-on. I had to try. And if I failed, I would still have the option of returning to shelter while the monster devoured her. I quickly dismissed that thought and went for it. The madman was about to descend upon the child, who was still lying motionless on the ground, when I got into position. For a half-second, I tried to line up my shot. Only six feet separated me from my target, but it seemed like an infinite length to me, the distance between life and death for a prostrate girl, her heart broken by her mother's tragic death and by the surge from the underworld that was surrounding her.

The shot rang out and hit the maniac right in the face. The blast was effective and left my opponent with a bloody stump, a mixture of bone, cartilage and burnt flesh in place of his head. He collapsed on top of the girl, who let out a sharp little cry. I threw myself at her, grabbed her wrist unceremoniously, and pulled her towards me, pushing the lifeless body aside:

"Hurry!" I shouted at her.

While my goal had been to reassure her in a soft, soothing voice, the urgency of the situation made me scream. I was convinced that she was going to stay on the ground, even more terrified, and that I would have to drag her inside; however, she got up almost immediately at the sound of my voice and grasped my wrist with her small hand, her frail fingers not long enough to reach all the way around it. I was turning to head back to the house when the nearest monster caught up to us. I quickly released my arm from the little girl's grip, grabbed the still-hot barrel of my rifle, and violently whacked the butt of the weapon against the madman's head. His jaw snapped with a loud crack and a red cloud of droplets. It wasn't enough, and with a grotesque smirk, the monster firmly grabbed the gun and took it with him as he fell. My weapon, that memory of my father, was lost.

I thought no more about it and left it in the hands of that blood-thirsty thing. The child somehow followed me as we desperately fled.

We quickly crossed the few yards to the back door and rushed inside.

No sooner had I closed the door behind us than banging was heard. The crazies gathered in front of the main entrance had been attracted by the gunfire and had circled the building in order to hunt me down. They weren't the only ones. One last glance through the small window in the door made me freeze with fear. Dozens of creatures were converging on the house from the fields. Not only was the rifle lost, but I had just rung the dinner bell for miles around.

The back door wasn't as strong as the one in front, and they would be inside soon. I ran with the child to the foot of the staircase.

"Take this, go up there, and hide," I said to the kid, who hurried up the stairs after grabbing the stove I was handing to her.

I hustled into the kitchen and got the lighter, finding it exactly where I was hoping it had been stored, in the cutlery drawer, tucked between two jackknives that I made sure to slip into my pocket.

Now I had to put my defenses in place to prevent the creatures, who would soon be invading the downstairs, from gaining access to the second floor. Installed in a recess, the small spiral staircase that led up there was so steep and narrow – which my visitors had often criticized after having hurtled down it on their butt cheeks – that it would be easy for me to seal it off.

My eyes then fell on the heavy, solid oak cabinet against the wall across from the stairs. I used it to store a whole bunch of old stuff, especially books and magazines. It had been years since I'd organized its contents; I just opened it up every now and then to pack in new things that were doomed to oblivion. It was so full and imposing that I couldn't imagine how I was going to be able to move it, and yet I had to: it was perfect, exactly the width it would take to block the stairwell.

With no hesitation, I threw myself down on the floor, placed my feet against the wall where the cabinet was standing, slipped my fingers behind the piece of furniture, and pulled with all my might. It moved. My ankle was stinging from the pain, and I had to stop myself from moaning with each effort, but I held on. I quickly repeated the operation on the other side of the cabinet so that it staggered forward, a few inches on one side and then the same on the other. It had almost arrived at its final destination, where it would completely block the access, when the banging on the door grew even louder. The little window had just been smashed, and I could distinctly hear horrible screeching noises coming from the creatures. I crouched behind the cabinet, sat down with my back against it, and put both feet against the wall before pushing with one last-ditch effort. The cabinet was finally in place.

I found myself stupidly cornered by my own strategy. In my rush, I hadn't even considered that it would have been better for me to have been on the other side of the obstacle. I was cursing my stupidity when I heard the door give way and the monsters invade the interior of the house.

Suddenly, my problem was gone, as my body found the solution on its own. I instinctively threw myself against the doors of the nearly six-foot-tall, heavy cabinet and hoisted myself to the top within seconds, sliding into the thin space above it. Somehow, I slipped through, and I let myself fall back down into the stairwell. A hand gripped my leg roughly, and with a frightened scream, I managed to pull myself free.

One of the monsters had already gotten under the steps and was trying to catch hold of me. I snatched the bag of supplies and ran upstairs as the crazies started attacking my barricade. They were banging on it vigorously but failed to make it move. Its base was weighed down by pounds of old books and magazines, and they certainly wouldn't be able to tip it over with no coordinated effort.

I had narrowly escaped, but I still needed to strengthen my defense. When I got upstairs, I dropped my bag and, without wasting a moment, grabbed whatever was handy and threw it into the stairway. Downstairs, the cabinet acted as a barrier, holding back the objects that were falling victim to my frenzy. The bigger things kept the smaller ones from falling between the steps. Very quickly, various pieces of the upstairs furniture were swallowed up in that space. Never had there been such a mess in my house. The floor was littered with torn papers, broken trinkets, shards of various shattered objects. I had thrown down almost the entire contents of the nearest room: shelves, books, lamps, picture frames, rugs, small furniture. Within a mere five minutes, in a non-stop, grueling back and forth, I had literally filled the stairwell. I had no confidence in the solidity of this barricade, but I hoped that, once they could no longer see a distinct passage, these creatures would cease their relentless persecution. Even so, I decided to seal off the upstairs landing, too.

I unhooked the doors to my bedroom and the one I had looted and stacked them so that they completely blocked the access to the steps. My hammer and nails did the rest, finishing the installation of this one last layer of protection. We were ready for the siege.

I slid gently to the floor in the hallway, my back leaning against the wall. A feeling of serenity invaded me within seconds at the thought of no longer being the immediate target of those monsters, and the stress was gradually dissipating. The fatigue I had accumulated thus far took over my body. All of that had only lasted a few minutes, and yet it felt like I had run a marathon or worked several days in a row with no sleep at all. My muscles were throbbing vigorously, and the large drops of sweat sliding down my skin made brown lines on my face, washing away the grime that had settled there during the commotion. The heat was not helping. I felt exhausted and disgusting and was suffocating on the inside. I was actually suffocating; realizing that I had been holding my breath since the moment I'd sat down, I swallowed a big gulp of air. I had gone into a kind of apnea to cut myself off from everything and allow some of the pressure that had been overwhelming me to melt away. I let my lungs reclaim their due. The air rushing in was stiflingly hot.

In the summer, I hardly ever slept in my bedroom upstairs, the temperature being so unbearable in there. I used to nickname this part of the house, located just under the roof and poorly insulated, the "greenhouse." I couldn't help but think that maybe I should reconsider that name and change it to "prison" or "mausoleum."

I put that ominous idea aside, got up, and headed to the bathroom at the end of the hall, where the tub was just starting to overflow. I needed to cool off and remove the layer of dirt that was covering my body. I turned off the faucet, putting an end to the light trickle of water that was dripping onto the floor tiles. I had arrived in time to prevent everything from being flooded and the false ceiling on the lower level from being stained. But I no longer had any reason to worry about that kind of problem. With the tub full, I now had about forty gallons of potable water. To drink, cook with, and wash with until help arrived and the government clowns finally decided to do something.

I grabbed a small basin from the white storage compartment under the sink, filled it with water, then pulled off my old T-shirt, which was soaked with sweat. It was torn in places, and my body also divulged these snags with several small scratches. They were all superficial, but it would be a good idea to clean them well. Now was not the time to risk an infection.

I moistened a washcloth and ran it over my face. Its freshness was pleasant and helped clear my head. My mind wandered as I tirelessly rubbed the cloth from my forehead to the crook of my neck in a soothing caress. I rinsed it off and was letting it drift over my face once more to remove the last layers of grime when I remembered I was no longer alone. In all the hubbub, I had completely forgotten that a child was hiding somewhere on this floor, as I had abruptly ordered her to do. Shirtless, I left the bathroom and, my mind muddled again, tried to find the kid. I called out to her:

"Little girl, you don't have to be frightened anymore. You can come out of your hiding place."

I didn't really know what to say, and I tried to use the softest voice possible, which was not easy with a long history of smoking behind me. I didn't dare yell for fear of attracting even more attention from our attackers, who were still making noise downstairs. After no response, I began to search every room.

There were only four on this floor: the bathroom, which had a small dormer window overlooking the interior courtyard but which got its light from a larger window, from which one could easily access the roof of the other wing of the house, which I used as a barn and storage area; the room that I had almost completely emptied to fill up the stairwell; the guest room, from which I had thrown the man into the void; and, finally, my bedroom, the largest room upstairs, which crossed the building from one side to the other and opened onto the other end of the hallway.

I was about to enter the guest room when I heard soft sobbing coming from my room. I moved forward slowly, crossed the threshold, and again heard the crying, which was trying to be as quiet as possible. It was coming from my wardrobe. Without opening the door, I sat down with my back next to it and tried to think of something to say. I was really uncomfortable in situations like this. I had never known how to comfort my loved ones during the most painful times in life. This little girl had seen her mother die under tragic circumstances and had been pursued by bloodthirsty monsters. The whole world she knew and probably cherished had also disappeared into thin air.

I chose to leave her alone for the moment and, most importantly, not to desecrate her hiding place. However, I wanted her to know that I was there and that I meant no harm to her. By saving her, I had kind of agreed to take care of her. It was a decision I'd had to make in the middle of the action, without even thinking about it for half a second, but it was still my own choice. And, even though I was a terrible psychologist, I was a man who accepted his responsibilities. I managed to mumble a few words:

"Listen, I know this is very hard for you, but…"

My words seemed to come out of my lips and dissolve in the air, they were so flimsy. I was reciting the same typical blah blah blah, except today I believed it even less than usual. My words were meaningless. Yet, I continued:

"It's going to be fine, don't worry."

I felt stupid reciting such bullshit to her knowing that over fifty lunatics were trying to reach the upper level of the house to devour us alive and that they would surely succeed. I had probably only prolonged her existence for a few hours, hours of grief and distress. But I couldn't do any better. I stood back up and, remembering that she was slightly injured, added before leaving the room:

"If you want to freshen up and clean your knees, there's a bathroom at the other end of the hall… There's nothing to be afraid of."

I left the room, aware that she would be staying in the wardrobe for a few more hours, time to heal her first mental wounds, which were much more painful than her scraped knees. I went into the guest room and collapsed on the bed, exhausted.

It wasn't even six o'clock yet, but I just wanted to stay there, close my eyes, go to sleep, never wake up, forget what was going on downstairs. Only a couple slats of wood separated me from the hell on the first floor, invaded by madmen who were uttering increasingly faint grunts. Periodically, the clatter of objects smashing on the floor echoed throughout the house. The noise was incessant as they were still trying to get upstairs. Despite my extreme fatigue, I was unable to doze off. The din was piercing my eardrums, and a feeling of insecurity was surfacing again in me. I could have put in earplugs, but even insulated from the sound of those monsters, my mind would not have been able to rid itself of the image of the carnage that these creatures had caused, nor forget what their only objective was now: to devour me, to devour us.

I needed to keep busy, to do something useful in order to distract myself from the situation, even if only partially. So, I decided to sort out how we were going to survive. While I still hoped someone would come to our aid, I knew very well that, being so isolated, I was certainly not a priority. If we were going to have to hold this siege for several days, I shouldn't have any doubts about my defenses. But I easily imagined the monsters would end up knocking over the cupboard, creeping up the stairs, breaking through my barriers, and flaying us alive. I had to prevent that.

Therefore, I proceeded to block the doors I had nailed to the top of the stairs so that any pushing against them would be ineffective. I immediately thought of the solid wood armoire that adorned the corner of the guest bedroom. It was perfect: sturdy, about the same width as the hallway, and tall enough to wedge the two stacked doors. I still had to manage to get it out of the room, as it wouldn't fit through the doorframe in its current position.

I set about emptying it completely to make it as light as possible. It mostly contained old clothes and a few pairs of used shoes. Linens that I would probably never use again but that I saw fit to keep. Just in case. In addition, I found some children's clothes in there that my nephews and nieces had forgotten during one of their parents' rare visits. I could see myself grumbling at the discovery of these abandoned items that had come to sully my home, but that day, I was pleased that I'd kept them, as they seemed to be the little girl's size. I placed them aside, on the bed.

I carefully took everything else out of the heavy armoire and put the contents on the floor without further logic. Once bare, it seemed naked to me, like the body of an old man that had been emptied of all his organs. It remained beautiful and rustic, though, built from noble, solid wood. All that was left was for me to move it a few feet in order to place it in the hallway. To get it through the doorway, though, I had no choice but to lay it down on one side. Standing up, I easily reached its filthy top, and as my fingers slid through the dust bunnies, I tipped it over. Its weight surprised me; it was much heavier than it seemed, and I dropped it roughly onto the ground. One of the piles of clothes I had created when emptying it dampened the fall slightly but didn't stop the whole house from resonating with a thud when it crashed into the floor's wooden slats. There was an almost immediate echo from below: the monsters moaned louder and tried with ever more tenacity to break through my defenses.

I felt like I was reliving one of the many sieges of fortified castles that marked the Middle Ages, when endless legions pushed their enemies to their limits, forcing them to make mistakes or to die from starvation. I hadn't starved to death yet, but I had just made a big mistake by stimulating the madmen's interest in me even more heartily. Moving the piece of furniture to fortify my rampart was becoming more vital than ever.

At this point, the armoire was resting on one of its sides. I cleared the clothes that were blocking the way and began to push it along the ground, well aware of the noise this maneuver was generating.

When I got to the door, I had to calculate the exact angle in order to get it into the hallway so that neither the doorframe nor the hallway wall would hinder its progress. After many tries, I managed to find an adequate trajectory and finally slid the piece of furniture into its final position. I laid it on its back and then found myself with a massive problem: lifting it back up. I absolutely had to straighten it out, or else only the lower door would be blocked. But even using all my strength, I could only lift the armoire a few inches. It was so heavy that I felt a sharp pain in my back every time I tried. I then decided to lift it in stages, holding it briefly and then immediately inserting something into the gap, widening the free space bit by bit.

I grabbed some objects of different sizes, mostly books, that had not already ended up in the stairwell. I gripped the edges of the armoire and, with my first try, managed to push it up a few inches. As my biceps protruded ominously, revealing veins swollen from the effort, I kicked an old dictionary into the gap. I repeated the operation, piling up several thick books and making sure the stack would not collapse. It was a tricky maneuver, but when the space was big enough, I slipped under the armoire, with my back against it, and to my thighs' great displeasure, managed to lift it. I wasn't athletic at all, but it was clear to me that a job as physical as mine had its advantages. The armoire now connected the two doors to the opposite wall, making it completely impossible to cross the hallway. The crazies could try to force it as much as they liked; they would have a hard time breaking down the stone wall the piece of furniture was resting against, especially since the stairwell's small space would prevent them from joining forces. I began to feel a sense of security again, accompanied by the triumphant bugle call of a duty accomplished.

Installing this final defense had taken me almost half an hour, and the effort, together with the heat that was not subsiding, had made me thirsty. However, placed in the middle of the hallway as it was, the armoire completely blocked access to the bathroom. Very fortunately, a connecting door made it possible to go directly from the guest room into the room that I had almost completely emptied and thus to gain entry to the sanitary facilities. This door had been locked for years since it was of no use to me. My comings and goings in this part of the house were limited to an endless journey between my bedroom and the bathroom, when I wasn't content to live exclusively downstairs to get away from the heat upstairs. I turned the small key that was resting in the lock on the door and opened it. It remained strangely silent; no squeaking was added to the cacophony being caused by the madmen. I went into the bathroom, snatched the glass I used to rinse my teeth from the white edge of the sink, and filled it up. I dipped it directly into the tub twice and drank the contents in one swallow. I slid the glass into the water one more time and moistened a washcloth before making my way to my bedroom, to a wardrobe that was shaking with sobs.

I made as little noise as possible as I moved around, trying to make our predators forget about us. However, I refused to take off my shoes in case we had to flee quickly. I could hardly see myself running barefoot, let alone dying in socks. This thought made me grin, but the little girl's sobs brought me back to reality. I had decided to let her cry and allow her to choose the right time to come out. At her age, I was sure she wouldn't let herself die. I just needed to try to build a climate of trust between her and me. Whether she liked it or not, and even though it bothered me to no end, I was responsible for her until someone else took charge of her. Her sobbing was still making me uneasy, almost as much as the screams echoing below and the incessant crash of blows raining down against the defenses I had erected.

I feared the monsters, but I was even more wary of this child. After what had happened to her, I knew she was bound to be unstable and traumatized. I needed to give her time. And if this wardrobe needed to be the foundation of her new life in this uncertain world, I would do my best to make it remain a safe haven. I had no love for her, did not know her, had no idea what her name was, and had barely gotten a glimpse of her, but I couldn't be completely indifferent to such a fragile being. I was often and with good reason called an old jerk, but living this way, alone, with little outside contact, suited me perfectly. I was not inhuman, though. Intuitively, I knew that this weakness could prove fatal to me and that I would be better off acting like a son of a bitch, like I had done thus far in my life. But I had not saved the girl just to throw her to the wolves, like I'd done to the man trying to climb up the front of the house. We would have to establish some kind of status quo while things settled down.

I placed the glass of water by the wardrobe door so she could grab it easily without spilling it. I laid the washcloth next to the glass, stepped back, and sat down on the bed directly across from the piece of furniture, not even six feet away. I cleared my throat and fixed my gaze on the large wardrobe. Anyone witnessing the scene would have taken me for a nutcase in the middle of a discussion with the furniture in his room, but in a world where madness had become the norm, a judgment like that would not have mattered…

"I brought you a glass of water and a wet washcloth for your knees. All you need to do is open the door to get them. I promise not to come near you and to leave you alone."

At the sound of my voice, the sobs lessened somewhat. I felt like I was taming an injured little animal. The more I thought about it, the more I told myself that I occupied the more comfortable position in this story. I was a self-supporting adult in his own home and felt like I was, for the time being, out of harm's way. As for her, the little girl was in an environment that was not at all familiar to her and in the presence of a man who must have seemed threatening and centuries-old to her. Indescribable sadness must have been overwhelming her, and I could only be a spectator to this heartbreak happening in the place where I always came to choose my clothes for the day. A choice that rarely took me more than thirty seconds, but a daily ritual that found a special meaning in such a situation.

Suddenly, the wardrobe door trembled slightly and began very slowly to move aside. A puny hand emerged, followed by a forearm, and quickly grabbed the glass and the washcloth before returning to its hiding place. Then, as if to thank me, the little girl placed the stove that

I had given her earlier, and that she had kept with her until then, out in front of the door.

My presence seemed to calm her down. The wooden door that separated me from her must have had a lot to do with it: unable to see me, her imagination could easily make me one of those old, protective wizards found in children's tales. Perhaps I had been transformed into a decrepit ancestor whose hoarse voice, not only full of wisdom but also of infinite sweetness, softened hearts. I had never thought of myself in that way, and to do so seemed unnatural to me. Still, I decided to stay in the room to inspect our provisions and keep the girl – or at least the wardrobe – company. Talking to her would occupy my mind, and hearing me would give her something else to think about, the hint of a hold to cling to in this New World. I picked up the bag and took inventory, listing everything out loud, like an old fool who had nothing but his room and his furniture for friends.

CHAPTER 3
THE ABSURD PARADE

Our living space, our bastion, now boiled down to four rooms, a single story of a small country farmhouse. A limited area for someone who was used to working in the great outdoors from morning to night and who, for leisure, did nothing but spend a few hours with his television set, an old cathode ray tube that would have made a good number of museum curators green with envy. Nevertheless, activity was not lacking. I fought the burden of confinement by keeping myself as busy as possible. Very early that morning – so as not to say in the middle of the night – at a time deemed appalling by the human body, I started to strengthen our line of defense by making sure that the armoire, which was now blocking the hallway, would be an unshakeable barrier. I tried to work in the utmost silence so as not to provoke the crazies, whose scratching had diminished somewhat. The day before, they had seemed to calm down a few dozen minutes after I'd stopped turning the second floor inside out and the little girl's crying had weakened in intensity. They still hadn't left, though.

Their presence was not in doubt; their plaintive moans had punctuated the whole night. In fact, they hadn't stopped since their greedy eyes had landed on us, and they knew we were right above them. I had no idea what part of their demented brains this information was stored in, but it monopolized all their attention. I was convinced: we were the one and only reason for their presence, and they would not leave until they had killed us.

By the early morning, their howling had not stopped, and worse, the creatures appeared to have gathered in the living room, just below us. They were drawn to our presence, as if they could somehow catch our scent or sense our warmth. They were there, planted under our feet, huddled together, intoning their macabre songs in chorus. Their vocal regurgitations pierced the floor and tore through our eardrums, enclosing our brains in an oppressive, perpetual embrace. The adrenaline rush that had kept me going the night before hadn't worked for long, but the fear remained. A dirty, sticky fear. The kind of dread that never lets go and, as soon as you close your eyes, thinks it's funny to paint, on the insides of your eyelids, all those dismal faces, with those relentless teeth, that are staring at you from a few inches under your feet.

The night before, shortly after midnight, after I had taken inventory of everything I'd been able to recover from the storage room, the little girl, still curled up in the wardrobe, had stopped crying and had given in to physical and mental fatigue. The sandman had not yet joined the ranks of that army of neurotics.

The glass of water ploy had only worked once; the pillow and blanket I had offered her were still outside the wardrobe.

As for me, sleep had seemed unachievable – it and I would not be on very good terms for a while. I couldn't bring myself to close my eyes, too afraid to open them back up to the spectacle of my own evisceration. So, I had remained lying on my bed for a few hours, trying to make myself very small on that soft island of apparent safety. Looking out the window at the shadows converging on the house, looming in the moonlight, I had gone over various possible scenarios, different possible outcomes of this misfortune. They all ended the same way. In a bloodbath. The blood of a man and a child.

And yet, I had decided to really take matters into my own hands. After all, by rationing ourselves and with the bathtub filled with water, we had enough food for about ten frugal days, a period that seemed long enough for our situation to improve. I was well aware that a rural area like this would not be the priority for the armed forces, if they were ever to take the place of the police to settle this matter, but I had high hopes that this mess was only local and that order would be quickly restored. I had no idea how wrong I was. This wave of frenzy had spread all across Provence, France, Europe, and even the whole world, taking with it the few scraps of intelligence that still remained in mankind. The predatory appetite was on the march.

I was amazed at myself for being so optimistic. Seeing things positively was not my greatest talent, and I easily could have continued to come up with scenarios involving my own death, but my companion was having a strange effect on me. Her presence pushed me to imagine a very different ending to our story. I had the irrational feeling that we could survive all of this, with or without help from the government. For the first time in my life, or at least in a long time, I had hope. I didn't really know what I was expecting, but this situation was starting to make me consider things differently.

In fact, I realized that this quivering serenity that was trying to find its way into me could be explained quite simply: I was finally doing something for myself. In just one day, I had found more strength to protect my life, and even someone else's, than I had in several years combined. My actions finally made sense to me. Everything I had done, even the most horrible things, was for me, for my life. The hours spent slaving away for a pittance, making the agri-food industries grow richer, without having the slightest sense of recognition, seemed far away now. How many people had my harvests fed? How many of them had even tried to imagine the man hiding behind what they were devouring? Probably none. I was these people's plaything, a foster father they would be ashamed to run into, a forsaken being whose life was meaningless. I loved my job, but I was finally seeing how it had alienated me. Now that I was fighting for myself, my every move, my every action took on meaning. Only one thing mattered to me: to survive. No matter what I had to do. I would survive.

Lost in my thoughts, I hadn't noticed the time passing by, and the sun had already reached its zenith. It was as if I were coming out of a daydream, but I hadn't been idle. Stay busy to avoid thinking? What bullshit.

During this mental absence, my body had gathered in my room, in an almost military procession cadenced to the rhythm of drums, a good portion of everything that could be useful to us. During this operation, I had completely cleared out the guest room, and our lair now included two rooms that were almost completely empty. I had positioned the tallest pieces of furniture closer to the windows out of fear that one of those things might discover that he has chimpanzee skills, but none of them were big enough to prevent me from seeing what was going on outside. I had piled up all fabric – sheets, pants, shirts, T-shirts – at the foot of my bed, and all these members of the textile family were tangled in a comforting mess. I had reserved one small shelf, on which I had carefully lined up all the food I'd collected from the ground floor. Each food item had been placed in such a way as to organize our rations: the canned ravioli stood alone in their row, while pairs of pasta and pâté swore loyalty to each other for the meals to come.

The sight of all this food, as uninspiring as it was, made my mouth water, and my stomach reminded me that my last meal had been over a day ago. Until that point, fear had been choking me, and I had been able to mobilize my body for hours without reaching its limits. My ankle had never stopped hurting, but the pain had become anecdotal in the face of the urgency of the situation, and I had suppressed it. Now, the return to some kind of routine left the door wide open to a wave of pain. The joint was still swollen and was throbbing again. A very poor reason not to eat, as the two bellies present in the room were claiming their due. The child hadn't eaten either, and I couldn't let her starve in her wardrobe.

I took the gas stove and set it up in the middle of the room, between my bed and the little girl's hiding place. I looked around for the stainless-steel reflection of a saucepan before realizing that, in my hurry, I had forgotten to kidnap one from the kitchen. I quickly searched the pile of items I had brought upstairs and found nothing that would do the trick. I therefore resigned myself to heating the cans directly on the fire. I wasn't sure how they would react to their hindquarters getting so hot, but I had no other choice. Quickly opened, the can of ravioli was the first to burn at the stake. Once empty, it would double as a pot for future meals, and I could also boil water in it.

It didn't take long for the first bubbling of tomato sauce to be heard as the ravioli splashed around in a bath that was getting hotter and hotter. A few discreet noises reached me from the wardrobe. The aroma rising from the stove had crept through the wooden wardrobe doors, and the little girl seemed to be showing some interest in the smell.

"I'm making some ravioli," I told her, a certain pride in my voice at the idea that my cooking, however basic it may have been, might awaken a damaged child's appetite.

Hesitantly, I added:

"If you want some, you can come out and get it. I won't hurt you. Or you can stay in the wardrobe, and I'll put a plate by the door."

A long silence followed my words, and as I realized that I had no plates or silverware, the girl gave a quick bang on the door. I took this response as an enthusiastic yes and placed a good plateful of ravioli in a metal saucer that I had picked up in my incessant comings and goings that morning; as for me, I would settle for the slightly blackened can. I put the makeshift plate by the door, right next to the pillow and blanket. The little girl moved, but the door did not open.

"I'm walking away, don't worry."

No sooner had I stepped back a few inches than a hand grabbed its booty before retreating to its lair. I was relieved to see that she had agreed so quickly to eat; the thought of her letting herself waste away forever in that wardrobe terrified me a little bit. I sat cross-legged on the floor and leaned back against the bed, soon adding my own chewing noises to the ones escaping from the wardrobe.

I found myself alone for the rest of the day, the little girl still not revealing herself after her metal lid, emptied of all contents, appeared outside the wardrobe. The time for her exit, for her first steps into this ravenous world, had not yet come. I just hoped I wouldn't have to force her out of her hiding place in an emergency, but I was sure our fortifications would hold up well.

I spent a good part of the afternoon tidying up what could be put away. I needed order to be calm. However, in such a confined space, my main activity soon turned into a nagging wait behind each window of our prison. I thus dedicated the end of the day to watching what was going on outside, regularly changing my observation post. Everywhere I looked, they were there. This was the first chance I'd had to observe them unhurriedly. Whichever window I spied on them from, the madmen wandering outside soon spotted me and came to stand just below, their arms outstretched miserably and their teeth chattering in the void. They opened and closed their mouths incessantly, adding a sinister concerto of clattering to their moans of pain and, no doubt, hunger. Molars against molars, incisors against canines. Their ravenous eyes stared at me with incredible intensity, and my slightest movement made their horrible eyeballs spin, eager not to lose sight of me.

There were about ten of them under the guest bedroom window, and their cries attracted even more. Some managed to get out of the house and joined the ranks of my observers, but most of the new extras in this ridiculous movie were coming straight from the road, from all those coffins on wheels that now lined my property. A real nest of sickos. The flow did not seem to want to dry up, and silhouettes continually emerged on the horizon, where the expressway stretched on.

They never lost patience, and all their attention was focused on me. As long as they could see me, they were doing all they could to reach me. They rubbed their fingertips briskly against the wall in the hopes of suddenly rising and sinking their nasty teeth into my flesh. Their threatening extremities were gradually being reduced to bloody stumps. The green of the nail polish of one of the monsters, who must have visited her manicurist not long ago, had mingled with the red of her flesh and was soon joined by the white of her bones. I found this spectacle delectable. Seeing these poor people, deprived of what made them human, flaying themselves like this on the walls of my own house should have horrified me, but deep down, it amused me. Watching these pieces of shit – who, after all, wanted nothing more than to feast on my body – wear themselves out in this way was perfectly fine with me.

When I got tired of seeing them clump together from one vantage point, I would go back to another room and sit on the windowsill, waiting for one of them to spot me and eventually round up all his buddies. I had rarely been so desired, and my admirers revered every one of my appearances as if I were a god. A god they would dream of serving for dinner. Never before had the offering of the body of Jesus to his faithful been taken so literally.

I was having fun making fools of them by changing places regularly. But, even though I was safe on my perch, I knew I shouldn't underestimate them. Their determination, their uncontrollable appetite, and the physical strength I had seen them display all seemed to me to be arguments in their favor. I couldn't let the absurdity of their actions and the ridiculousness of their appearance make me forget what I had witnessed a few hours earlier. Yesterday, these village idiots had slaughtered everyone in their path and infected still-healthy people with a single bite. I had seen the violence just one of them was capable of and found it hard to imagine what such a large group would do to me. I probably wouldn't even have time to become one of them, their fangs would tear me apart so fast. That might be a good thing.

I fixed my eyes on the crowd. In that despicable horde, everyone had their own little physical peculiarity, a ticket to gain entry to the monster fair. Some had been partially devoured by their peers before becoming one of them and exhibited missing or unusable limbs. Others – like Mr. Tomato, his face studded with shards of glass and his eye sunk into its socket – displayed horrific facial features. Missing a piece of his cheek, one of them wore a double smile as his bloodied molars were visible in the middle of a gaping wound; another one had both his eyes gouged out. The majority of their throats were wide open, as if, like ferocious beasts, these monsters instinctively aimed for the jugular in order to swallow as much blood and flesh as possible before their victim, their delicious meal, arose in their own quest for a tasty morsel. There was only one word to describe them: grotesque. Dismally grotesque.

When it was time for dinner, I repeated my little cooking trick and, after making some pasta in the ravioli can from lunchtime, I asked the girl if she would rather come and eat with me or stay in the wardrobe. Her answer did not change. A slight knock against the wooden door alerted me that she preferred home delivery. So, I put her metal saucer in front of her little den and hastened to add a glass of water. After offering her a drink the night before, I had completely forgotten to bring her more. To be saved from the clutches of psychopathic monsters just to die of thirst in a wardrobe… How ironic! I was terribly angry with myself. I had spent a good part of the day observing those things and amusing myself, and at no time had I thought that the little girl might need me. Quite uncomfortable, I stammered a few words as the glass and the plate disappeared into the wardrobe:

"I can fill it again if you want, if you're still thirsty, I mean. We have plenty of water."

I paused, then quickly added:

"Forgive me, I forgot about you this afternoon… You understand…"

Suddenly, I couldn't find my words anymore. Why did I feel the need to justify myself to a kid I didn't even know? I was exasperated, ready to let irritation get the better of me, but I tried to control it.

I could only blame myself. I was the one who had rushed out into the danger to rescue her, and I had vowed to take responsibility for her. She could stay in the wardrobe; I wouldn't let her die of hunger, let alone thirst, now.

"Don't think about it anymore," I added. "I promise never to forget about you again. Have your meal in peace and quiet; I'll stop bothering you."

To my surprise, those last words were almost immediately followed by two quick knocks, as if she were asking me, in her mute way, to continue. I thought about it and said:

"Do you want to listen to me talk?"

One little knock.

"What could you possibly want me to say?"

Of course, there was no reaction. To answer yes or no to this question would have been quite an achievement. A little bewildered, I thought about what I could say. I had no idea how to address a child who couldn't have been more than seven or eight years old.

"Listen… My name is Patrick, and I'm a farmer. I'm the one who grows the wheat in the fields. I also have corn plants, and it's thanks to me that the stores are always full."

I could sense how stupid my words were, but their content wasn't important. All that mattered was that I spoke, as if my presence had finally become something reassuring to her.

"I'm fifty-seven years old. Yeah, an old man. You are in my home, well, in my wardrobe… I have lived here all alone for a few years…"

I continued in this manner, telling her a whole bunch of trivial things, from the most personal to the most general, in a voice loud and distinct enough to cover our predators' odious screams. I found myself feeling sort of at ease talking about everything and nothing like this, and I only stopped when the rare noises that came from the wardrobe were replaced by soft, rhythmic exhalations, like a monotonous music box. She had fallen asleep. The lethal boredom of my conversation had calmed her down, and she was able to let herself go to sleep. It was going to be much harder for me.

The night was indeed very difficult again. My body was constantly oscillating between the need to rest, and thus re-energize, and the instinct that told it to stay awake and listen carefully. Being attentive was of no comfort to me, however. On the contrary. I so longed to be able to get away, if only for a few minutes, from the incessant noise of the crazies. They had now stopped trying to demolish our barricades on the stairs, but they continued to moan. Most appeared to be standing still, waiting for us to make the slightest movement so they could track us down. Some were still under the windows, gathered in small groups, all copying each other's clumsy attempts to climb the walls. It was wasted effort, but the distinct sound of their fingers rubbing against the front of the house terrified me at this point. That ominous noise amplified the horror of their cries, and time and time again, I tried to stifle it by sliding my head under the pillow. There was nothing to do; I couldn't sleep. My senses remained on constant alert even as my mind began to fail. I didn't know how long I would be able to endure this auditory torture before horrifically mutilating myself so as not to hear them anymore.

In this cacophonous hell, time was losing all meaning. It seemed to fly by peacefully during the nighttime racket, finally free of the chains that held it slave to mankind. The hours meant nothing to me anymore, and I just watched them pass without much interest. I already knew that the day I had just lived was bound to be repeated endlessly. We were cornered, and there seemed to be no possible way out, other than madness. The next day didn't even interest me since I had already experienced it today. Whether it was day or night, our situation was not changing. Of course, the howling was less intense at night, but the darkness had the perverse effect of making our hearing better. I tried observing the hands of my watch, which, with their perpetual movements, had become one of my favorite distractions. I stared at their high-speed pursuit, hoping my ears would give up and finally let my eyes gently unfurl the veil of their lids. Finally.

∗∗∗

I awoke suddenly. I had finally slept for a few meager hours. My heart was racing, and I lay there for a couple more minutes to calm down. The sun's rays were beginning to break shyly on the horizon. Stretched out on the bed, where it was becoming unbearable for me to remain, I peered outside. The sight of my fields caressed by the delicate, grazing light of dawn brought an immediate end to my anguish, and my heart ceased rattling my rib cage. However, seeing the body of the little girl's mother – a barely discernible, disjointed puppet that had finally fallen off the hood of the camper van – quickly brought me back to reality, and I jumped out of bed. In my haste, the floor made a loud squeak. An immediate echo was heard.

As I had feared all night long, with no other goal than to wait for help, the day was a pale imitation of the previous one. I was on the lookout for human activity outside, with little result, and began to think the army was taking a while to react. My farm was regularly flown over by military planes, but since the monsters had arrived, the sky had remained strangely calm. Blue and peaceful.

The crazies were no longer amusing me. I repeatedly threw various unnecessary objects into the crowd that had formed under the bedroom window, to their utter indifference. I hit one of them in the face, but he didn't even seem to notice. Drowned in the horde of his degenerate contemporaries, he continued to stretch out his arms towards me, frequently clacking his teeth.

Only the day's two meals brought me any comfort. Like the day before, I found myself talking about everything and nothing in a long, nonsensical monologue. In response, I only got some more or less vigorous knocks on the wardrobe door.

The young girl remained holed up in the wardrobe. I had to wait until the morning of the third day for my companion in misfortune to finally come out of her hiding place.

I was standing in front of one of the windows. My body was having a hard time masking the annoyance that had come over me since becoming convinced that no one would be coming to our rescue. I had been foolish to believe that a commando unit would be dispatched to come save me.

The number of madmen now squatting downstairs and roaming around the house left no doubt: the army had other fish to fry. The unbearable mess that was Marseille was surely a real Mediterranean hell by now. I was imagining the metropolis being ravaged by hordes of lunatics, its main streets strewn with corpses, which sometimes rose to go seize a new victim, when a thin, uncomfortable voice pulled me from my thoughts.

"They're zombies."

I was much more surprised by what I had just heard than by the long-awaited presence of the little girl outside of the wardrobe. I might not have been fond of horror films, preferring much lighter programs, but I was a man of his time, and her words immediately resonated with me. In my mind, I saw the images that we were regularly inundated with on television news shows of all those idiots dressing up as corpses and parading through the streets. Zombie walks. The little voice was right. My house was under siege by zombies. We were witnessing possibly the greatest zombie walk in history, except that makeup remover wouldn't be enough to put an end to it.

Once the surprise of this lexical discovery had passed, I slowly turned around. The little girl was standing there, a few yards away, halfway between the wardrobe and me. Despite the gentleness of my movement, she retreated slightly as my face entered her field of vision. I could read in her eyes that I was a vision of horror. I hadn't shaved for three days; thick black and white hairs had appeared on my stretched skin, making me look like a scruffy homeless man. Worse, monumental dark circles, evidence of my struggles with sleep, were plastered under my eyes. My disturbing appearance, like that of a sick creature, must have been just as frightening to the child as the monsters around us. Yet, what she must have read in my eyes was hardly any different.

Despite the washcloth I had given her, her condition was devastating. Her whole body was soiled, and I quickly realized that it was not just traces of food. Locked in the wardrobe for the past three days, she'd had no choice but to satisfy her natural urges where she had been spending all that time. Once again, I was terribly angry with myself for having neglected her like that, for not even thinking for a second about the insane effort it would have taken her to stay in her hiding place. I should have forced her to come out.

I was about to suggest that she go wash up when she said, in her frail, trembling voice:

"They're going to eat me, like my mom."

I sensed how painful it was for her to broach this subject.

"Your mom wasn't..."

I did not finish my sentence. How could I tell her that her mother hadn't been devoured by these things but run over by someone who was still well aware of his actions? After all, she was in the same room as a man who had committed the unforgivable himself. I couldn't be one to judge the driver of the camper van, but I also couldn't make the girl lose all faith in humanity. She would be better off if her mother died in the clutches of those monsters rather than at the hand of man.

"They won't eat anyone else… I'm here now," I picked up again.

She stared at me with her big blue eyes, walked over to me, and gave me a hint of a small smile.

"Okay, Mr. Patrick."

I was glad she remembered my first name. My long monologues over the past two days hadn't been as pointless as I had imagined, in the end.

"Follow me. You need to get cleaned up."

I crossed the room to lead her to the bathroom. She tried to take my hand, which I instinctively pulled away. She jumped at the intensity of my reaction and stepped back again. The slight smile that had graced her face a few seconds ago resolutely faded, and her expression did not mask her concern.

"You surprised me, I'm sorry. Come on, let's go."

Despite my apology, our hands did not meet. I was not prepared for so much trust, and her interest in me made me uncomfortable. In the hallway, I categorically forbade her to go near the armoire that was blocking access to the zombies.

After a detour through the old guest room, we were in the bathroom. I dipped a plastic basin into the tub. The water was starting to get lukewarm, the result of the intense, strong sun that was so typical for June. I dipped a washcloth into it and turned to the child.

"I don't think you would object to washing up a bit."

The little one looked at me awkwardly, as if she had become aware of her condition and the smell emanating from her body.

"I'll leave you alone. Take your time. You can use that soap and the water in the basin. Most importantly, you must not touch the water in the bathtub; that's our reserve. Understood?"

She didn't respond immediately, as if she were gauging the strangeness of the situation she'd found herself in. A large bathtub full of crystalline liquid was inviting her to come soak in it and get rid of all her dirt – all that was missing for a most enjoyable bath were some toys – and yet, she had to be content with a small basin. She nodded anyway. I left the room then, taking with me another container that I had just filled.

"Take your time. You can close the door, but don't lock it. I'll come back with some clothes."

I returned to my room and inspected the wardrobe. She had un-hooked most of the clothes that had been suspended there, letting the bare hangers dangle limply with no reason for being. She had made a cozy nest for herself. Some of the clothes had worrisome yellow traces on them, though. I opened the window and quickly got rid of all the laundry. No sooner had it fallen to the ground than the horde came to trample it, rendering it permanently unusable. Tearing my gaze away from that pathetic spectacle, I emptied my container of water inside the wardrobe and awkwardly began to clean it. The result was not perfect, but I had high hopes that the odor that had started to permeate the space would disappear. It would have to, especially if the little one was going to go back in there and hunker down, as I was convinced she would. I set up a clean blanket and several pillows for her, hoping that she would now come out in the case of pressing needs.

This task accomplished, I embarked on a new mission: finding my nephews' and nieces' clothes.

CHAPTER 4
THE METAL SONG

A week had passed since the world had been committed to this asylum. The straitjacket of confinement was suffocating, and the little girl and I only wanted one thing: to be able to go outside freely and enjoy the refreshing gusts of wind that were having a tough time getting inside the house. A week without a drop of rain or a thunderstorm. At night, the temperature only fell a few degrees, leaving us permanently at the mercy of the oppressive and arid atmosphere on the second floor.

Each day was getting harder to bear, especially since the water in the bathtub was now around eighty-five degrees. Suffice to say that consuming it was no longer a pleasant way to quench our thirst; we were only drinking it out of necessity. Two days earlier, the clear, cool water coming from the tap had been replaced by a dirty liquid carrying, in its flow, multiple more or less disgusting impurities. As I had instinctively predicted, the water service had shut down very quickly when confronted with this outbreak of madness. The station technicians had certainly preferred to get back to their families for one last hug, but perhaps some of them were busy ravaging my first floor. What could be more normal than that?

I was mostly worried about our food reserves. We had no more than three days of provisions left, and if no one came to our aid in time, we would have nothing to subsist on but hot water. I knew there were a few cans lurking in their cupboards downstairs, but that meager pittance, that few days' trip to the land of culinary delights, was unattainable. I could hardly see how to go get them without signing my death warrant. Several dozen zombies were still squatting downstairs, and they didn't seem to want to leave the premises. At times, one of them would find the exit and stroll tirelessly around my property before returning to the dark, smelly interior of the house. There was nothing I could do.

There was no way I was just going to cross my arms and wait to die after so much effort. I had never counted on anyone in my entire bitch of a life. Putting my fate in the hands of a fictitious convoy of soldiers who might come and free us from our unwavering prison seemed like a mistake I should not make. If I were going to survive, I would have to do it on my own. Therefore, there was only one solution left for us: to try to escape from the house, to flee as far away as possible. The very next day.

Over the last four days, the little girl – whose name I did not know, perhaps because I hadn't asked her – had increased her outings beyond her kingdom. She now agreed to eat with the wardrobe door open and sometimes went on an expedition without me always knowing why. Even so, she spent most of the time curled up among the pillows I had placed in the wardrobe. I did not know how she managed to endure the heat that must have reigned in that confined space. I had tried several times to explain to her that she should not lock herself in there like that, at the risk of being cooked like in an oven. The image had struck her as funny but not at all convincing. Faced with her systematic refusal to listen to me, I decided to bring her water regularly. Warm, but hydrating.

During one of our meals, she told me everything she knew about zombies. As bizarre as the source of her knowledge was – she had spent hours watching her big brother play video games – the vast majority of it turned out to be true. With complete indifference and a desire to overstep their mother's orders, he didn't care that his little sister was seeing extremely violent scenes. As a result, sometimes she would suddenly leave her brother's room in tears, terrorized. Still, it was never long before she squeezed through the doorway again, hungry for thrills.

According to her, zombies were dead people who attacked everyone and were easily avoided due to how slow they were. The best way to kill them was to aim for the head, and above all else, you had to make sure not to get bitten, or else you'd become one of them. She also did not fail to tell me about the bizarre origin of zombies and how they resulted from scientific experiments carried out by a horrible corporation. She seemed to take a certain pleasure in it, and in the midst of the many anecdotes permeating her tale, a clear and precise image emerged of what was in my house downstairs. Real zombies, whose description fit almost exactly: a very real fiction.

Those whom I had taken for a bunch of crackpots, before understanding that madness had nothing to do with it, were definitely dead. Their wounds, each more serious than the next, left no doubt. As their bites had proven time and time again in the first hours, they were contagious. On the other hand, I doubted their slowness, remembering how some of them raced madly to seize their prey, but I had to admit that, in the days following the outbreak, they had indeed adopted slower paces and much more uncertain gaits. I didn't have much education, but I could well imagine their blood clotting after they died and eventually becoming an unyielding brake on their movements. They were all wandering around uneasily, nonchalantly dragging their mortal remains. They wobbled periodically, and their coordination seemed no more advanced than a young child's. Perhaps a completely different reason explained their condition, and there was no proof that, face to face with their victim, they would not still be able to move quickly. I didn't want to check, nor did I want to see if a blow to the head was indeed the best way to get rid of them. I would find out soon enough.

That day, after opening a new jar of pâté that would serve as a source of protein for the next two meals and cooking some pasta, I told the little girl that we would be leaving the house the next morning. I feared that my decision, which was certainly very sudden in her eyes, might seem completely crazy to her. However, she accepted it with a simple nod, without even asking me any questions. Where were we going to go, what were we going to do? I wouldn't have known how to answer. The only priority was to find a way for us to escape in one piece, without getting bitten.

Between mouthfuls, I gave her the task of gearing up for our departure and being ready to go. Having failed to dig up any toys for her, I had kept her busy those last days by presenting everything I asked her to do as a mission of extreme importance. This way, even the most mundane things turned into real epic quests in her eyes, which her childhood imagination could easily populate with legendary creatures and probably... cannibalistic monsters. For my part, before developing an escape plan, I had to find something to protect ourselves with, if only summarily, in order to deal with the eventuality of hand-to-hand combat. If we ever managed to get out of this place, it would be stupid to die a few hours later in a zombie's clutches for failure to be sufficiently equipped.

Out of all the clothes I had gathered in the early days of the invasion, not many felt thick enough to withstand the zombies' rotted-out fangs. No doubt wool sweaters and other lighter materials would be of no use up against one of their fierce jaws. Their parched teeth would have no trouble slipping between the fibers of the fabric to plunge into our flesh. My motorcycle jacket seemed to me to be the best solution. Even though its black leather had been cracked by time, it was still going strong, and the burgundy elbow patches that made me so proud were still firmly in place.

I still remembered the day I bought it, almost forty years ago. Right after I'd gotten my motorcycle license, I had rushed to the bike store to get the most expensive biker outfit, thus squandering all the savings that had been so hard to amass working weekends on the farm with my father. I had sweated for hours to get that money, but spending it in that way had been one of my greatest joys. The next morning, as I was pulling up at the high school on the motorbike a friend had let me borrow, all eyes were on me. I spoke to a whole bunch of new people, and many had smiled at me, but it didn't last. My friend had taken back his machine, and my parents had refused to buy me anything on two wheels. I was angry with them for several weeks, cursing their back-ward thinking, but eventually I gave up, and my brand-new jacket ended up in the armoire. Until now.

It still had that animal smell that had made me choose it. In fact, it had hardly changed at all. On the other hand, the weight of the years had been much crueler to me. It was impossible for me to pull up the zipper, each side of the jacket being separated by an insurmountable mountain of flesh, and my arms were being hugged tightly in the too-narrow sleeves. My musculature of the time had given way to a bulkier mixture of fat and tired muscles. My very physical work had helped keep my body in shape, but age and a certain love for beer had saddled me with some nice love handles and a plump belly. Dressed like this, I looked ridiculous with my spare tire bulging out of the jacket, but it was the most suitable garment: my arms and my back were protected. To hell with the ridiculousness. I was convinced that what would have been considered an eccentricity just a few days ago could very well save my life. The burden of social norms had drastically diminished, and now, as light as a feather, it would no longer mean much to Man. The practical and the useful would take precedence over the aesthetic. A dictatorship was coming to an end, and only what would allow me to survive seemed worthy of existence to me. Death to futility.

For the bottoms, I opted for heavy jeans. I covered my prominent stomach with one of the monochromatic T-shirts that filled my wardrobe. I deliberately chose the color that least matched the black and red of my jacket, in yet another gesture of insubordination towards good taste: a hideous neon green. However, it wasn't long before I replaced it with a black T-shirt, out of fear that the zombies would spot me too easily – at least if their appetites were able to pierce the opaque veil covering their expressionless eyes. No sense taking the risk just for the sake of provocation.

As I expected, I didn't have anything good for the little one. I had already given her everything that was her size. The Mickey T-shirt and the little green Bermuda shorts she had been wearing for the past few days were the most suitable. Knowing that she would be so unprotected really worried me, and I would have to do everything possible to keep her out of immediate danger.

When it came time to think about our weaponry, I rapidly gave up on making my own weapons with what was lying around upstairs. As good a handyman as I was, all my ideas seemed pathetic when I thought back on all the paraphernalia in the wing of the house that served as a warehouse. Nothing would be as sturdy as what was in there, and I would rather entrust my life to tools I trusted than to an old plank riddled with nails. I could imagine hundreds of ways to use them in my quest for vengeance, wielding my mace with all my might, rhythmically chopping with my ax, throwing my pitchfork as if it were a javelin. Like a warrior in Thermopylae, I could see myself resisting successive waves of enemies, letting my wrath fall on anyone who dared invade my property. I swiftly shook off these absurd thoughts, reminding myself that I first had to find a way to access this warlike cornucopia before going into battle. I tried to put myself in the shoes of the greatest military strategists before realizing that my enemies had no plan of attack. They were guided by their hunger, their thirst for destruction: my only chance would be to use this blind frenzy to my advantage.

I rushed to my bedroom window. Banging against the floor and screaming at the top of my lungs, I tried to get the zombies' attention. The little girl opened the wardrobe door a crack and, thinking I had lost my grip, closed it again almost immediately. The zombies didn't take long to converge under the window, though. They didn't care about my apparent madness; all that mattered to them was plunging their vile faces into my bowels, in a delectable bath of flesh and organs. They did not seem to be in a position to be choosy, either, since every day, new creatures came to join our attackers, as if all the walking human buffets in the region had been picked clean.

When there were enough of them, around fifty, I walked as quietly as possible to the bathroom and peered outside. A good dozen of them, probably the slowest ones, were still squatting in the yard, but they were stubbornly making their way towards the outside of my room. However, just moments after my hullabaloo ended, the crowd was already starting to disperse and circle the house once again in search of any access to the upper floor. Within five minutes, the enemy troops had redeployed and covered all the possible exits. Still, their behavior gave me some hope. I was convinced that I could manipulate them, and that with loud, constant noise, I could keep them away from the adjacent barn long enough for our escape from the house-turned-prison.

Then, a light breeze from outside tickled my face before transforming into a much more violent gust that made the leaves of the oak tree in the yard quiver. Nature had just brought the solution to my problem, and if I could count on it when the time came the following day, the wind would play a song of liberation for the little girl and me. Convinced that it would not let me down, I decided to build the largest mobile ever seen in Provence. A mobile that would make the zombies' dirty ears vibrate when the time came for us to escape.

I retrieved several sheets that had accumulated in a corner and entrusted the little one with the task of cutting them into long strips. After showing her what I expected of her and asking her to be careful with the pair of scissors I had given her, I gathered together as many metal things as possible. I set my sights on whatever might work, adding once again to the chaos and devastation that reigned upstairs – especially in the bathroom, where I violently pulled out the plumbing. After about an hour, with the afternoon just beginning, all the elements were ready. The girl had quickly gotten bored with her job, and I ended up cutting the last strips of fabric. All that was left was for me to put everything together so that the wind could easily knock together the different parts of the whole.

I started by building a structure from the slats of my bed, which I had taken apart, and some nails that I still had left. Sticking out from the top of the wardrobe while being put together, the mobile looked like a giant, disturbing hand. At one end of the wooden bed frame, slats went out in all directions like twisted, misshapen fingers. The little girl hurriedly came out of her hiding place when it started shaking with each of my hammer blows. Every time I hammered in a nail, the sound was echoed immediately from below as a large number of zombies moaned. Even after a week of their ominous concert, I still wasn't used to their groaning; unlike the steady, soothing song of the cicadas, which I very easily forgot, this made me feel irrepressibly disgusted. Each scream made my blood run cold. The symphony for life being intoned by the hammer and nails, iron against iron, was masked by the gloomy song emanating from the dry, putrid throats of the zombies.

I didn't stop, though, and the girl decided to help me. At intervals, she handed me new strips of fabric that I attached in different places on the slats. It wasn't long before they, like fishing rod lines, were dangling various metal objects that I had hooked onto their ends in one way or another. My construction, like a macabre tree straight out of

Tim Burton's imagination, looked terrifying. As I propelled the first parts of the mobile against the others, it initiated a repeated swinging movement that produced a powerful noise: the creature finally came to life. The metallic clinks multiplied and amplified as inertia pulled them together in a loud dance. Silence quickly returned as the last pendulums stopped, hanging limply in the air. I was hoping the mistral wind would be strong and steady enough to bring this life-saving chime to life, long enough for us to sneak into the barn and flee.

I then went into the bathroom, where I wet my whistle with a tall glass of hot water. It was very unpleasant, and I wanted to spit out that repugnant liquid in which all kinds of bacteria would soon be growing. The idea disgusted me, but not as much as that of ending up as a desiccated mummy. With my lips moist, I took a deep breath of air before opening the window and letting a heinous scent forcefully enter the room and worm its way into my nostrils.

I tried to contain my gagging and climbed over the windowsill, placing my foot on the tiled roof of the barn, which formed a wing perpendicular to the house. I moved forward a few feet with a firm, determined step, turned around, and winked at the little girl, who was watching me. Leaning on the windowsill, she looked worried. I reassured her, explaining that I was used to acting like an acrobat whenever, after a particularly violent storm, some tiles shattered, leaving thin streams of water to penetrate inside. I always hurried to replace them, anxious that the hay I stored in the barn would rot and rob me of a significant portion of my income. Spring had been particularly wet last year, and the few fields I had left fallow had provided an incredible amount of grass. The haystacks I had piled up in there almost reached the top of the barn.

I placed a foot on either side of the ridge of the roof. The slopes were pretty gentle and had never impressed me, but when the dead began to accumulate on both sides of the building, calling for me to fall with their incessant moans, my presence up there seemed crazy to me.

The fall probably would not have been fatal, but my predators' sharp fangs, which left no doubt as to their effectiveness, would have soon finished the job. Frightened and with my lungs full of a pungent, disgusting smell, I crouched down and crawled on all fours. I didn't dare turn around for fear the little one would read the fear on my face. My fingers gripped the edges of the tiles forcefully; my blood wasted no time in flowing back, leaving my hands like two pale, cold vises. My limbs shaking and aching, I finally got to the far end of the wing, about thirty yards from the bathroom window. Under the roof, in this precise spot, my hay was waiting for me.

I was convinced that the piled-up haystacks would make it easy for me to descend into the barn. I sat down on the central ridge and began to remove the tiles one by one. Although they were nested within each other, I had no trouble dislodging them from their spots. Some, damaged by time, were falling apart on the edges, and an ocher powder promptly covered my fingertips. After a few minutes, a mound of a dozen tiles sat by my side. The whole thing was unstable, and when one tile slipped and crashed down below, I decided to get rid of all the others. What was the use of heaping them up like that? I grabbed the first of the lot and, with all my strength, sent it flying towards the zombies who had gathered at the foot of the building. It made a wide curve and spun around before disappearing into a scrum of arms, all outstretched in my direction. The zombies didn't even seem to notice my attack. Those my projectile had hit were tirelessly stretching their gaunt limbs towards me, moving their broken fingers with a repulsive crackling sound. I started again and multiplied the throws. I hit several of my targets squarely in the face, but the tiles just shattered on their bony skulls and ended up in pieces on the ground. About ten minutes later, the zombies were walking, unconcernedly, on a thick carpet of rubble, and I had stripped a large area of the roof.

I studied the cluster of gamy meat that wasn't taking its eyes off me and managed to make out a few superficial wounds on some of them, scratched and torn by shards of tile. I could have spent the next few hours bombing them like that, but the arsenal on the roof wouldn't have been enough to deal with those vermin from beyond the grave.

Several wooden rafters, spaced four inches apart, made it still impossible to access the interior of the barn. I had only grazed its skin, and I would have to debone it in order to get inside. I stood up and waved my arms in the direction of the girl, who had not stopped watching me and had even let out a shy laugh when my high-speed projectiles were knocking zombies to the ground. She responded to me by waving her little hand mechanically. I shouted at her:

"Can you bring me my hammer, please? It's next to my bed!"

She didn't have to be told twice; her small brown shock of hair disappeared in a flash inside the house. I cautiously walked back to the window, trying not to imitate the tragic fate of the tiles. She arrived long before me, hammer prominently displayed, a big smile on her face. Seeing her look so happy thrilled me, and I caught up with her faster than I would have thought. She proudly handed me the tool, which I took, thanking her.

"What are you doing?" she asked me.

I was delighted that she was finally getting more comfortable with me, even if she refused to call me anything other than Mr. Patrick. I replied:

"I'm preparing our escape. Tomorrow morning, we will go through there."

"Through the roof!" she exclaimed, as if the thought of entering somewhere through the roof seemed like just one more anomaly in this new world.

"Yes, through the roof. I hope you like acrobatics."

She thought for a moment and, without responding directly to my words, added sadly:

"And will we go find Arnaud and Papa?"

I really wasn't expecting that question, and I hadn't had time to think about what we would do once we were away from here. I didn't know if it was out of cowardice or because I really believed it, but masking all my emotions, I told her that we would. Hesitantly, I leaned over and kissed her on the forehead. This gesture surprised her, and she smiled at me again. Embarrassed, I turned on my heel and headed over to the gaping hole that was tearing through the barn roof.

Removing the nails that held the joists was much easier than I'd imagined. I whacked each rafter away from the main beam with the hammer and then pulled it off. Very quickly, a space about twenty inches wide was cleared. It was ideally placed, since a haystack was just about three feet below it. It would be a breeze for me to drop onto it and then reach the ground using the crude staircase created by the pile of hay bales. I hoped the little one would be able to do that, too. With my help, it probably wouldn't be insurmountable. Everything seemed ready now.

Before heading back to the house, I waved at my tractor through the opening.

"I hope you're up for the great escape, pal."

Its red hood, covered in a thick layer of mud in spots, gave me a big smile, and I was immediately reassured. Everything would be fine; this old friend of mine would never let me down.

CHAPTER 5
FLAMES OF RESENTMENT

The good thing about the apocalypse is that alarm clocks are unnecessary. When the sun's rays finally decided to dawn on the horizon and bring some color back to the world, I had been awake for a long time. I was no longer managing to relax enough to give myself over to a deep sleep; as my brain idled during the long hours of waiting each night, my body always remained vigilant.

The lack of rest was taking its toll on my physical stamina, and it was getting increasingly difficult to keep my thoughts clear. Yesterday had worn me out, and my few moments of slumber had not been enough to recharge my batteries. So, although well aware of what to expect today, my mind kept drifting off.

My presence in this world seemed like a distant mirage to me, and it took a superhuman effort for me to manage to slowly sit up in the bed, my vision blurry. Now was not the time to flinch; I needed to get a grip on myself quickly and focus on the next few minutes. Nothing could be left to chance if I didn't want us to be served up to the zombies.

The bag I had packed the day before sat proudly beside the bed, the fabric tightly stretched by its contents, like a protruding torso. I had stuffed everything I could in it, favoring containers I could put some water in. Food, some medicine, clothes, and a bar of soap rounded out our gear. A small backpack accompanied the bag; I had taken care to fill it with the lightest items so that the little girl could carry it easily.

The wardrobe door was ajar and revealed a slender foot. I stared at it for a few seconds then got up. My knees manifested their disapproval by creaking loudly, but they quieted down after a few steps. I dragged myself to the bathroom and plunged my face into the tub. The contact with the hot water was unpleasant and failed to clear my mind. My head felt like it was being bathed in a sticky, clammy substance. I pulled it out hurriedly, sending drops of water flying all over the room and letting small waves form on the surface: an old stranger was looking at me through the turbid water.

He looked tired and, notwithstanding the ripples that made his face quiver, I could make out two dry, blue eyes, sunk in their sockets. I took a step back; then, seeing only the top of the stranger's head, I moved forward again. He was still staring at me. He suddenly seemed very familiar to me: the surface of the water had regained its peacefulness and now clearly reflected my face.

I turned hastily to the mirror above the sink and discovered a decrepit old man. In just a few days, I had aged ten years. My face was hollowed out, and a thick beard was starting to form. My eyes were the scariest. Encircled by heavy, bluish circles and thick eyebrows, they made me look insane. Shocked at my appearance, I let myself fall to the ground.

Tears flooded my unhealthy eyes. I hadn't cried in years, and yet, I found myself unable to hold them back. For once, I was overwhelmed with sorrow. An infinite sadness invaded me, and my body seemed to want to express all the misery in the world. I didn't know if I was crying for myself, for the end of a world I hated, or for that poor little girl who had no hope of survival except for an old man who was as repulsive as he was useless. Head in my hands, I definitively surrendered to this pain that was gnawing at me, letting heavy tears run down my face. Suddenly, a delicate skin brushed my forearm.

"It's going to be okay, Mr. Patrick."

These words were like an electric shock, and I swallowed one last sob as I turned my head towards the girl. She was looking at me with big, wet eyes. Her face distorted with grief, she repeated:

"It's going to be okay, Mr. Patrick."

She collapsed in turn, and for the first time, I saw her cry. Until then, the wardrobe had served as a pretext for my cowardice, and I had left her to purge her grief alone. Her desperation had the effect of a big cup of coffee after a hangover, and getting a grip on myself, I pulled her into my arms. This gesture came to me naturally, and I felt the need to protect her more than ever. We shared that embrace for several minutes, and as she calmed down, her face buried in my chest, I began to pull myself together. I gently stroked her hair and whispered to her:

"Yes, it's going to be okay. So, are you ready to go find your papa and Arnaud?"

She slowly pulled away, keeping her small hand on my arm. She looked deeply into my eyes, as if judging my ability to help her find her family, and stated distinctly:

"Yes."

"Then, let's go," I replied.

I stood up and, after running my hand through her hair one last time, headed to my bedroom. The mobile was still hanging from the top of the wardrobe. I cleared the space between the window and the piece of furniture and began to push it. Each jolt made the pieces of metal dance at the end of their strings in a ballet of spindly, hanged men. My forehead was quickly getting covered in sweat as the window slowly got closer. A few minutes later, and after several breaks, the fingers of the chime finally protruded through the opening. The metal elements hung limply, not showing the slightest movement: it was still early, and the wind had not picked up yet.

The wait was painful and exasperatingly long. I kept moving, going from one observation post to another in the hope of seeing any sign that the wind was coming. From the bathroom window, I stared at the treetops looming on the edge of my property a few hundred yards away. Motionless and impassive in the face of my nervousness. From the bedroom window, I gazed at the golden expanse of my fields, as still as a Van Gogh painting. A sad snapshot that condemned me to wait patiently in suffering. Only the zombies, with their slow, jerky movements, broke the monotony of this tableau. They were everywhere. Some were circling the house perpetually, hungry satellites orbiting their meal. Others came and went senselessly with a maddening idleness.

All I wanted was one thing: to finally take action and stop thinking. The image of the old man that the water in the tub had reflected back at me haunted me as soon as I closed my eyes or took the time to calm my nerves. To escape his gaze and forget his ominous presence, I replayed the plan on a loop in my head and dragged myself from room to room for no apparent reason. If the wind finally decided to pick up, all would be well. I was convinced of it.

For her part, the little girl was proving to be incredibly patient. Sitting on what was left of my bed, her legs dangling in the air, she waited calmly, simply glancing at me every now and then. My edginess didn't seem to affect her. However, when a slight metallic noise came from outside, she screamed with joy:

"There it is! It's here!"

I had heard it, too, and I rushed to the bathroom window. The world was finally coming alive. The tree branches began their dance, while the ears of wheat quivered impatiently in anticipation of the spectacle they were about to witness: our escape.

Ten minutes later, fierce gusts arrived and made the giant mobile moan. Luck finally seemed to be on our side, and almost all the zombies could now be found under the bedroom window. They were stretching out their arms towards the pendulums in the hope of grabbing hold of them. With each metallic clink, the horde let out an angry growl. Hundreds of nefarious fingers twisted towards the sky, writhing like the ferocious jaws of a school of piranhas. To them, the sound that was echoing through the fields was synonymous with life, and their impatience was growing as they jostled and trampled each other. The weakest zombies – the dead bodies of children and of those who had lost the use of some of their limbs during their transformation – found themselves crushed under the weight of the hungriest ones. Indifferent, they tirelessly stretched their emaciated limbs towards the mobile. The call of hunger was stronger, and the pack, united by this insatiable appetite, responded in unison.

I watched them for several minutes through the couple-inch gap that remained between the top of the wardrobe and the upper edge of the window. Standing on the bed and leaning on the dusty wood, I was careful not to make a sound. I held my breath when the metallic song stopped and the zombies, like grasshoppers with amnesia, began to disperse again. Luckily, the mobile was quickly coming back to life, and it was no more than a minute before their interest was aroused again. Reassured, I got off the bed and sat down next to the little one. She already had her backpack on.

"I guess now is the time to go."

I stood up and grabbed my overly heavy bag. I had no idea what we would do once we left, but I imagined us wandering the country roads in search of food and water. The thought of rushing headlong into the unknown like this made my blood run cold, and I refused to do so without being well-equipped, even if it meant putting a heavy, crushing sack on my back. Only my survival and the girl's were pushing me to launch myself into this madness. I didn't know what the next day would look like, or even if I would see it, but I was sure of one thing: staying here meant certain death. We had to go for it today. I had to summon the courage and accept living from day to day, leaving behind me those long years of Soviet planning of my life. The clock of time had been rewound, giving way to a new paradigm, a broken pendulum that marked an insane world where the dead hunted the living. Now was the time to leave, the time to take control of my destiny, at least for a few minutes. My hand closed around the little girl's shoulder.

"So, let's go."

We made our way discreetly to the bathroom window. A few zombies, too far away to hear the wind chimes, continued to roam the fields, dragging their bodies slowly and flattening the ears of wheat. I hoped that they wouldn't see us and that our silhouettes, perched on top of the barn, wouldn't interest them. I stepped over the ledge and reached my hand back inside. The little one was planted a good three feet from the opening, as if the thought of crossing the roof had taken all her strength away. She was looking at me wide-eyed.

"Don't worry, we'll go together. I will stay behind you. Nothing is going to happen to you. Okay?"

By way of response, she took a small step forward and grabbed my hand. Her tiny fingers displayed surprising strength, and her grip left little in doubt about the fear she was feeling. I pulled her towards me, slipped my hands under her armpits, and hoisted her up to get her through the window. She let me do it, but her feet had barely touched the roof tiles when she gripped the windowsill firmly, determined not to take one more step.

I had not considered this situation even though I myself had been frightened during my crossing. I cursed my stupidity, but I didn't have time to think about it anymore. I took the little girl in my arms. Getting her out of the house had seemed easy to me, but now her weight felt like a terrifying burden. My huge backpack, which could throw me off balance at any moment, my paunchy stomach, and carrying the girl probably made me the most pathetic tightrope walker in history. From a distance, my figure must have looked like a trembling Michelin Man who had decided to end his life in a fatal fall.

Now motionless, the girl had buried her face in my neck, which she was holding tightly. Overwhelmed by the weight of my load and the weight of the responsibilities that flowed from it, I started walking as the mobile continued to make itself heard. Whenever the zombies moaned in chorus, my steps became more uncertain. The terror that had overcome me the first time I did this filled me again. Even though I knew no decomposing mouth was waiting for me below, my muscles refused to obey me. They had contracted, as if from a cramp, and every movement became torture. I dragged myself along hazardously and painfully, my gaze fixed on my feet. Each stride was agony, but the breach in the roof eventually appeared. I felt like I'd been through the wringer. I gently knelt down and sat the little girl on the ledge.

"Hold on tight. I'll go down first, and then you will join me. Okay?" I said to her between two gulps of air.

I sat down next to her and slowly slid into the barn's cool, dark interior, onto the top of the first haystack. I crouched down, ready to begin the descent, when the stack was suddenly knocked off balance by my weight. Sensing that I was about to fall, I tried to grip the edge of the hole, but my unstable perch buckled under my feet. In a final attempt to catch myself, I dug my fingers into the dense, dry blades of bundled grass, but all I managed to do was take them down with me. The fall only lasted a fraction of a second and, after bouncing off another, particularly hard bale, I fell heavily to the ground. The bag cushioned the impact, but my back started throbbing terribly, right where one of the cans of food had crushed my flesh through the fabric.

The little girl couldn't help but scream when she saw me tumble down, but that was the least of my concerns. Not only had the bales of hay in the stack collapsed to the ground with a thunderous noise and knocked over many tools with an absolute racket, but access from the roof had become impossible. Panicked, I threw my bag against the tractor, which I had almost hit when I fell.

I glanced furtively towards the hole, from which a worried face emerged, and rushed towards the small, dusty window that overlooked the inner courtyard. My heart jumped in my chest when I saw the pack of zombies crawling determinedly towards the barn. The mobile had ceased to interest them, and the promise of a fresh, wriggling meal was guiding them towards us. We were trapped.

I grabbed the bunch of keys that was hanging from a rusty nail to the right of the window, just next to the huge iron hinges on the barn's double-wing doors. I quickly located the key to the tractor and slammed it into the ignition.

The moans were getting closer, and the crunching of the gravel in the yard was becoming more and more worrisome. I dashed under the opening in the roof.

"Throw me your bag! You're going to have to jump!"

The girl's face went white, and she began to cry.

"I can't, Mr. Patrick."

I didn't have time to argue, and panic gave way to anger. I shouted:

"You want to kill me, is that it? Do you want to end up like your mother, devoured by these monsters? Don't you want to see your father and your brother again?"

Her sobs had redoubled in intensity, but they seemed like a harmless murmur what with the howls from the courtyard making the walls of the building shake.

"Jump!" I yelled at her. "I'll catch you!"

Suddenly, her bag crashed at my feet. But she had disappeared. For a few seconds, I thought she had given up all hope and gone back to the house, but out of the blue, she threw herself into the void. In a fraction of a second, her body came out of the darkness and landed in my arms, shaking with sobs.

I wasted no time. I set her down on the tractor's thin bench and loaded our bags in the back, where I usually put a cooler with a few cold beers when I had to work in the sun. It was a small tractor with thick black wheels, taller at the rear than in the front. At that precise moment, I regretted not having chosen the model with a cabin that the salesman had tried to get me to buy. The promotion had been attractive, and the merchant's speech almost convincing, but I had preferred to opt for a traditional model. The one my father probably would have chosen, too. The vehicle seemed naked to me with its simple seat and long, mud-covered hood. All the zombies would have to do was reach out their arms in order to wallow in a culinary orgy.

With a knot in my stomach, I rushed to the back of the barn and grabbed a heavy bolt cutter and a rusty shovel. I took one last look at the workshop sprawled behind the stockpile of straw and then ran to the door.

A chain held the two panels closed. I had no choice but to cut it, the padlock being on the other side, shaking as the zombies approached. The pliers' teeth fiercely bit into the iron of the chain, which soon collapsed to the ground with a metallic clatter, ringing the dinner bell for the undead who were now gathering just a few feet away. I left the door closed and swung the shovel into the back of the tractor. As I was about to start it, a crazy idea crossed my mind. I hastened over to the gas can that was lying next to the hayrack and poured its contents onto the straw. The liquid quickly soaked into the hay, and the smell of the fuel choked me for a few seconds. The little one was cowering on the bench seat, and I could feel the weight of her wet eyes on me.

I pulled my lighter from the front pocket of the bag and summoned its flickering little flame with a quick touch of my thumb. I quickly ignited a stalk of straw and threw it onto the gasoline-soaked hay. Upon contact with the liquid, fire broke out, and thick smoke began to waft as I got back in my seat and turned the key. The engine sputtered, and then it filled the barn with a loud, reassuring sound that barely managed to cover the crackle of the spreading blaze. I stepped on the accelerator without releasing the clutch, letting the tractor rumble in response to the groans of the walking corpses, then jerked us forward.

Despite our vehicle's lack of power, the two doors separated violently as we crossed the threshold, throwing the first zombies to the ground. The horde was right in front of us, ready to swallow us.

I grabbed the shovel with my right hand and started a ninety-degree turn, holding the steering wheel firmly with my other hand. Then, like a knight wielding a flail on his noble steed, I whirled my makeshift weapon sharply above my head, slamming it down rhythmically on the arms reaching towards us. The girl made herself as small as possible and pressed her face against my thigh, her eyes closed. The wheels bit into the ground as I floored the tractor. The creatures howled and scratched their claws in the air as we sped through their fingers. Within seconds, we emerged from the putrid mass, but two zombies were standing in our way. They had suddenly appeared at the corner of the barn, probably attracted by the commotion that had just occurred. Going along the wall, I could not avoid them without getting the vehicle dangerously close to the crowd of the dead. With the pedal already to the metal, I plowed into them. The first one, a young man around twenty whose T-shirt had been completely torn off, was flipped over by the collision, and his unnatural existence ended under the tractor's wheels. The second one, much more energetic, managed to cling to the hood, his blank gaze fixed on me.

When we reached the end of the building, I initiated another right-hand turn, towards the woods that extended beyond my fields, fleeing as far as I could from the cursed road. Despite the violent change of direction, the zombie was still holding on tight, trying to pull himself up towards us.

A thick black cloud was emerging from the barn now, and I could already feel the blazing heat taking control there. I had no time to lose. I wedged the steering wheel between my knees and, letting it go for a few moments, grabbed the shovel with both hands and slammed it down on the parasite's head several times. His teeth dug ferociously into the bumper, leaving long scratches there, before breaking away from the eager jaw of the corpse, who soon met the same fate as his companion.

The slow but determined horde continued to gain ground a few dozen yards away, in a chase scene the cinema never would have wanted. The zombies were advancing painfully, like disjointed puppets, while the hero, an old man with a prominent gut, charged ahead in his race car at twenty-five miles per hour. James Bond would have died of laughter.

More monsters were getting dangerously close when suddenly, all of our attackers were knocked down like bowling pins. The explosion was terrible and knocked the wind out of me, a piercing hiss ripping through my ears. Surprised by the magnitude of the shock, the little girl jumped in terror beside me, gripped my pants tightly, and held on. My mind and my body both shaken, I stopped the vehicle and looked behind me.

The fire had reached the propane tank, which could not withstand the terrifying furnace that was the barn. The damage was considerable. The barn had been strewn all around in a shower of flaming debris. A great void sat where the building had been, and the flames were now devouring the attached house. The roof was crumbling under the damage from the fire, and soon there would be nothing left but the stone walls.

I felt a cruel twinge in my heart when I saw the oak in the yard being eaten away by the blaze. Its magnificent foliage was replaced by a sad, grey veil where the fire had fulfilled its lethal function. The coolness of its shade and the song of the birds that came to take refuge there would be nothing more than a distant memory, another one consumed in this madness.

"Forgive me, my old friend," I told the tree before restarting the tractor, as the nearest zombies were already getting back up.

The horde, on the other hand, had been carried off by the blast, reduced to ashes. None of them were left. A slight smile appeared on my lips: I had destroyed the squatters who had come and turned my life upside down. If I could no longer enjoy the tranquility of my home, no one could, and especially not a bunch of vile corpses.

I hit the accelerator and headed for the forest. A track opened its arms to us, inviting us to flee. Far from the past, far from the road, far from the fire that had spread to the fields and was growing in intensity.

CHAPTER 6
AT THE FOOT OF MY TREE

We were going as fast as we could through the woods. The tractor's wheels were being guided by thick ruts dug into the clay soil on either side of the path. Jolts shook every part of our bodies as the machine, on its last legs after the chase, grunted louder and louder.

With one arm hooked under mine, the little girl couldn't stop herself from looking behind us to make sure she had indeed left behind the hell that had spread in front of her eyes. The blaze had spiraled out of control, and the strong, violent mistral wind was fanning the flames determinedly. The fire was spreading across my fields as the wind blew sparks into the distance, widening the extent of the inferno. Fortunately for us, the gusts were blowing in the opposite direction of our escape, pushing the flames towards the road.

Hardly a summer went by without some sicko deciding to play the sorcerer's apprentice in the forests of southern France, thus providing the media with one of their favorite perennial stories. I knew how easily and quickly acres could go up in smoke.

Flooring it, I intended to put a large distance between the front line of the blaze and us. A few days earlier, I would have been truly ashamed of becoming a member of the crazed arsonist club, and yet, I had no remorse. I was well aware that the fire would ravage everything in its path and leave nothing but smoldering ashes behind it, but I still rejoiced to see it get rid of a large number of zombies. No Canadair firefighting jet would be taking off from the airport in Marignane to put an end to the flames' fury and these infernal creatures' torment.

At times, unsteady grey figures emerged from the dark trunks of the pines and moved hopelessly towards us. I had hoped the woods would be completely deserted, but some zombies had invaded them as well, dragging their rotten carcasses with difficulty between the thickets and the tree branches that had the audacity to get too close to the ground.

I remained vigilant, watching for any suspicious shadows, fearful that they might attack us by surprise.

The route plunged into denser, thicker vegetation. Two heavy coats of foliage and branches framed the path: the ideal place for an ambush. A concept that the zombies would be unable to put into practice by joining forces. Lucky for us...

The land, which had been flat until then, abruptly began a steep climb, and the tractor's wheezing got worse. The poorly oiled mechanisms in the motor began to struggle severely, and the vehicle was having a hard time moving. Every yard was torture for it, and when we finally arrived at the top of the hill, a light cloud of vapor was billowing out from under the hood.

A gap in the vegetation allowed us to see the orange roofs of a farm down below. Seen from here, the fields of wheat and sunflowers that surrounded it were magnificent, but the view was spoiled by slowly-walking silhouettes. I saw a dozen of them and wondered if any of them had had the pleasure of devouring that old bastard Jules, the owner of the farm, who always found a way to return the cooperative's vehicles in deplorable condition.

The path came out in the middle of his fields. We thus had no choice but to head towards the zombies that were wandering there, waiting for prey. Coasting, I let the tractor ride quietly down the hill, ready to take off like a shot when we came out from among the trees. Carried along by its own weight and ours, the old machine descended at high speed. The irregularities in the path tossed us in all directions, and the little girl clung to my arm as our hindquarters periodically bounced off the seat.

As we approached the fields, with my muscles tingling, I shifted gears and took advantage of the vehicle's inertia to propel us forward. We had emerged from the protection of the trees, and the crops were spread out on either side of the path. The view was clear, and the zombies were far enough away for us to pass through without any inconvenience. Drawn out of their wandering torpor, they had nevertheless started coming, their eyes fixed on us. We only had a few hundred yards to go before reaching the forested hills beyond which the village where the little one had told me she lived was located.

We were arriving at a crossing, which led to the farm on our right, when without warning the tractor stopped. Like a wounded animal, harassed by an endless hunt, the machine had dropped dead. The burning hood again let out a shimmering cloud of vapor. Incredulous, I turned the key in the ignition, convinced that the vehicle would restart without any difficulty. But, at death's door, the engine remained silent. I glanced around us. The zombies were getting dangerously close. A dozen of them were converging from the surrounding fields as a much larger number, attracted by the tractor's final gasps, left the interior of the nearby farm. The building seemed to be spewing out entire legions of the dead, ready to seize any potential prey. They never thought it would be served up on a platter.

Fear gripped my stomach, and the adrenaline rush, which had kept me going during our breakaway, was having no more effect. I attacked the starter, vigorously turning the key, unable to keep my mind clear. I couldn't come to terms with this situation, which was worthy of the biggest dud of a movie: the tractor breaking down at the worst possible time, leaving us exposed within reach of a new horde of zombies. I was trying to convince myself that this scene would end up on the cutting room floor, that the hero wouldn't perish in such an absurd way, and yet I remained immobile, my eyes riveted on the approaching preda-tors. I was staring at the nearest zombie, a man in his forties dressed in canvas pants and a bloodstained, short-sleeved shirt, unable to look away from his ripped-open carotid artery, when my eyes caught an indistinct movement alongside the tractor. Lightning quick, an oval shape raced down the path in the direction of the forest before coming to a stop.

"Mr. Patrick!" she cried several times with all her might.

The liveliness of the thing drew me out of my vegetative state, and the face of the little girl, heavily loaded with her backpack, took shape instead. I turned, grabbed the strap of my bag in one hand, the shovel in the other, and ran to join her.

Then, the forty-something year-old blocked my way and threw himself onto me. The speed of the attack caught me off guard, and I fell to the ground with my attacker in a cloud of dust. The shock knocked the wind out of me. A foul smell entered my nostrils as the monster opened its filthy mouth wide, just inches from my face. I didn't give him time to finish his deadly kiss and pushed him away with all my strength. He rolled onto his side and tried to get up: way too slowly. Already standing, I took the handle of the shovel in both hands and struck the edge of the tool against my assailant's skull. The iron sank into the rotten flesh like a sharp ax, splitting the cranium in two with a blood-curdling crack. The zombie lay motionless, finally brought back to his natural state of death. With my foot resting on his vile face, I freed the shovel, taking with it part of the corpse's decomposed brain.

My backpack had rolled to the ground; I loaded it on my shoulders and made my way over to the little one. The attack had brought me back to reality. I left the tractor behind me with no hesitation, not even looking back.

"Run!" I yelled as I neared her.

She didn't have to be told twice; she accelerated in the direction of the forest. I caught up with her in a few strides. Her bag was bouncing and slamming hard against her lower back with every step as her short legs struggled to keep up with my pace.

"Wait, give me that," I said, grabbing the top handle of her bag.

She slid out of the straps immediately, looked behind us, and instantly resumed her run, a look of distress on her face. I didn't have to turn around to know the zombies had gotten closer; their moans were growing constantly louder.

I wished fear could give me wings, but the weight of my cargo negated the effect of any biochemical processes that would have allowed my body to outdo itself. All I could manage to do was trot painfully, my gaze staring straight ahead at the little girl, who was running with a new ease, as if in a schoolyard. By the time she got to the edge of the forest, we had only gone about a hundred yards, and my heart was about to explode in my chest. My forehead was covered in sweat, and my clothes were soaked. I took a break, placing my hands on my thighs to catch my breath. With my mouth wide open, I inhaled long gulps of hot, suffocating air.

The zombies could only win at this little game of cat and mouse. Neither heat, nor fatigue, nor dehydration, and even less so physical pain would put an end to their hunt. They would advance patiently, never stopping, until we were completely exhausted, accepted our sad fate, and let ourselves be caught. Our only chance was to put as much distance as possible between the horde and us, in the hope that they would eventually lose track of us.

The fields we had just crossed occupied the bottom of a valley between two hills, and the path that stretched in front of us went up slightly. It had been dug directly into the side of the hill and was bordered by a high, almost vertical embankment made of stone and clay. At the top, there was a dense tangle of roots. We could take advantage of such rough terrain: the zombies, with their poor motor skills, would be unable to keep up with us.

I straightened up and ran straight towards the slope. My boots sank into the crumbly clay, and despite my momentum, I only climbed about six feet. I scraped the ground with my right foot, creating a tiny avalanche of dirt pellets below, and dug out a small step that I leaned on to stabilize myself.

The little one approached me without a word, casting worried looks behind her incessantly.

"We're going to climb. Give me your hand."

I threw her bag and the shovel up the embankment and leaned towards her, holding out my arm, all while making sure I didn't become unbalanced by my own load.

"Hold on, I'm going to hoist you up to the top."

She stepped back a few feet, then launched herself at me, both arms out in front of her. I grabbed her wrist and pulled her to me; then, one hand on her back, I helped her go up the slope.

"Climb, go on."

She tried to move forward, but the ground gave way under her feet as mine slowly descended towards the path. On all fours, like an amateur mountaineer, she attempted to climb, but the holds she was clinging to slipped through her fingers. With great effort and thanks to my constant pushing, however, she was getting closer to the first roots. The zombies had already made up for much of their lost time and were only twenty yards away. The distance that separated us was visibly shrinking.

As the girl slipped again, I gave her a final push, and she finally managed to find a solid hold.

Off balance, I hurtled down the embankment and fell flat on my face on the path. The mob, only fifteen yards away now, seemed to speed up as they approached their prey.

Refusing to give in to the panic that had almost cost me my life a few minutes earlier, I got up and ran in the zombies' direction. Seeing me coming, almost able to catch me, they let out a moan in unison. A monstrous ode sung by a single entity ruled by the god of Hunger. But, when I turned around and ran away at full speed, the cries escaping from their frustrated mouths intensified. I sped towards the clay slope and managed to propel myself up to the roots in three strides. I grabbed one of the roots, but – with my vision suddenly clouded by the effort – I wasn't able to react when it broke on one side. For all that, I hadn't let go; I was holding it with both hands, like a fragile rope about to drop me into the rotting hell that awaited me at the foot of the slope. Completely exhausted but refusing to drop the dead weight that was my bag, I couldn't hoist myself up. Each movement loosened the root more.

All of a sudden, my eyesight stabilized, and my gaze fell on the girl's horrified face. The corpses were trying to climb the embankment, bringing their gaunt hands closer to the bag's straps. In a last-ditch effort, and with the sole desire of erasing that terrified expression from the face of my companion to the apocalypse, I managed to grab hold of a thicker root and pull myself up to the top. The operation was a miracle, and I lay on the ground, trying to catch my breath and calm myself down. This madness was going to kill me in the long run.

With my cheek pressed heavily against the thorn-covered, black earth, and the rest of my body completely slack, emptied of all strength, I inhaled deep breaths of air. I lay inert, like a whale stranded in the middle of a forest in Provence. Pain was coursing through every single one of my muscles, yet I felt like I was floating outside of my body, my exhausted mind concentrating on minor things and forgetting the scraping of the zombies who were trying to reach us. My attention focused on a drop of sweat that was beading on the edge of my scalp and slowly sliding down the arch of my brow before accelerating, crossing my entire forehead and disappearing into the ground. Long after it fell, I continued to feel its track on my skin, a thin groove with blackish edges laden with grime.

I don't know how long I stayed there, stretched out like that, letting my thoughts wander freely, but when I finally pulled my torso off the ground, the little girl was sitting down a little higher up. She was staring at the dead who persisted in climbing the slope. Whenever one of them managed to lift its heavy, blood-filled legs high enough to move up the embankment, it slipped and crashed into its peers, creating scree. An impressive mound of freshly turned dirt had already formed down below, the fruit of the horde's vain efforts. No monster had yet come up with the idea of looking for another means of access; they were all milling about where the distance between their prey and their greedy gobs was the smallest. Their stupidity condemned them to be on a forced diet, which made me quite happy.

As I regained lucidity, the zombies' proximity became my first concern again. Pressing on one knee and using my hands, I raised my heavy carcass. The pain was still sharp and would turn into terrible aching in the days to come, but thinking about the future was a luxury I could not afford. The little one had stood up as well.

"All good? Are you ready to go?" I asked her with a forced smile.

She stared at me for a moment then, lowering her eyes, replied:

"I was scared."

"Me, too," I added spontaneously.

It was the truth. I had never felt such fear and didn't have the strength to hide it. She took a step forward and extended her hand towards my face. Wary, I leaned forward without a word. She awkwardly ran her fingertips over my cheek.

"You had some dirt," she murmured timidly.

This surge of tenderness left me speechless, and I patted her hair on the sly before taking her hand and leading her towards the top of the hill. The zombies expressed their anger in an outpouring of cries of rage as they saw our silhouettes disappear between the trunks of the oaks and pines that lined the slope.

On weak legs, we climbed the hill without a word, then slid to the bottom of a valley before ascending yet another hill. The density of the vegetation made our progress difficult but considerably reduced the probability of coming face to face with a zombie. The many scratches on my face – souvenirs from the thorns on the junipers that were abundant on this southern side – were quite paltry compared to the fate one of the living dead could have in store for me.

Several hours had passed since our meeting with the horde when we came to the end of a particularly grueling climb. When we got to the summit, there was little doubt that we would not be going any further. My thighs were on fire, and my hands were shaking in a disturbing way. No longer having the strength to lift her head, the little one hadn't taken her eyes off her feet for a long while. It was only six o'clock, though, and the day was far from over. If we hadn't encountered the horde, the trail certainly would have already led us to the village. But our state of fatigue would not permit us to continue our journey, and I preferred to camp here, high up, rather than take the risk of collapsing deep in a valley where the zombies could get to us much more easily.

I slipped off my bag with a sigh of relief and leaned back against the trunk of a gigantic evergreen oak tree. The little girl had continued to move forward, as if walking had become an automatic reflex imposed on her exhausted body by a brain that was disconnected from reality. She turned around when she heard the muffled sound of the bag hitting the ground.

"We'll stop here," I said, motioning for her to come back towards me. "I don't know about you, but I can't take anymore. I won't go any further."

I wanted to ask her if everything was okay, but I already knew what she would say. What good are these stupid civilities in a world where the answer is bound to be *absolutely not?*

I undid the bag and pulled out a water bottle that was deformed from the impact of my various falls. We had already drunk half of it, but my throat was still dry from thirst. I held it out to the little one, who threw herself at it. I watched her take a long sip and then a second, not able to tell her to be careful. I took back the bottle, which had significantly less in it now, and put it away without even wetting my lips. Suddenly, the girl turned to me, looking agitated.

"I drank too much. I need to pee," she complained, hopping from one foot to the other in an unexpected burst of energy.

For the first time since the start of this madness, all my anxiety disappeared into thin air, and I roared with laughter. And when she stared at me sulkily, annoyed by my reaction, I laughed even harder. Very quickly, carried away by my outburst of good humor, the little one stopped pouting and joined in my euphoria.

I hadn't laughed like that in a very long time. It had taken the end of the world and the death of probably several million people for me to allow myself a few minutes to enjoy the present moment.

My usual seriousness having returned, but with my cheeks still all flushed, I rummaged in the bottom of the bag and pulled out a roll of toilet paper.

"Off you go! Whatever you do, if you hear or see anything, you call me and you run away, got it?"

She nodded and disappeared behind me, leaving me alone at the foot of my tree. I was wondering how we would spend the night – sleeping on the ground and out in the open didn't really entice me – when the little girl cried out my name.

I shot to my feet, ignoring the protests from my muscles, tore the shovel from the ties that held it to the bag, and hastened in her direction. My heart was pounding but immediately calmed down when I saw the girl, unharmed, in her panties, her pants lowered in an absurd fashion.

"Mr. Patrick, look!" she exclaimed, pointing at a dark mass between the trees: hanging between two pines, a wooden treehouse patiently awaited its future tenants.

"I'll leave you to your business. I'm going to go get the bags," I told her as I walked away.

Luck was finally smiling on us. The structure appeared to be in pretty good condition, and we could sleep without fear of being slaughtered in our sleep by a lone prowler. I sat back down against the evergreen oak, allowing a few minutes to pass before gathering our gear and rejoining the little girl.

She hadn't lost a minute and was already exploring the foot of the two pines.

"We can go up that way," she yelled to me when she saw me coming. "There's something like a ladder!"

The floor of the cabin was about nine feet above the ground and was supported by several fairly thick beams, securely screwed into the trunks of the twin trees. It was most likely the work of an adult: probably a hunter's shack. The memory of my father in his fatigues crossed my mind, but I immediately pushed it away.

"I'll go up first, and if all goes well, we'll settle in for the night."

Several planks had been nailed directly into one of the trunks and acted as a ladder leading to an opening in the floor. More acrobatics on this insane day.

Despite the pain in my legs, I easily reached the entrance to the hut and stuck my upper body through the hole. The place was much more spacious than I had expected, maybe 45 or 50 square feet. A real palace in our situation. The fitted-out area was completely enclosed by walls made of planks, except for a narrow horizontal window that looked out onto an open expanse at the bottom of the hill. The perfect place to slaughter partridges and other winged game. I hoisted the rest of my body up inside.

I couldn't help but smile when I saw the empty bottles stacked in a corner, lying under the lustful gaze of a woman revealing generous breasts. Hunters had always had the art of cultivating clichés. I snatched the image from the wall, not without giving it an interested glance, and tossed it into an empty cartridge box lying at the far end of the shelter. I didn't know if the sight of that poster would have had any effect on the little girl after the trauma she had suffered, but I preferred not to have to explain why it was there. I stuck my head through the opening. The girl was waiting impatiently at the foot of the ladder with her backpack on.

"It's perfect!" I told her with a big smile.

She already had one foot on the first rung when I added:

"Wait, I'm going to come down to help you."

Standing under the ladder, I waited for her to enter the cabin before grabbing my bag and joining her. She had started to unpack a few clothes and was stacking them as a sort of pillow. Mental fatigue was suddenly added to my muscular distress, and my body became very heavy. I took off the motorcycle jacket, which was stuck to my soaked T-shirt, and rolled it into a ball. After sentencing me to suffer even more from the heat all day long, it was only fair that it should allow me a good nap.

I took one last look outside, and in the distance, I could make out the ocher roofs of the buildings in the center of the girl's village. My brain wanted to stay awake and plan our next move, but exhaustion got the better of me, and I fell back gently against my makeshift pillow.

CHAPTER 7
FUNEREAL HORN

I woke with a start. The long, plaintive moan had pulled me out of my slumber. I hadn't slept so well since the onset of the carnage: my eyelids had remained tightly closed the whole night long, letting my body regain strength. The tranquility of the forest and my exhaustion certainly had a lot to do with it.

Reinvigorated, I stared at the thin rectangle of light that the narrow window was projecting onto the floor. The sun had almost reached its zenith already.

My mind still foggy from the long rest, I made sure the little one was still there. She was sleeping peacefully, at the other end of the cabin, in the fetal position.

A growl, loud and distinct, reminded me of the reason I woke up, and I rushed to the opening. A zombie was standing at the foot of the shelter.

When he saw my head pop out, he moaned again and stretched his arms out towards me. I couldn't believe one of those bastards had bothered to come and stalk us this far. How had he spotted us, and how had he managed to climb the hill? I looked at him intently. He must have been in his twenties, maybe a college student or some slacker from this mediocre new generation before his transformation. Unlike his fellow maniacs, his body appeared to be devoid of physical injuries, and the wide V-neck of his T-shirt hinted at unharmed, grey-ish skin. His movements, although imprecise, were a lot less jerky and much livelier. His impatience was growing, and he began to scream continuously. I turned around to grab the shovel and almost knocked over the little girl, who had approached, dragged from her torpor by the howling.

"Good morning," she said, sticking her head through the opening.

"Good morning," I answered her simply as she pulled back, a look of disgust on her face.

"Mr. Patrick, are you going to kill him, like yesterday?" she asked me, as if this were just one trivial matter among many others.

Uncomfortable, I reflected for a moment:

"He is already dead. But yes, I am going to kill him."

Mentioning the word "kill" was painful. For the first time, the face of the man I had cowardly thrown into the void when it all began hadn't haunted me that night, and I didn't want to remember that moment any longer. In any case, taking out zombies was not murder: you can't kill what is already dead. It was good. A necessity.

I grabbed the handle of the shovel, already anxious about the idea of getting closer to the monster. I had no problem saying I was going to take care of him, but the reality was different.

The situation was really not to my advantage. Despite the length of the tool, I had to venture onto the ladder in order to reach him. Yet another acrobatic maneuver that my young, slender body would surely accept without difficulty. Yeah, right.

I was terrified at the thought of sliding through the space because I already knew that my corpulence would prevent me from seeing where I was stepping. I hated doing things blindly, especially if my life depended on it. Having no other choice, I went through the opening anyway, after figuring the zombie would be unable to reach the final three rungs. That left me about two and a half feet to position myself and hit him with the fatal blow. The tip of my shoe groped at the tree trunk and quickly found the ladder's first wooden plank. With three-quarters of my body still inside the hut, I crouched down and stuck my foot out to the second step. With my torso surrounded by the floor, I was having a hard time seeing the zombie, but I could hear him redoubling his efforts down below. I tried to bend my chest in order to get my head clear, but the space was way too tight, and my agonizing joints were screaming bloody murder at this pathetic contortionist act. Going down one more tier was imperative, but it scared me. I had guessed that the creature was incapable of reaching the next rung, but I was suddenly unsure of my analysis of the situation. My ankle could already feel the insolent pressure of the monster's claws, and my whole body was shaking at the idea of being dragged to the ground.

The little one had sat down cross-legged, her head in her hands. Her fingers were digging into her cheeks and pushing up her freckled cheekbones, making her look like a mischievous mouse.

She was smiling at me.

"It looked easier yesterday. Too bad the tractor broke. We would have crushed him!"

Her determination struck me. She was not afraid. She was counting on me, and her face radiated genuine confidence. She didn't seem to care that her hero was a chubby old man acting like a chimpanzee. She believed in me.

The third rung now seemed like an easily attainable step. I had to have faith in myself. I slid through and crouched down, both feet on the wooden bar, my head finally outside the shack. The position was uncomfortable. I gripped the first step tightly, my fingers tucked between the plank and the bark of the pine tree. I asked the girl to give me the shovel, and the handle immediately appeared through the opening. With my right hand, I grabbed it almost at its end, thus ensuring sufficient reach to attain my target. The tool felt surprisingly heavy to me. I fervently hoped the zombie's skull would make the same remark. Unfortunately, the floor limited my range of motion. I was reduced to just being able to bring the shovel down on top of my enemy. Sensing that the fingers holding me up were losing their confidence and becoming covered with a slippery veil of sweat, I tightened my grip around the wooden handle and hit the zombie a first time. I couldn't miss him.

He made no attempt to dodge the attack, and with his arms still up along the side of the trunk, he took the full blow. His head snapped backwards but almost immediately came back into place, oblivious to the affront it had just suffered. With difficulty, I brought the shovel back up towards me and repeated my assault several times. The top of his face took on a weird shape and color, but none of my blows broke his skull. I didn't have the strength. I probably could have continued like that until the repetitive shocks had the desired effect, but the tightness of my muscles was limiting my ape-like skills. Resting in the cabin was also out of the question. I didn't want to risk having more zombies arrive during that time.

I turned my head towards the opening and, not seeing the little girl, made my decision in a flash: I pushed with all my might against the board and threw myself into the air towards the slope. The fall lasted only a fraction of a second, and the carpet of thorns covering the ground partially cushioned the impact. However, I couldn't hold back a scream as a stinging pain shot through my injured ankle. I didn't have time to think about it. I lifted the shovel above my head and, now free in my movements, dealt an extremely violent blow to the zombie, who had immediately pounced at me. I wasn't lacking in strength this time. The corpse collapsed like a marionette whose strings had been severed by an evil puppeteer.

Hearing me scream, the little one also let out a cry before calling to me as loud as she could, powerless to look outside.

"I'm fine," I replied to reassure her, my eyes glued to the remains on the ground.

He was the first creature I could observe so closely without having a whole army of them on my back. I quickly surveyed his body and found no signs of wounds or bloodstains, except for the top of his crudely bashed head. How had he transformed? I had seen dozens of people being attacked by zombies before they became one. They had all been bitten, but this man hadn't been. I then remembered Mr. Tomato and his accident: he hadn't been a victim of zombie fangs either, and yet... A shiver ran through me at the idea that they might have been contaminated by an airborne virus, but I quickly abandoned this hypothesis.

A medical degree was not necessary to know that a virus, no matter how aggressive it was, could not survive in a heap of rotten flesh without a blood supply. These creatures' hearts were no longer functioning, evidenced by their ridiculously puffy lower limbs in which their blood had pooled. Gravity was doing good things by impeding their movements in this way, even though they were still moving and, for some, climbing hills. Hunger was making them capable of anything.

I was considering other explanations when the little girl's voice interrupted my train of thought.

"I can't move your bag, Mr. Patrick; it's heavy. We're leaving, right?"

I took my eyes off the corpse, almost immediately forgetting my concern. Whatever the origin of this aberration, only taking action mattered now.

"Wait, I'm coming. You're going to hurt yourself."

My ankle was throbbing terribly again. I winced in pain as I climbed the ladder, but I put on a neutral expression as I entered the hut. The girl had already packed our things. One of the sleeves of the motorcycle jacket was hanging from my awkwardly closed bag. I hadn't even put it on to take care of the zombie. What an idiot.

I hadn't planned to break camp so late, and the closer we got to the village, the more unbearable the heat became. The forest was much less dense as we went along, and the sun's rays were beating down on us. The black leather of my jacket was white hot and burned my skin. Summer had never seemed so hot and dry to me. The world had already shed all its tears of sorrow, and the ones from the sky had long since dried up. Mankind deserved no more than a few drops, a barely refreshing shower. The survivors could very well burn in their Earthly purgatory.

The village was not very far away. I could make out the county road leading there. It crossed the plain that stretched out at the foot of the hill, without any obstacles in its way. On either side, grapevines were carefully lined up as far as the eye could see, still unaware that their young branches would never be pruned again. In a few years, it would be impossible to move between the rows without having to cross an ocean of greenery. A few villas and the thick hedges that surrounded them broke the monotony of the landscape. They seemed deserted. Just like the road. Its asphalt glistened in the sun, free of any vehicles.

Notwithstanding the heat and the distance we had traveled since leaving the treehouse, the little girl hadn't complained once and was walking forward with a determined step. Her father and brother were waiting for her at the end of this winding path. She knew it.

I was afraid she was deluding herself, but I still held out hope that they were there. It was the only way we could get some order back in this world. For me to be alone again. With no responsibilities other than my bitch of a life.

"Tell me, where do you live exactly?" I asked her, starting to think her directions might be helpful to me.

"Not very far past Kevin's house," she replied casually.

"Kevin's house?"

"Yes, the big house along the road right there," she said, pointing to one of the isolated dwellings in the middle of the vineyards. "Mine is a little further, at the end of a small street."

A few hundred yards away, just before the entrance to the village, a residential area broke the lines of the fields of vines with its cramped buildings.

"Let's go, then. We'll get back on the road. I don't see anyone, but stay on your guard."

We began our descent towards the county road, eager to walk on less hostile ground. The soil in the vineyard had been turned recently, and large clods of dry earth rolled under our feet, torturing my still aching ankle, but our faces no longer had to fear the malicious slapping of branches. We were making slow progress, but I was having a harder and harder time containing the little girl's excitement. I kept grabbing her by the shoulder to make her slow down.

"Relax, will you?" I scolded her sharply as she accelerated again.

Attracting attention was the last thing we needed to do. Not so close to our goal. I tried to take her by the hand, but she pulled it away abruptly. She stopped and stared at me for a few moments without a word, her brow furrowed. Her gaze seemed to be challenging me: she had no more use for a stranger like me in order to get back home.

I wondered why I continued to hinder myself with such a burden, but I fell into step behind her anyway. My legs were hurrying after her on their own. Why was I following this insolent kid? I didn't need anyone.

Once again, I was acting the way society, with its codes of conduct, told me to. It had patiently instilled in us that only monsters were capable of abandoning a child, and I wasn't a monster. But the corpses had come back to life, and our civilization was dead and buried. You would have had to be crazy or desperate to encumber yourself with such a dead weight; I was neither of those things. Not yet. I was actually walking her home as a rare representative of Humanity, not as an individual. The species had to be saved, right? A few more minutes to go.

"Wait for me. I'm sorry for talking to you in that tone, but we have to be careful."

She slowed down without replying, and I caught up to her in one stride.

"Let's get back to the road."

We dove between two rows of vines perpendicular to the county road. I was tall enough to get a panoramic view of everything around us, but the little girl's vision was limited to a long corridor: glittering green walls, an azure ceiling, and a black horizon streaked with white.

We quickly arrived at the asphalt. The temperature was even hotter there. The tar had melted in places, and it stuck to our shoes. We had passed the house of the famous Kevin by about fifty yards, and the road was leading us to our final destination. Still out front, the little one followed the white line down the middle of the road. I had no trouble keeping up the pace, but she had definitely forgotten my reprimand. All of a sudden, she began to run.

"Stop! Wait!" I yelled at her as I tried to catch up with her.

At this speed, each step was true agony for my ankle. She got out ahead of me quickly and suddenly disappeared. A large building stood on the left, and a white and red sign marked the entrance to a street about ten yards away. The little one had dashed off there.

High hedges demarcated the small lots that surrounded the houses. Like the little girl in the vineyard, I was stuck in a tunnel full of unknowns. Double-locked gates took shape between the branches of the hedges; recesses allowing homeowners access to their garages emerged between two trees. The street was narrow. Inhospitable.

Still, I continued to drag myself along, and I left several villas behind me before catching sight of the girl. She had frozen in the middle of the street and was staring at one of the houses. I joined her in no time at all, with a knot in my stomach.

"Why did you take off like that?" I asked her, having a hard time masking my anger.

"Why is Papa's car open?" she whispered.

I turned to the object of her interest: a poorly parked, red family station wagon. The driver's front door was wide open. The girl's father must have been very much in a hurry when he got home. He'd had every reason to be, with no word from his wife and daughter when the world went nuts. The vehicle had come to a stop across the entrance to the garage near the gate that provided access to the yard from the street. There was no sign of life.

"Huh? Why is it open?" she repeated, her body shaking like a leaf.

I had no answer for her. None that she wanted to hear.

"I'll go take a look first, okay?" I said, taking her hand.

She did not shy away.

"You're going to stay in the car and wait for me to come back," I added, pulling her towards the station wagon. "You're going to lock yourself in there, and if anything happens, all you have to do is honk the horn to let me know. Okay?"

She climbed in without protesting and limply pressed the button to lock all the doors. All her energy had evaporated. Her father must have taken great care of his car if a simple open door would put her in such a condition. But I shared her concern.

I headed for the front door after a last look at the little girl, whose pained face barely protruded from behind the wheel. I knocked three times on the door, which opened directly onto the street, and waited for a few seconds. No one came. I knocked again. A long silence answered me. Had they left in another vehicle, or were they terrified and did not dare come open the door?

I walked past the station wagon again, avoiding the little one's gaze, and tried to open the gate that gave access to the patio attached to that side of the house. I pulled the lock by sliding my arm over the steel mesh door and went in. Child's play.

The yard had a real charm despite its small size. Although deserted, it resonated with intense activity. The flower beds were neatly tended and were buzzing to the rhythm of the insects that busied themselves there. Much like mine did years ago, the girl's mother appeared to cherish the Felicia daisies and their little blue flowers. They were everywhere. In their terracotta pots, some of the delicate plant's stems had even invaded the brick barbecue. A long wooden table, shaded by a white umbrella with its canopy wide open, presided in the middle of the yard. I imagined the little one's family getting together here on the weekends and enjoying the time spent together. But all of that was just ghostly bits and pieces from the past.

I walked along the side of the house, staying on the small concrete path that led to the patio, which two large, glass doors connected directly to the interior of the house. One of them was ajar. A very bad sign. I advanced calmly and stuck my head through the doorframe, not knowing what else to do. The temptation was way too strong, and just like in every bad horror movie ever made, I couldn't hold back these words:

"Is someone there?"

The house remained completely silent. I put my bag down outside and pulled out the hammer I had stored in it. If I were to encounter anything inside, the shovel would be too unwieldy. I entered the building, my fist tightened around the handle of my weapon. Everything seemed to be in order, as if the owners had not yet returned from work and the children were still at school. When I saw the front door, though, I realized that something was really wrong: an impressive bunch of keys was hanging from the lock. The key to the station wagon was there. Why had the little girl's father taken the time to close the front door behind him but left the patio door open? Had he abandoned the house and the car in a rush?

Despite the tension that was growing as the number of rooms to explore diminished, I continued to inspect the ground floor. Deserted. A heavy silence hung over the house. Everything was still.

The slightest creak made me jump, and the many mirrors lining the walls of the living room never lost an opportunity to play tricks on me. The steady but rapid beating of my heart echoed powerfully behind my eardrums as I moved from room to room.

I quickly found myself in the kitchen, the last place I hadn't yet searched. It was just as neat and tidy. Everything seemed perfect. The interior of the house was nothing like the yard I had entered through, which was resplendent with life and steeped in memories; everything inside was rigid, like a dismal staging at some furniture seller's. An empty shell whose soul had flown away with its inhabitants' personalities.

I couldn't help but peek in the cupboards. They were full of food. What a godsend. I closed their doors slowly and went to the bottom of the stairs, directly in front of the main entrance.

"Is someone there?" I repeated, certain there would be no answer.

If the little girl's family had been here, they had left a long time ago. I climbed a couple steps and stopped. I had heard something.

"Is someone there? Don't be scared; I'm not infected," I tried in vain.

Heavy drops of cold, slimy sweat were starting to bead on my forehead. Was it just a figment of my imagination, or simply the house creaking?

I squeezed my weapon firmly and continued my ascent, legs shaking. Each step was a victory over fear. I had promised myself not to let it overwhelm me again, but I continued to prove to be cowardly. My bravery remained a mystery; I was capable of jumping from the top of a ladder onto a zombie but was paralyzed at the thought of entering a deserted house. I was having a hard time understanding myself.

I moved along the wall, and as I was about to reach the landing, another muffled noise – a sort of gurgling sound – startled me.

"If someone is there, answer me!" I yelled, gradually losing my temper. "I have your daughter with me! So come on out!"

I only wanted one thing: to see the girl's father come running towards me with a bright smile on his lips, get his child back, and put a happy end to my babysitting adventures. But nothing seemed to want to happen as planned.

"Your daughter is with me, you hear? Your daughter, damn it!" I screamed at the top of my lungs as I hurled myself onto the landing.

The noise suddenly became much clearer. Someone, or something, was scratching behind one of the five closed doors upstairs. I took a deep breath and slowly walked over to the room where the scraping sounds were coming from. Just a few steps, and I no longer had any hope of finding the little girl's father and brother alive. Maybe it wasn't one of them, but a zombie was behind that door. I was sure of it.

Aware – or whatever the appropriate word for these things – of my presence, he was scratching his fingernails continuously over the wood. His moans were weak and plaintive, interspersed regularly with disgusting gurgles. He couldn't have been very fresh and had probably lost a lot of his blood before transforming. In any case, that was what the reddish pool that had leaked under the door was suggesting. The father's blood, or the son's?

I got a few inches closer. The knob suddenly moved, but the door remained motionless. I took one step back and raised the hammer over my head, ready to throw myself at my victim or to run away if courage failed me. I didn't know which action I should take, but I was sure of one thing: running away and telling the little one that her father and brother were gone was unthinkable. She would definitely want to come inside, and I wouldn't be able to forbid her from approaching this room. I absolutely had to verify who the zombie was. I clung to the hope that it was a desperate neighbor who had taken refuge here. His family had to remain unharmed. It was his duty.

I took one step forward and kicked my good leg hard against the door. It moved about four inches. That was it. Something was blocking it. The zombie didn't waste a second: almost immediately, his hands appeared in the crack and started to writhe. His dry, bony fingers closed in on themselves and then unfolded like the talons of a bird of doom. I didn't move; I watched those unsightly limbs twist through the opening. The zombie's face was hidden by the door, and I could only make out a bit of his shoulder.

I got some more momentum and hit the door a second time, far from the creature's claws. Under the impact, the door moved back another four inches, enough for the zombie to thrust its hungry maw through the gap. A young man with shoulder-length black hair fixed his glassy eyes on me: the little girl's brother. I gagged at the idea that this thing was the child's loved one. His throat had been severed, and a gaping wound formed a second mouth for him. It was wearing a frightening smirk. I couldn't tear my gaze away from that wound as the zombie kept squirming, trying to squeeze through the crack.

The door was just beginning to open wider from the corpse's pushing when the sharp, unforgivable peen of the hammer first met his skull. I felt the blow all the way to my shoulder, and the dead man collapsed to the floor. I stood there for a few seconds, a crazed look in my eyes, before I flung myself down on the ground and hit the body again.

"Why? Why?" I shouted in rage.

I was terribly angry with him for giving up so easily. Had he let himself be tricked by the zombies in the same way? Not even fighting back. I cursed him for his cowardice, which reminded me of my own; for not being there to comfort his sister; and for being one of the dead, among so many others. I let my exasperation and despair explode, and the blows rained down on him. When I regained my composure, a terrible shame assailed me. I had reduced the boy's face to an indistinct heap of rotten flesh and slimy liquids. The smell was horrible, but the sight was even more terrifying.

I got up and pushed the door open with both hands. A bed was lined up against the wall at the back of the room, under a large window; the sheets would work well to wrap the body. I went into the bedroom and yanked them off the mattress. I thought nothing worse could happen when, as I turned around, all the horror of the situation hit me in the face. There was a corpse, with a long blade in its hand, lying behind the door. The blood that had stained the floor was not the little one's brother's, but this man's. Not much was left of the body, its limbs having been devoured to the bone in spots.

I reconstructed the family drama that had played out in this room a few days earlier. I imagined the kid's father coming home in a panic, grabbing a knife, and discovering that his son had turned into a zombie. I saw him struggle with all his might before succumbing to the bites from his beloved child. The images that paraded through my mind turned my stomach. Grief was starting to take hold when a loud noise roused me from my self-pity: the car horn.

I rushed to the window, which overlooked the driveway, and glanced down. A creature was glued to the car window on the driver's side. I forgot about my gruesome discovery and hurried out of the room, tumbling down the stairs and grabbing my shovel as I exited through the glass patio doors. In just a few seconds, I was heading out the small gate from the yard, my weapon ready to do its job. The horn continued to sound, loud and uninterrupted. The thing had its back to me and was banging against the window of the station wagon. I brandished the shovel, but as I brought it down towards my target, he threw himself swiftly to the ground:

"Hey, wait! Hold on!" he cried.

A survivor.

CHAPTER 8
GREY DANDELION

Forgetting about the stranger, I dashed to the car.

"Open up!" I shouted to the girl.

Gripped by panic herself, she unlocked the door. Before she could pull the handle, I had already opened the door and grabbed her hand. After going past the gate, I turned briefly to the man, who had stayed on the ground.

"Don't just sit there. Hurry up, and lock the door behind you," I ordered him as my eyes fell on the flood of decomposing heads advancing down the street.

This horde must have formed not far down the road, in the village, and wasted no time when the little girl's horn started blasting.

I dragged my protégée into the living room and waited for the stranger to run through the patio door before closing it.

"What the hell was that! What got into her, honking like that?" he said, glaring at me.

I had no desire to explain myself, and faced with my silence, he added:

"We need to barricade ourselves upstairs. Let's go up and..."

"We're not going upstairs," I interrupted him in a dry voice.

The little one had moved behind me, and I could feel her gaze weighing on my back. The man did not seem to agree with me.

"It's the best thing to do. They won't be able to climb up there if they come in."

I knew that much better than he thought, but taking refuge upstairs remained out of the question. Faced with my lack of response, he turned and headed towards the stairs. I grabbed him by the shoulder.

"I said, no one's going upstairs."

He brutally pushed my arm away and looked at me furiously.

"What's your problem, Grandpa? You wanna die?"

A violent urge to hit him rose inside me, but a light touch on the sleeve of my jacket held me back:

"I want to go upstairs, too," said the girl, pinching the leather of my jacket between two of her fingers.

"Even the kid agrees, Pops," the stranger added without wasting one second.

I looked her straight in the eyes, unable to tell her the news, my mind racing all over the place. Seeing the devastated expression on my face, she understood.

"They. Are. Dead?" she asked, detaching each word, transforming her question into a simple enumeration, devoid of any intonation.

Once again, a long silence was my only response, as my lips moved silently.

"Hey, who's dead?" the man asked before adding, to the little girl:

"Is this your house?"

Seeing the little one's ashen face, the stranger's jaw twitched, and he began to scratch his cheek mechanically.

"Fuck," he mumbled, unable to restrain himself.

The girl was not crying. She remained motionless next to me, staring into space. I wanted to talk to her, to console her, but once again I didn't know what to say to her. "Your parents, and probably everyone you know, are dead, but don't worry, you'll be fine." There was nothing I could tell her without lying, without changing the truth. Even the greatest speakers and the most gifted embellisher of words would have had a hard time getting her to swallow that all was for the best in the best of all possible worlds. So, what could I have done? It was the stranger who broke the silence:

"Don't worry, it'll be fine..."

He broke off when the little one turned her back on him and headed into the kitchen. I watched her walk away then followed suit. I didn't want her to lock herself in some piece of furniture again. We were not safe here.

When I got there, she was kneeling on the floor and rummaging through one of the cupboards under the large counter. I stayed in the doorway and watched her. She pulled out a large white bowl with a pastel blue floral pattern and placed it on the table. Seeing me, she bent down again and added a second one.

I was projected years into the past where, on Sunday mornings, I had gotten into the habit of having breakfast with my daughter before going to work. She always insisted on serving me and making everything. These were some of the rare moments we spent together. Before she left...

The little one opened the door to the fridge and jumped back, attacked by a foul smell. The power had been cut here, too, and a steak that was lying on a simple plate had started to decompose. The smell only held her back for a couple seconds. She grabbed a bottle of milk from the refrigerator door. But, after unscrewing the cap, she made another face and tossed the bottle into the large trash can that adorned the corner of the room. The smell emanating from it hadn't convinced her, either. She rummaged under the counter and took out a new carton of shelf-stable milk, carefully checking the expiration date. She was resourceful for her age, and it wouldn't have surprised me if she used to make her own breakfast before going to school. My daughter was much older when she started taking care of our little Sunday dates. Until she turned ten years old, her mother used to do everything. Before she left, too...

The child filled both bowls, one a little more than the other, and pulled out a package of chocolate cereal. She sat down and invited me with her eyes to do the same. I gently pulled out the chair and took a seat across from her. As the little one started shaking cereal into the milk, I watched the mischievous dog on the box waddle around. The animal stopped its dance and moved towards me, licking his chops. I grabbed the package the little girl was handing to me and happily served myself. I let out a hollow laugh when I saw that the manufacturer was bragging about using French wheat. He might have to wait a long time to buy more. I was probably one of the last farmers in France, and to top it all off, my fields had burned down.

We had certainly earned this breakfast. But, as I brought the bowl to my lips, there was a thud. I pushed my chair back violently and rushed towards the living room. I had been distracted. Had the zombies managed to get inside? From behind the glass patio doors, I peered outside. The sight of the deserted yard reassured me. Nothing had disturbed its peacefulness. They hadn't gone through the gate. But the living room was empty, too: the man had disappeared.

I made a quick tour of the downstairs, making sure that the zombies lurking on the other side of the windows facing the street didn't see me. No trace of the stranger. He had gone upstairs. I returned to the kitchen, where the girl continued to eat as if nothing else mattered to her.

"I'll be right back," I said simply, before heading back to the stairs.

The house was still so quiet. I felt like I was reliving the same scene a second time. I had no desire to go up to the second floor and confront the corpses, but I was afraid of the man most of all. I didn't know what his intentions were.

"Is someone there?" I asked without much conviction.

A voice answered me, though.

"Shh!"

The man's face appeared at the top of the steps.

"Come look at this," he whispered.

I climbed the stairs, hoping he wouldn't lead me near the bodies. I didn't know what he was up to, but I was ready to defend myself: my fist was clenched around the handle of the hammer, which I had slipped into my belt.

The stranger had his forehead glued to the window I had first seen him through; I was again forced to face the corpses, which were patiently waiting for me at the entrance to the room. I walked over to him, unable to tear my eyes from the carnage. The sight of Arnaud's face, which I had reduced to mush, made me gag.

The man, indifferent to the spectacle, did not seem to notice and motioned for me to come closer.

"Look. I think they just knocked that thing off," he said, showing me a pile of dirt and debris at the foot of the gate.

One of the wall-mounted flowerpots that decorated the two pillars framing the entrance to the yard had been knocked over by the clumsy movements of the zombies, who had gathered near the car. The post on the right was bare, and the dead were trampling on the remnants of its hanging basket. The creatures had not seen us and were wandering around the poorly parked vehicle. They weren't even trying to get in. You would have thought they were a swarm of drunken bees. They were dragging themselves around in all directions and jostling each other, without any reasoning behind their movements.

"Let's not stay by the window. They're going to see us," I whispered, even though I was convinced that the zombie's moans would drown out the sound of my voice.

"We better go back downstairs," I added.

"What about them?" the man asked, indicating the two corpses with a lift of his chin. "The dude with the knife had fun. Did you see the other guy's face?"

I felt a violent urge to yell at him, to tell him that he couldn't talk about the dead that way; but who was I to tell him off like that? Just minutes earlier, I had let my anger express itself without restraint on the corpse of an innocent teenager. My monstrosity was matched only by this world's. I disgusted myself almost as much as the remains of the two men strewn across the floor, two putrid piles of rotting meat. The little girl's family.

"Could you…"

"Okay," the man interrupted me. "I'll take care of them. Go on back down."

He picked up the sheet I had torn off the bed and walked over to the bodies. As he bent down to pick up the father's emaciated carcass, I turned on my heel and fled from the room, my face a deathly pale.

The little one had finished eating and was putting her bowl in the sink when I entered the kitchen.

"Your cereal is going to be all soggy, Mr. Patrick," she said.

I smiled and took my seat again. The milk had soaked into the flakes and become engorged with chocolate, taking on a strange coffee color. I lifted the bowl to my mouth as she resumed:

"I want to see them."

Her tone left no doubt about her determination. I let the chocolate slide down my throat, savoring its sweet taste before responding bitterly:

"No, you can't."

I expected her to insist, to ask me why I was refusing, but it was her tears that forced me to justify myself.

"I want you to have good memories of them, okay?"

I got up and walked around the table, drawn to the refrigerator door. A whole bunch of photos, which I hadn't noticed when I first discovered the room, were stuck to it with magnets. I gently removed one and crouched down next to the little girl, who was sobbing harder now. I placed the picture in front of her, stroking her hair.

"I want you to remember them."

All four of them were sitting in the living room: her mother, her father, her brother, and her. It wasn't an extraordinary photograph, nor one of a month-long summer vacation spent by the sea and forgotten as soon as school started again. It was a simple photo, a snapshot of their life. The parents, seated on the sofa, exchanged knowing looks, while the girl, at their feet, piled up wooden toys on the coffee table with a beaming smile. Arnaud, sprawled beside his mother, made a funny face, a hand-held game console on his knees. I had no idea who had taken this photo – surely a member of their family – but I was convinced it was going to become one of the most important things in the world for the little one.

"Your family is here. Not up there. I want you to keep this photo and never lose it."

She turned towards me and, her face covered with tears, threw herself against me, wrapping her arms around my neck.

"I promise," she whispered in my ear between sobs.

At the same time, the stranger entered the room, his hands hidden behind his back. They were covered in blood. He walked around the table and approached the sink. He turned on the faucet and cursed.

"Dammit, I'm never going to get used to this."

Deprived of water, he sprayed his hands with dish soap and rubbed his fingers briskly. Very quickly, the foam, which had been transparent initially, became saturated with the last traces of the corpses and took on a blackish color. The man cleaned himself up for several minutes before wiping his sticky hands with a paper towel.

The whole time, the little one kept crying into my neck.

He sat down facing us, rested his elbows on the table, and placed his head in the crook of his arms for a few seconds before lifting it up:

"My name is Karim. Sorry about earlier," he said sincerely.

"It's okay, I think we're all on edge. I'm Patrick," I replied.

Karim couldn't have been more than thirty years old. His small size proved that, as was the case with me, the most athletic were not the only ones capable of surviving the worst disasters. His T-shirt hardly masked how thin he was; his long, slender arms protruded like two twigs ready to break at the slightest effort. His dark eyes, sharp and battle-hardened, betrayed a real quickness of mind. Thick eyebrows traced the contours of the arches and melted into his olive skin. His gaze landed on the little girl, and he asked:

"What about you? What's your name?"

Surprised, I realized I had never thought to ask her for her name. The fact was, I didn't need a name for her. She was the only survivor with me, the only one to hear my words. I'd gotten the feeling we understood each other without speaking. I received proof of this when, not hearing her respond, I noticed she was staring at me, her eyes red with tears, as if awaiting my approval to reveal her name to this stranger. I gave her a slight nod, smiling.

"My name is Emma," she said in a whisper, between sobs.

"Emma, Patrick, I am very pleased to meet you."

I was amazed to hear him display such politeness, especially after the aggressiveness he had shown earlier. But I could understand his loss of composure after narrowly avoiding a deadly shovel attack and the disgusting fangs of a horde of zombies. He had apologized. Not me. I wasn't the type to be friendly off the bat, but Karim seemed honest to me, and he hadn't renounced his humanity like I would have expected from other survivors.

"I would like to extend my sincerest apologies for the shovel."

"No need for us to be so formal. You missed me; that's the main thing, sir."

I wasn't sure how I should take the fact that he had called me "sir" despite him suggesting not addressing each other formally. Did having the abs of a shut-in and white-peppered hair automatically place me in the old man category?

"Then you can be informal with me, too," I replied simply.

"Do the two of you live here?" he asked, looking at each of us in turn.

"No, this is the... Emma's house. We had just arrived when the horde showed up."

"Sorry again, it was hot on my heels. I wanted to hide out in one of the houses when I saw Emma in the car. I'm glad I ran into some new survivors."

"New survivors?"

A glimmer of excitement crossed Karim's eyes:

"You thought you were the only ones?"

"You're the first person we've met who hasn't tried to eat us, at any rate," I replied bitterly.

"There's about thirty of us who found refuge at the school."

"Thirty!" I exclaimed, not knowing if I should rejoice or lament.

I was happy to hear that other people had survived. The little one would surely find someone to really take care of her and maybe make some friends.

But knowing that so many people were still alive brought me back to a couple days earlier, when I was still just an ordinary pawn on the chessboard that was the world. A time when the kings and their edicts dictated our actions. I rather preferred being a bishop, almost free to move around. I had lost everything with the arrival of the zombies, even the little things that I cared about, so what was the point of getting close to a relic from the past?

"I was out looking for food when the horde stumbled upon me. I ran as far as I could to get them away from the school. That's how I ended up here," he continued, tapping the table with his fingertips.

"What about you? Where were you guys before?" he added.

"At my home, on the farm. We had to leave it."

Seeing that I wasn't going to expand on what had happened, he got to the point of this discussion.

"You should come with me to the school. You'll be safer. Plus, the more of us there are, the more we can..."

His hesitation betrayed his doubts about the future, but he recovered quickly.

"The happier we will be, quite simply."

I wasn't sure I wanted to go with him. I had no desire to put up with questions from the other survivors or take part in their collective actions, but Emma left me no other choice when she pushed back her chair and stood up:

"My teacher might be there," she said, her mouth outlining a fleeting smile.

Of course, that was her school. She would surely know a good number of the survivors. She would finally be reassured.

"What's her name?" Karim asked her.

Emma closed her eyes to think. Sometimes, for a child, the answer to such a question was not obvious.

"Ms. Bleuet!" she exclaimed when the name came back to her.

I was afraid Karim's face would darken and announce a new horror to the little girl, but a big smile appeared on his lips.

"Christine is doing very well. I'm sure she'll be happy to see you again."

Karim stood up, too, then turned to me, fully aware that now, we would go with him no matter what.

"Patrick, it'd be best to go there now. Let's take the opportunity to bring whatever might be useful to us."

He was right; it would be good to get out of there as soon as possible. I was not prepared for another siege, and I questioned my ability to cohabitate with another adult in such a situation. I smoothed down Emma's hair.

"It's decided, then. Let's go," I said.

She smiled briefly again, but as I got up to get my bag and stock up on groceries, she grabbed my hand and looked me deep in the eyes.

"We have to bury Arnaud and Papa before we leave."

Her request caught me off guard, and it was Karim, who had not moved, who replied:

"Don't worry, I'll take care of it."

The young man left the room and returned with my shovel. Instinctively, my arm reached out, and my hand gripped the handle of the tool firmly.

"I'll dig. Both of you, get ready to go."

Addressing Karim, I added:

"We were already carrying fully loads; I hope you planned ahead."

"No problem," he said, dashing off again towards the living room.

"You can get things from your room when Karim says you can go upstairs, okay?" I said to the little one, uneasy.

She nodded.

"See you later, then," I sighed as I headed for the door with my heavy burden as interim gravedigger on my back.

I retrieved the bunch of keys, which was still hanging from the lock, in the hopes of finding the one for the back door that I had spotted while taking the tour of the house. I didn't want to risk stepping through the patio doors again, even though I was almost sure the zombies wouldn't see me.

Mostly, I had noticed, through a downstairs window, a big pile of sand outside. It almost completely covered the narrow strip of grass that bordered the east side of the house, along which a whole pile of construction equipment had been stored, only separated from the small, pretty yard by one of the corners of the building.

I made my way to the back door and, after several attempts, finally hit upon the right key. I turned it gently in the lock and, taking a deep breath, pushed the door open just as slowly. The hinges creaked as if this entrance was rarely used, but no creature, attracted by the noise, appeared in my field of vision. I leaned through the opening and checked both sides. The area was empty. And even better, it was out of view, sandwiched between the side of the house and the thick hedge that surrounded the residence. I slipped into the stifling air, appreciating the welcome shade from the shrubs, in spite of everything.

As I had hoped, the ground next to the pile of sand was soft; it was a mixture of gravel and soil, unlike the clay that was typical of Provence, which would have given the best pickax a hard time. I didn't have to excavate a very deep pit, anyway. It wouldn't be difficult to cover the bodies, at least what was left of them, with the sand. I didn't intend to dishonor the little one's dead with a low-quality grave that the slightest storm would tear open, but we had to face it: we had other priorities. To start with, surviving and not finding ourselves completely surrounded.

By the tenth stroke of the shovel, big beads of sweat were already streaming down my forehead. The repeated friction against the ground rid the tool of the traces of dried blood that had covered it since its visit to the depths of the zombie's brain. Each shovelful tore up a large clump of compacted sand and quickly enlarged the pit. When I deemed my work done, Karim was already there, two big, soiled packages behind him in the hallway. Caught up in my thoughts, I hadn't heard him.

"I asked Emma to fill up my bag with canned goods while I brought the bodies down," he explained. "I got another set of sheets to hide the stains when they are buried. I think she wants to be there. Can we get started?"

I nodded, then hesitated before helping him put the two corpses at the bottom of the hole. I tried to push the image of Arnaud's face out of my mind by imagining it was just two heavy bundles of dirty laundry. But you can't get rid of a memory like you can a simple stain. As he had suggested, Karim spread a clean sheet over the bodies. The smell was troublesome, but there was nothing we could do about it. At least we were outdoors.

"Is everything ready on your end?" I asked Karim.

"If Emma is done with the cans, I think we can get going."

"I'll go get her, then."

I returned to the kitchen, where she was busy filling Karim's bag. It was already pretty full, and she was hesitating between a can of fruit in syrup and a can of green beans to top it off. I let her think about her terrible dilemma a little longer before interrupting her thoughts.

"Emma. We're about to get going. Go on up to your room quickly, then come say goodbye to Arnaud and your father," I said to her in the softest possible voice.

She jumped up and placed the can of fruit in the bag.

"Go get your bag; I'll take care of Karim's. I'll wait for you at the back door."

As she dashed off, I grabbed the handle of the bag and pulled it towards me. She hadn't been stingy with the cans. I hoped the young man's load wouldn't slow us down.

We met up again at the back of the house. The little one was already in the doorway when I arrived. Motionless, she was staring at the white linen, her family photo in her hands. I placed a hand on her shoulder.

"Would you like to say a few words?"

I had never been comfortable at funerals. Not that anyone would feel like a fish in water – like a corpse in formalin, rather – in such a situation, but all the lamentation and often hypocritical sharing of condolences had always annoyed me. But when the girl stepped forward and, before beginning to speak, crouched down to pick a dandelion that had had the audacity to grow next to the house's foundation, I felt like I was where I needed to be.

"Papa, Arnaud… You can count on Mr. Patrick to take care of me. I will never forget you. Or Mama. I love you."

Coming from such a little girl, this funereal eulogy was a magnificent thing, and I was more than touched to be mentioned in it even though I was still, luckily, part of the world of the living. I stifled my emotions and grabbed the shovel I had stuck in the pile of sand. I gently covered the sheet, a cloud of dust rising with each shovelful. The white of the fabric quickly disappeared, and a small mound formed. No one said a word. Only the sound of the earth and my noisy breathing broke the silence. Finally, the little girl placed her flower on the heap, its yellow petals silhouetted against the grey of the sand. She turned to us:

"I want to go to the school now."

CHAPTER 9
THE RIFLE'S SMILE

By the time we came within sight of the school, a large group of zombies had entered the small square in front of the main gate. Usually frequented by the students' parents who were coming to pick up their children, a much less joyful procession was now gathered there. The dead pressed against the bars, crushing each other, playing at who would be the first to invade the school's interior courtyard.

Held together by a simple chain, the two doors of the gate were showing signs of weakness as the zombies' pressure increased with each push.

About a hundred yards away, we watched the scene from our hiding place behind a dumpster that had wound up on the side of the small road leading to the school, which was a little further down. The school building formed a large U around a big playground. The zombies had gathered at the opening of the U, where a wire fence and a metal gate were holding against their ferocious assault. Thick bushes stretched along most of the fence, preventing the walking dead from approaching. A few creatures had crept through where the shrubs' heavy branches did not reach, but most of them were clustered in front of the entrance. Combined like this at an access point, they proved to be much more effective, and they were exerting an increasing force against the gate. Karim looked concerned. It must have been the first time such a massive horde had attacked the school's last fortification.

He had managed to get us this far without any problems, avoiding the narrow streets and skirting the village as much as possible, only to unveil to us a Garden of Eden about to be desecrated by the taint of Death.

I was beginning to think it would be best to retrace our steps, before the racket being caused by the zombies attracted more of their peers, when several men appeared at the corner of the building further down, coming up on the zombies from behind.

"Ah, finally, there they are. Let's go," said Karim, whose eyes had regained their usual gleam.

The young man slipped his hand under his large T-shirt and drew out a hatchet. The article of clothing's size had allowed him to conceal his weapon. Seeing it appear so suddenly gave me the shivers. Because of all the detours, we had covered a long distance before reaching the school, and at no time had he seen fit to have his weapon in hand. Did he not trust me?

He proudly brandished his ace in the hole and started running towards the school. A dozen men had taken their places behind the zombies. They were a motley troop, a ridiculous little militia. Their battle gear was truly comical: some had come up with real armor for themselves and were wearing motorcycle or bicycle helmets and had put on several layers of clothing. One of them even had elbow and knee pads, which were way too small for him.

Their weaponry was not much more impressive, considering one of the combatants' garden rake or the frying pan a short man was holding with both hands. One of the strangers, however, had a rifle. But it was hanging behind his back, held in place by a large leather strap as the man waved a long machete in front of him.

When the first zombie saw them, he pounced on them with a powerful groan that stood out from the others. The battle was starting.

The small group's efficiency surprised me. Without hesitation, they rushed towards the zombies who still had their backs to them, beating, crushing, pummeling the backs of their skulls with their warlike arsenal. Within seconds, they had reduced the enemy's troops by more than half.

They regrouped, apparently under the command of the man with the gun, before dispersing again to strike the last zombies, making sure to always stay out of their reach. Karim participated in the end of the fight, slicing open the skull of a creature he had slipped behind with a quick, precise movement. Twenty-three corpses littered the ground, and none were human, or at least not still human.

The young man gave a hug to one of the survivors and began chatting with the one who seemed to be the leader. He promptly pointed in our direction. It was time to step into the scene or to turn on our heels.

"They're strong," said the little girl, who had not missed one bit of the massacre.

I hesitated, torn between the desire to run away and the desire to lead the little one to safety with the strangers. I had the odd feeling that if I went down that little hill, I would definitively lose my freedom. The presence of other survivors meant interrogations and heavy, questioning looks. Hell. The girl's voice pulled me out of my thoughts.

"Come on, Mr. Patrick!"

She had already walked a few feet and was motioning for me to join her. Karim was waving his arms, as well. Once again, she had decided for me. I joined her.

A few of the survivors greeted us, while most were already carrying the zombies' corpses behind the building. Karim was waiting for us in the middle of the small courtyard. Beside him stood the man with the rifle. The latter took a step towards us, a smirk on his lips:

"I hope you enjoyed the show. It's not every day that we have an audience at our performances."

I was as surprised by this manner of addressing me, not sure if the man was reproaching me for not intervening, as I was by his deep, hoarse voice. Not having any desire to justify myself to this stranger, nor to flatter him, I settled for staring at him. The little one had grabbed my hand and was standing slightly behind me. The man met my gaze, his eyebrows slightly raised. Feeling the tension setting in, Karim stepped in.

"Gerald, this is Patrick and Emma."

He was about to continue the introductions when the man suddenly moved towards me. I took a step backwards as he vehemently put his hand on my shoulder.

"Well then, welcome, pal. I'm sure we'll get along fine."

He turned to Emma and reached out to ruffle her hair, but she hid behind my back. If the child's reaction upset him, Gerald didn't let it show.

"You are very shy, my little lady," he said simply.

In an instant, the time it took for that first meeting, my fears were already starting to materialize. I didn't know who this man was, but I was convinced he would be nothing but a source of trouble. I hated people who acted overly familiar right off the bat and didn't hesitate to resort to physical contact to back up their words: a former salesman, surely. I hated salesmen.

He withdrew his hand from my shoulder and motioned for us to follow him.

"Karim, make sure they get rid of all the corpses. I'll take a tour of the premises with our new friends," he said to the young man, without turning to him.

Karim nodded at me as if to tell me that everything was fine, and I fell into step behind the man, pulling the little girl by the hand. I couldn't take my eyes off the rifle swinging at his back. It was the spitting image of my father's. Except it wasn't lying in the middle of a burned field. Consumed by fire and useless.

We walked briefly along the hedge and then around the building that delineated the corner of the courtyard. A large security door, the kind that can only be opened from the inside, was guarded by a grey-haired woman. When she saw the girl, she took a step forward, a broad smile on her face, but she immediately stepped back to block the door as it began to close.

She called out to us.

"Emma!"

Hearing her name, the little one emerged from behind my back and peeked towards the source of the sound. She then started running in the direction of the emergency door, passing the man with the gun. She was no longer afraid of him.

"Ms. Bleuet!" she cried.

I never imagined that one day I would see a child launch herself at her teacher like this. The news on TV kept telling us that our school system was mediocre, the educators incompetent strike-lovers, and the pupils each worse than the next. The scene unfolding before my eyes, however, tended to prove the contrary. The woman knelt down and took Emma in her arms. She was crying and stroking her student's hair affectionately. Gerald didn't stop; he went through the door.

"Save the reunion for later, Ms. Bleuet. We have our work cut out for us."

He turned to me and added:

"Come on in so I can show you around."

I wanted to protest, to ask him to give Emma and her teacher a little time, but Ms. Bleuet got back up and motioned to the little girl to cross the threshold.

Of course, she obeyed. I followed her, giving the teacher a slight nod in response to her warm smile. We entered a large, covered playground that extended from the courtyard. It was deserted. I had expected to find a good number of the survivors Karim had told us about, but there was no one there. Not one kid having fun. Not one adult watching.

"We avoid venturing into the schoolyard. We don't want to attract their attention," Gerald said, as if he had anticipated the question I wouldn't have asked him anyhow. "Everyone is inside."

We crossed the courtyard. A long row of trees planted in the middle of it created a large, shaded area where hopscotch games rested peacefully. Ironically, on one of them, the top square, which is called "Heaven," was almost completely erased, while the first square, or "Purgatory," seemed to have been repainted recently. The still visible white lines seemed to indicate the path that Gerald was taking, straight towards the buildings.

He placed his hand on the doorknob of one of the classrooms and turned around to face me.

"I'm warning you, we haven't had time to clean everything up yet."

He opened the door wide, and the smell of death made me choke immediately.

"Do we really have to go in there?" I asked him as the girl hid behind my legs.

Without answering, he walked through the room until he reached the hallway it opened onto.

"Enter!" he said firmly.

Behind us, the other men were starting to come back. They had obviously finished getting rid of the bodies. I preferred to postpone the introductions and therefore pulled the little one along with me. Then, I noticed that the windows had been covered with newspaper. The light struggled to pass through them, bathing the room in a sepia tone. However, it did not soften the dark, dreadful color of the stains that covered the walls, floors, and furniture. Some of the desks had been knocked over, and others had been pushed to the sides of the classroom, but almost all were covered with large scabs of clotted blood.

"This is where I killed them," the man said in a clear voice, articulating exaggeratedly.

He stared at me, plunging his two dark eyes into mine, and added:

"All of them. By myself."

I felt an uneasiness taking hold in me but tried to hide my concern. He was testing me. I had to stand my ground, make him understand that he would never control me. I tore my eyes away from the dreadful sight and joined him in the hallway. The little one had let go of my hand and was standing in the middle of the room, shaking with grief again.

"This is my friend Margot's class," she said, her whole body trembling.

I returned to her and took her in my arms, carrying her away from that scene of horror. Heavy tears were rolling down her cheeks. I was about to wipe them away when, out of the blue, a foreign finger did it for me.

"It was my daughter's, too" said Gerald, his face expressionless.

He withdrew his hand and moved down the hall.

Motionless, I watched the man walk away, imagining what he must have been going through the past few days. Despite the horror of his revelation, I still couldn't shake the strange feeling I'd been having since I first met him. There was something about him that didn't sit right with me, no matter what hardships he'd had to get through.

Trying to clear my mind, I started to follow him. He was already several yards ahead of me. I was again caught off guard by the sight of the rifle that kept swinging on his back. The end of the barrel swayed in a wide arc, a more sardonic smile than the Cheshire Cat's.

The light that was entering the hallway was also subdued by newspapers that had been taped to the windows lining the exterior facade. The dark corridor ran from one end of the building to the other, forming one branch of the school's U-shape.

The silhouette of a zombie, who was walking alone on the street, suddenly stood out against a window to my right. I tried to ignore this terrifying Chinese shadow puppet theater as Gerald, who had turned around, raised his index finger in front of his mouth.

I stroked the little girl's hair to calm her sobbing and slowly walked forward. Voices were suddenly heard at the other end of the hall: the survivors who had taken care of the zombies outside had evidently come inside through another entrance and were heading towards us. Gerald silenced them with a brief "shh," but the zombie was already banging on the windows. He slammed his palms against the glass, weakly but repeatedly.

Gerald moved in our direction, passed us without a word, and joined the group. I didn't hear their discussion, but two men put on their makeshift soldier gear and ran back where they had come from. The rest of the troops, Gerald in the lead, came back towards us. I did not see Ms. Bleuet among them. When they got to us, he put his hand on my shoulder again, his face cold and unfazed.

"Let's go," he said, pushing me gently.

I followed him to the end of the building; the other survivors were bringing up the rear and whispering to each other. The corridor made a left turn, the walls surrounding it forming a perfect right angle. Gerald veered off and stopped almost immediately in front of a double-leaf door. He gave me a half-smile and said:

"Welcome aboard."

He pushed the two doors aside, and a whole bunch of voices flooded the hallway. About twenty people were seated in the large, white-walled room that stretched before my eyes. The place was spacious and had a much higher ceiling than the hallway. The overpowering June sunlight entered the room through large rectangular panes that extended its entire length about nine feet above the ground. Some chairs and round tables, as pale as the walls, had been piled in a corner.

The school cafeteria had been completely rearranged, and apart from a few tables that had remained in place, it no longer looked like a dining area at all. Rugs were lying all over the floor; some of them were isolated, with heavy bags overflowing with stuff beside them, and others were grouped into small islands.

One of the men was lying quietly on his rug in a corner of the room, his back leaning against the wall, a book in his hands. But like everyone else, he had ceased his activity and was watching us closely. I felt like an alien, the last man on Earth, even though only nine days had passed since this madness had begun. They were not used to seeing new survivors every day.

Gerald walked away without a word and went to a small platform on the opposite side of the room. It, too, had been converted, and far from hosting children's end-of-year shows, it was accommodating its new tenant's few possessions on its boards. Gerald sat down cross-legged, his gun resting on his knees. He was staring at me. I quickly forgot his heavy gaze as most of the other survivors – those from the small troop and from the cafeteria – approached us. I put the girl down, my elbows aching from carrying her that far, and tried to get my bearings there in the middle of this flood of new faces. The short man with the frying pan was the first to really capture my attention.

"You are the first to join us in a week; we didn't think we'd see anyone else," he said in a voice that hardly masked his pessimism.

"The army will be coming soon," said a woman in her thirties, her eyes outlined by two huge, dark blue circles. "We just need to be patient."

"Do you really think they give a crap about us?" retorted a second man about the same age as her. "They're all staked out in the big cities to protect the politicians. We're nothing but useless hicks to them."

"If it's been like this in the big cities, they're all dead by now," the short man added.

"Why don't you shut up for a bit," the young woman cried, visibly at the end of her rope, before bursting into tears. "There must still be someone out there for us…"

Two older people I hadn't noticed yet pulled her aside from the small group, pushing her away like a temperamental child with no business in the middle of an adult discussion. They walked her over to what must have been her new bed – an old mattress, thicker than the other rugs – and sat down with her, trying to comfort her.

"Sorry about that," said the man with the pan. "I'm Thierry."

"Patrick. And she's Emma," I replied.

Everyone else then introduced themselves. I caught a few names – a Stéphane, a Magalie, a Raymond – but I knew I would soon forget them all. I'd never been very good at remembering people's names. I was even worse at being the center of conversation.

One woman, probably in her seventies, wearing a floral dress and reeking of perfume, offered to show Emma where she could get settled. The little one looked up at me, and I nodded to her that she could go; she let herself be led away, saying nothing. I then became the one and only subject of interest.

"Did Karim bring you here?" asked the man named Thierry.

"Yes, it was him," I said, trying not to meet the speaker's gaze.

"You were lucky. You could have still been alone."

Knowing perfectly well that frankness would not be welcome at this first discussion, I refrained from telling him that I would have preferred to have been left alone, unencumbered by other people. I had no other choice than to agree.

"Yeah, we were lucky…"

"Are you and the kid from the village?"

"No. Well, I'm not. This is Emma's school."

"Ah…" he said, looking at the ground.

My answer had hit home. Seeing Thierry troubled and the others remaining silent, I seized my opportunity.

"I'm going to go rest," I said, leaving the circle as one of the men, whose name I had already forgotten, stepped aside to let me pass.

No one held me back. They remained grouped together all the same: the time had come for the debriefing about the new guy. Good or bad first impression, I didn't care.

I joined Emma, who had started to unpack her backpack, helped by the lady who had taken charge of her.

"Your granddaughter reminds me of my daughter when she was still in school," she told me with a smile, her lips as ridiculously made up as her eyes.

"He's not my grandpa. He's Mr. Patrick," Emma said.

The woman looked at me strangely, her brow furrowed, then apologized for her mistake.

I nodded to her that it was fine and put my bag down next to Emma.

"Everything okay?" I asked her stupidly, considering just a few minutes before, she had learned of the deaths of some of her schoolmates.

"Yes," she whispered. "Giselle said I can sleep here. It's weird sleeping in the cafeteria. But she said everyone is sleeping here. And you're next to me."

"Well, if you want to stay here," interrupted Giselle. "Maybe you want to sleep somewhere else since she's not family."

The woman appeared to be bothered by my lack of kinship to Emma and wasn't hiding it. I really must have looked like a monster to elicit such a reaction. Maybe she was right, after all.

"Emma is the one who will decide," I said, scratching my beard.

"Here is good," the little one said with no hesitation. "Like in the cabin."

I smiled at her briefly, remembering how waking up in the treehouse that morning hadn't been the most pleasant thing.

"It's decided, then."

I sat down next to Emma and helped her get the last few things out of her bag. Feeling useless and ignored, Giselle rose to her feet, freeing up the rug Emma had assigned to me.

"I'll go get some water for the child," she said before turning on her heel.

As she walked away, the little one chuckled:

"She smells like cheap cologne!"

I laughed in turn, happy to see that my nose wasn't the only one to have suffered the affront of Giselle's olfactory offense.

"Ms. Bleuet also smells like perfume," added Emma.

I was surprised to see her in such a good mood again. Meeting up with other people seemed to be doing her some good. I was glad I'd taken it upon myself. I just didn't know how long I could last. I unhooked the shovel from the bag, put it down next to my rug, and then leaned against the wall. Even though he was seated at the far end of the room, Gerald was still staring at us. I turned towards the girl so as not to see him anymore, but I could still feel his eyes on my back. I sighed and said to Emma:

"I hope we'll be good here."

"Ms. Bleuet will take care of me, too. She's nice."

She slid down onto her carpet and stretched out, a small wall of cans between her and me. Suddenly, she got back up:

"Why haven't you unpacked your bag, Mr. Patrick?"

The answer was obvious to me, but I didn't know what to say to her. Fortunately, at the same time, Ms. Bleuet entered the room. The perfect pretext not to answer.

"You rest; I'm going to go talk to your teacher."

CHAPTER 10
THE INSATIABLE FLOOD

"He's not really in charge. He just took matters into his own hands very quickly. I feel like it suits everyone a bit anyway. But no… There is no real leader," Christine replied with no real conviction.

Since I had approached her, she hadn't stopped rubbing her hands together and was constantly avoiding my gaze. She was not enjoying this conversation, but I needed to know what I had gotten myself into. I nodded, even though she was staring down at the ground and couldn't see my gesture, then added:

"Just now, he told me he'd killed them. All of them."

A short moment passed before Ms. Bleuet looked up at me. A veil of tears clouded the green of her irises. She ran a hand through her greying hair and, with pursed lips, looked briefly at the platform where Gerald was lying down. Looking horrified, she said to me:

"No, I don't want to."

When she turned around to cut the conversation short, I gently placed my hand on her shoulder.

I held her back.

"You need to tell me what happened. For Emma."

I spoke these last words with a bitter taste of remorse in my mouth. She didn't deserve such cheap blackmail.

The little girl's teacher turned her chest back towards me and, as a tear as heavy as the sorrow on her face trickled down her cheek, whispered:

"Please don't force me to talk about it. I have to go take my shift," she added.

I was surprised to hear that they were so well organized, and my curiosity took over.

"I'm coming with you."

Without saying anything, she walked over to the door, which she held open for me. I glanced at Emma, who seemed to be sleeping already, and left the cafeteria. It was much cooler in the corridor, and the light was less aggressive there. Christine left in the opposite direction to the one we had arrived from a few minutes earlier. I followed her, a couple steps behind.

I regretted insisting like this, but my worried mind couldn't shake Gerald's words. "I killed them. All of them." I only wanted one thing: to get out of there and not be stuck in the midst of these strangers. But, since I was incapable of making the decision on my own, I needed a good reason to find the courage to leave. Gerald's strange behavior was the only excuse that stood out at the moment. One that my cowardice could cling to, finally letting me take off without looking back. Without shame.

I had never had the slightest problem telling people what I thought of them, let alone acting like a jerk around those I couldn't stand. My scathing frankness had often left indelible marks on my relationships with others. Far too often.

I didn't know Christine, but I refused to behave that same way. I was certainly garbage, but not the last of the scumbags. Eventually, she or another survivor would surely tell me what had happened. The sooner the better, though, as I didn't feel like spending an eternity here.

Ms. Bleuet suddenly disappeared into the darkness of a room to her left. I paused in front of the entrance. My nostrils greeted the heavy stench of urine in the air with disgust. When Christine opened the door at the far end of the long, narrow room, the light rushed in, eager to illuminate the urinals that lined the wall with its ghostly whiteness. Worse than a public restroom, diligently maintained at least once a year, this place was disgusting. Convinced that their stay at the school would be short-lived, the survivors had taken no care of the place, leaving a foul-smelling, soaked floor and urinals stuffed with soiled paper. Why bother pissing straight when you're not at home? Exasperated by the mediocrity of the survivors, I went out into the courtyard.

"How classy," I said to Ms. Bleuet, who had started to climb the first rungs of a wooden ladder that was leaning against the front of the building, three short feet from the entrance to the boys' bathroom.

"Have you never been to a campground?" she replied, continuing her ascent.

"No, but I've been in the crapper at a bar before," I told her amusedly when she was almost at the top.

Despite the lack of zombies ready to devour me below the ladder, I found the climb to be more difficult than it had seemed. I needed a rest, too. My ankle was no longer the only thing hurting, and many of my muscles – far more than I could have listed – were in continuous pain. Driven by the desire to know more, I hoisted myself to the top of the ladder. Christine's little joke had relaxed the mood; maybe she would end up giving in.

The flat roof of the school was covered with gravel. Metal vents of various shapes emerged here and there, without apparent logic. Two tired, white, plastic lawn chairs had been set up in a corner behind a low wall that rose about three feet above roof level: the perfect place to watch the street without being seen. I imitated Christine, who had stooped down to get to the observation post discreetly, then sat down next to her after she took her spot.

We had an unobstructed view of the vineyards below the school. On slightly sloping terrain, they ended where the fences of the villas in a small residential area began their work of dividing up the world. Two parallel roads, which stretched out on either side of the fields, flanked the dwellings and extended all the way to the school. One of them – the one I had arrived on a little earlier and where the parents used to park, back when picking up their children was still one of their concerns – went right past the small courtyard that the playground gate opened onto. The other one timidly climbed the slope until it lay at the foot of the side of the building on top of which we were now located. Both streets were deserted. Not one trace of zombies.

After I'd seen so many of them in one single day, this sight was not reassuring at all. Quite the contrary.

For about ten minutes, while Christine remained silent and observed the street with a vacant look in her eyes, I scanned the surroundings in search of the slightest movement. Everything was still. Once again, the mistral wind was nowhere to be found, and the landscape was motionless. The world seemed to be holding its breath in anticipation of a tragic outcome.

The leaves on the vines, still green despite the sun's heat and the relentless drought over the last few days, were paralyzed at the ends of their branches, and the sky was forced to display a pure blue. There was neither a cloud nor even a plane to mar this monochromatic painting with a few white streaks. Most worrying, however, was the complete absence of birds. No furtive black dot came to stain the sky. The soundtrack to this lifeless spectacle was even more overwhelming. It was non-existent. Much like the birds, the cicadas, which usually began their incessant din at this time of year, remained silent, hidden in the ground. Christine cleared her throat, finally getting us out of this suffocating silence.

"What about you, then? How did you get here?"

The tables had turned. It was time for me to answer her questions. With her, though, it was a different ball game. I didn't feel forced, and the legitimacy of her request motivated me to share my story. After all, I had arrived out of nowhere with her student. Me, a total stranger. She had the right to know. It wasn't some sleazy curiosity that was prompting her to interrogate me, but her genuine interest in Emma.

Omitting all the parts about an old farmer's wanderings through a zombie-invaded Provence, and without being as evasive as she was, I began to tell her about Emma's recent days. My character was there, a simple witness to the drama that was playing out in the little girl's life. The words, which formed on their own as I summed up the days we'd spent together, amazed me with their simplicity and their power. Christine started to cry when I described how I met Emma after her mother's accident. She interrupted me to thank me for taking care of the child and asked me to continue. She wanted to know everything. But as I was about to tell her about our terrifying escape from the house, a foul odor flooded my nostrils. Much worse than the one in the bathroom. I couldn't help but retch. Despite the omnipresence of this smell of death for the past several days, a stench of such magnitude still upset my stomach easily. Christine, who had obviously smelled this macabre fragrance, said to me:

"It must be the mass grave. We threw all the bodies behind the building. I know we should burn them, but..."

I raised my arm and interrupted her. A light breeze was sweeping over the top of the hill the school was built on, bringing with it plenty of noxious air, but not from the corpses below. I took in a big mouthful of that foul air and, holding my breath for a few seconds, with my arm still in the air, stared at the top of the hill. I glimpsed movement around the corner of one of the villas along the road. But it was the monstrous noise that suddenly rang out, conclusively putting an end to the silence that had been hanging over the school's surroundings, that confirmed my doubts: a horde was approaching.

Accompanying the army of monsters, the first ranks of which were already appearing between the buildings, the gusts of wind were growing stronger, carrying that cadaverous aroma with an ever more certain enthusiasm. The blowing, heavy with a pestilential smell, increased the fierceness of the wails. The hair on my arms was standing on end. I was terrified once more. Was I going to find myself trapped by these creatures again? My muscles stiff, I threw myself to the ground and pulled on Christine's pant leg so she would do the same. Paralyzed in her chair, it took a few seconds for her to react and drop to my side. Both of us lying down, we dared not make the slightest sound. Gravel had penetrated the palm of my right hand. It was bleeding profusely. I wanted to turn it over and remove the intruders that had sneaked into my flesh, but Christine was gripping it tightly. Her fingers, with their cadaver-white knuckles, were shaking uncontrollably and making the gravel roll around in my wound.

My fear was such that the pain seemed like a vague, distant sensation. Unlike the zombies, whose groans were still escalating, terror had robbed me of the ability to express myself and cry out in pain. My ears, on the other hand, had no trouble discerning, amid the dead's macabre melody, the screeching of gravel. A man who had been the lookout on the other side of the roof was racing towards the ladder. The monsters spotted him immediately and moaned in unison. I could easily imagine their sinister faces turned in our direction. I bit back a curse and vowed to deal with that jerk if I ever got out of there. Alive or dead. I'd be happy to devour him, then regurgitate him before swallowing him again, if the zombies were to convert me to their cause.

Very quickly, the sound of their beating on the walls and windows of the school added to their cacophony. Christine was on the verge of panic. Wide-eyed, she stared at me, her face as pale as her fingers. She was crying silently. Something in her gaze told me she was ready to get up and throw herself into the middle of the ocean of the dead. Just to get it over with. I gently shook my head and tried to reassure her without uttering a word.

Then we heard a scream, and the banging intensified. The mass of creatures kept flooding the walls of the school. From the roof, through the rain gutter, I could see the tops of the skulls of some of the living dead. The flow was non-stop, and every zombie I saw pass by was immediately replaced by another abomination. The school was being besieged by a veritable strike procession. A republican demonstration the likes of which had never been seen before. A coming-together of all political parties, all faiths, all sexual orientations, all skin colors. All united under one single banner: hunger, the desire to devour us. A true apocalyptic tolerance.

But as the screaming increased downstairs, I realized I was mistaken. We were actually witnessing a parade that only military dictatorships had a way with: a morbid march of fully brainwashed soldiers. We were the ones opposing a newly established order that, without bothering with envelopes hurriedly tossed into an ordinary ballot box, had taken over the world. The members of our resistance had only one role to play. We were the food supply. We were doomed, unable to endure so much hatred. Maybe they didn't really hate us. These sad, corporeal shells were surely not conscious of their actions. They were simply responding to an irrepressible need, an orgiastic urge for the flesh of the living. There was nothing we could do. Overnight, they had all begun preaching a new religion, that of an eternal feast, and nothing other than death – the real one, the one where the maggots can do their work in peace – could convert them back to reason.

Seeing the blank look in my eyes, Christine loosened her grip and lifted her hand to my face.

I smiled stupidly at her, without letting her touch me, and took the opportunity to free my palm from the turmoil of the gravel. I rolled over onto my back and gazed into the vastness of the sky.

I could have stood up and tried to help the people who were stuck down there, but this scene was far more calming. The zombies just had to smash one window downstairs to be able to use their gaunt fingers to pluck the few survivors, fruits far too ripe from having resisted until now. What could I do about it? I'd had my fair share of catastrophic situations. I was shielded here on the roof. And if they invaded the school, hunger and thirst would certainly bring an end to my repugnant self, but that mattered little to me. My fear had gotten the best of me. I preferred to stay here and let the others fend for themselves. They were all adults. Well, almost all of them.

I then imagined old Giselle pushing Emma towards the corpses to gain a few more seconds in this cursed world. This vision brought me back to reality, and the pain in my hand exploded as Christine placed hers on my shoulder. She whispered:

"We have to go help the others."

This world was desperately insane. It wouldn't allow me even a moment of cowardice anymore. Is surrendering to the beauty of the sky too much to ask? It kept pushing me to make decisions that were nothing like me. How could things as monstrous as these zombies have changed me so much? I had to risk my skin for strangers yet again. Or was this just for Emma? A few days ago, learning about the massacre of the entire staff of the school wouldn't have affected me one way or the other. And now, I was ready to follow Christine, to rush headlong into what was already shaping up to be carnage. I would have preferred to die emaciated on this rooftop.

I stood up, the usual creaking of my knees sounding timid compared to the cries of the zombies, and held out my hand to Christine. She grabbed it immediately, and I led her towards the ladder. When we got downstairs, I noticed that the zombies had not yet completely surrounded the school. The gate, which was completely clear, gave a glimpse of one last possible escape. But the world – Christine's determined grip – once again decided for me, dragging me through the bathroom.

It was panic inside the school. A few survivors were rapidly moving desks out of the nearest classrooms. A barricade had already been summarily erected. Luckily, the portion of the hallway in front of the door to the cafeteria was all concrete. The dead were busy with the windows a few yards away, a stone's throw from the fragile barrier. Their banging made the windows shake and echoed ominously throughout the building.

We ran to join the group that had set themselves up behind the crammed desks. Having been lain on their sides and stacked on top of each other, they offered minimal protection, but their thick wooden shelves were the same width as the hallway and completely blocked the entrance. Seeing me arrive, one of the three men grabbed me by the arm:

"You, stay with us."

He handed me a heavy hammer, keeping the sharp machete hanging from his belt for himself, and without paying any further attention to me, added:

"Christine, I think Gerald needs you inside."

She immediately turned on her heel and rushed into the cafeteria, leaving me alone with them. I had no time to protest: the noise that everyone had been dreading was heard as a window exploded into a thousand pieces a few yards from the barricade. The glass fell in a sparkling rain, but this was immediately followed by a cascade of filth. The first things, pushed by their comrades, crashed to the ground in the corridor, their bodies torn by the sharp edges of the shattered glass. They had no time to get up, collapsing under the weight of other zombies who rushed through the breach. Within seconds, more than a dozen creatures had entered, and they kept on coming.

Outside, the closest ones had ceased their assaults and were heading for the opening, jostling one another. His face dripping with a foul substance, one zombie had managed to extricate himself from the swarming mass of dead people that had formed under the shattered window and was advancing towards us. Their single, long wave of attack would soon come crashing down against our pathetic dyke.

One of the men ran off, leaving his post before even the slightest bloodshed. I wanted to imitate him, but the survivor to whom I owed the chance to be part of the first line of defense put one of his hands on my shoulder and the other on that of the second future martyr.

"Guys, if we don't stop them here, we're dead. We're going to die at any rate, so we may as well kick some ass beforehand."

I was sure of one thing: this man had not been in the military. More likely, he was obsessed with American war movies and thought he was like the badass sergeant, but those few words convinced me more than any other speech.

"We'll bump 'em off one by one, okay?"

With these words, he unsheathed his machete and stood at the center of the barricade.

"And try not to take me out in the process," he added.

I took up a spot on his right. The stacked desks were level with my shoulders, leaving me with a clear view and perfect range for the hammer. The first zombie, the slobbery one leading the way, crumbled under our apprentice sergeant's blade. A large opening separated his skull into two almost equal portions. With a slight tremor, his body slumped against the barrier. It wouldn't hold up for long if they managed to congregate within reach of the desks.

The second one arrived almost immediately, without even waiting for his ticket number to be displayed behind us. He threw himself at the barrier, where he was greeted with a violent blow from a metal bat. He joined the first body on the ground.

By all logic, the third one was for me. I aimed at his skull with all my might, and the head of the hammer carved a deep crater into his forehead. But the thing kept coming, pushing violently on the barricade as it thrust its filthy fingers towards my face. I ducked to avoid him. My neighbor immobilized him with a second blow to the head.

"Get up," he cried in panic.

Within seconds, we were almost swamped. Several zombies were arriving side by side, each one's face more horrible than the next. My colleagues' blows were raining down on the monsters. The hallway no longer looked like an elementary school corridor. The few drawings displayed on the walls were covered with the black, foul-smelling blood of the living dead. The peeling paint had been replaced with pieces of torn flesh.

Five zombies were already lying at the foot of the desks by the time my hammer blows rejoined the two other survivors' strikes. A dense wave of corpses was assailing us. They continued to pour in through the opening and pile on top of each other. But it wasn't long before we realized that their numbers might just be fortuitous for us. Each collapsing body was an additional obstacle for these stumbling things. As they got to the carcasses, not one could stand firm against the jostling from his buddies, and they were all collapsing pitifully to the floor. As they fell, their skulls presented themselves to us with no defenses, far enough away from the dreadful protection of their claws and fangs. We didn't miss a single opportunity.

Soon, a pile of dead bodies almost as tall as the stack of tables stood in front of us, as my joints cried out in pain. Despite their numbers, the hallway was far too narrow for the zombies – who continued to enter the building – to move the foul mass of their comrades who had died for infamy. Instead, they clumsily climbed over the bodies until they came within range of the fatal blow and became a new brick in our wall of death. But hunger was still getting the better of them, and they hoisted themselves towards us tirelessly, digging their blackened nails into the flesh of the corpses in the wall.

We kept repeating the same sequence, taking turns slaughtering a monster while one of the other two pushed the corpse back to widen our rampart. A mixture of the smells of death and sweat hovered around us as our defense grew thicker.

At the other end of the hall, a similar barrier had been erected, but no zombies had broken into the building over there. They had all headed for the breach in front of us. I was wondering where all the others had gone when five men, led by Karim, burst out at the end of the corridor, coming straight from the bathroom. When had they left?

"Move, all of you! We have to block all the doors in this wing of the school!" he yelled, looking worn out.

The men pushed aside the useless barricade of desks and spread into the building. Karim was walking towards us when the door to the cafeteria opened, allowing Gerald, rifle in hand, to appear in the crack.

"Damn it, Karim, they got into the courtyard," he said in a voice as monotone as ever.

"There was nothing we could do. There were too many of them. The gate didn't hold. Three guys got nabbed."

He let out a long sigh and continued:

"We absolutely have to block all the doors that open to the courtyard. Well, the ones in the other wing. That side is fucked," he added, indicating the direction to us with a tilt of his head.

"Okay, help the others lock everything up, then. I'll send some people," he confirmed before slipping back inside the cafeteria.

A metallic noise was heard, as if he had just locked the door behind him, the bastard. Karim came over to us as we continued to slaughter new monsters.

"Thanks, guys. You saved us on this one," he said. "Gerald sent us directly into the courtyard; he wanted us to secure the interior. Holy crap, what a massacre."

He glanced at the bits of corpses sticking up from the top of our barricade and suppressed a gag.

"We'll talk later," our sergeant blurted as he eliminated a new opponent with a precise machete strike.

"That idiot Gerald has forgotten that if they get through here, we all die."

At the same time, the door to the cafeteria opened, and several people, mostly women, rushed out: Gerald was holding the door for them. The small group headed off and split up in the other wing. Karim ran after them. I called out to Gerald, who was watching them leave:

"What's going on inside? You can…"

Machete man cut me off just as the other survivor smashed a climber's skull.

"We don't give a damn! What did you tell them so they wouldn't come and help us?" he shouted at Gerald.

The latter ignored him and made like he was going to go back into the cafeteria. But the sergeant was just getting warmed up:

"Son of a bitch, just because you bumped off your kid and her little friends doesn't mean you can get away with whatever you want, you bastard."

It all happened very quickly. As my turn came to slaughter another creature that had pulled himself up to us, Gerald reached us and grabbed the survivor by the collar.

"You'd be one poor, dead asshole without me," he spat in the sergeant's face, his nose just inches from his opponent's.

"Go fuck yourself," he replied, pushing Gerald away with both hands.

Gerald looked at him defiantly for a moment, then turned around. The tension was palpable, and my colleague and I were having a hard time focusing on our zombie attackers.

"Disgraceful father," the man murmured when Gerald started to walk away.

Gerald whirled around and rushed at the sergeant, screaming like a lunatic. He grabbed his face with both hands and pushed him up against the barricade. Gasping for breath, the man tried to catch hold of something and threw his arm out behind himself: black teeth, dripping with a viscous liquid, closed around his hand. He hastily pulled it back and immediately understood.

"Asshole!" he bellowed, hurling himself, machete raised, at Gerald, who had taken a few steps back.

We had no time to do anything. The sergeant's head disappeared in a reddish cloud. The barrel of Gerald's rifle was pointed in our direction, savoring the death of its latest victim.

CHAPTER 11
DESCENT INTO HELL

It seemed like I had been slaughtering the increasingly rare zombies who managed to climb the wall for hours when two men, burly but shaking like leaves, came to replace us. In a few words, my companion and I explained the process to them. Smash. Push. Repeat. Not really rocket science, even for a half-wit bodybuilder.

With sticky shoes that were covered in the sergeant's blood, which had formed a thick pool on the tile floor, I straddled his body and walked back to the cafeteria. I'd had to use my left hand to kill the zombies, the deep wound in my right palm being much too painful for the tool's hard handle. I couldn't feel my arm anymore. Only a giant mess of withered, suffering flesh.

Almost all the survivors seemed to have gathered here, deserting the wing of the school where they had barricaded the entrances to the courtyard. Apart from Karim's team, which was clustered together in a corner of the room, I was the only one covered in blood. But it wasn't just zombie blood on my face. Far from it.

I kept moving, my eyes downcast, and joined Emma – who, despite my increasingly horrid appearance, hugged me when I sat down next to her. Giselle was there, too. I could feel her small, dry eyes watching me.

"You okay?" I asked the little one.

She lifted her head off my forearm and looked at me. Her eyes were red with grief and fatigue. She must not have slept more than a few minutes before the horde arrived.

"Are they going to stop someday, Mr. Patrick?"

"I don't think so…" I replied, way too tired to lie to her again about what was in store for us.

"You'd be better off comforting her instead of spouting off horrible things like that," Giselle suddenly broke in.

A contemptuous look crossed her face, and she continued:

"At least Gerald knows what he's doing. You wouldn't have taken care of that poor Eric. The poor man. Fortunately, Gerald was there to put an end to his suffering."

I quickly turned to the platform where Gerald had set up his stuff. He was there, seated, his rifle still between his legs, staring at me as he nodded to a woman he was talking with.

"Gerald said he would be honored, even though no one really knew him. Along with the three men who died in the courtyard…"

She narrowed her eyes and, looking disgusted by her own words, whispered:

"There's probably not much left of their bodies."

A strong urge came over me to get up and drag her over to the decapitated body and tell her about how Eric had gotten bitten, but I restrained myself. I had seen what Gerald was capable of.

"You're right," I said quite simply, turning my back to her.

She sneered and returned to her business, as futile as it was. Surely, she needed to powder her nose again. I wondered what story Gerald could have told after he killed the sergeant. He had obviously put himself in the best light. He disgusted me and frightened me at the same time. I was maybe twenty years older than him, and yet I felt like he was controlling this whole situation with a lot more experience than I had.

I thought about Eric's words again. How could Gerald have massacred a bunch of children, including his daughter? I imagined the terrible scene: a man rushing into a classroom overrun with zombie schoolchildren and slaughtering every last one of them. However, the images that came to mind were not of a desperate father but of a madman indulging in orgasmic carnage. That idea horrified me. He hadn't hesitated for a second to kill Eric. Had he shown the same determination when faced with his own daughter?

To bring myself back to reality, I gave Emma a hug and leaned back against the wall. I wished we hadn't gone with Karim. Maybe we could have stayed in the little girl's house and waited for the horde to go away. We'd had enough there to keep us going. Instead, we were stuck inside this damn school.

I could hear the zombies moaning continuously outside. I could even make out the sound of their feet dragging against the tar in the courtyard, as the ones who had entered through the breach were ransacking the classrooms in the invaded wing, looking for a way through.

The night spent in the treehouse, in the quiet of the forest, seemed so distant to me. My body lay on the mattress, motionless and aching, my hand struggling even to stroke the girl's hair. My mind continued to wander from one terrifying idea to another, and yet, sleep finally found me: scared, bloody, and slumped over.

***

I woke up in the middle of the night with no idea what time it might be. The heat had finally dropped, despite how many of us were in the cafeteria. The loud, rhythmic breathing of the sleeping survivors was now joining the sound of the zombies' groans. Instinctively, I turned my head towards Gerald's mattress. It was empty. My heartbeat quickened, and my fatigue dissipated instantly. My sleepy eyes regained their sharpness and scanned the room for the man.

Emma had turned over and was sleeping with her head resting against her small backpack. She finally seemed peaceful. I stood up as quietly as possible, my limbs heavy and aching. I stepped over several survivors and, guided by the moonlight, made my way to the door. It was not locked. I pushed one of the panels gently and entered the hallway. Two figures were guarding the barricade. Neither of them was Gerald. I walked over. In the dim light of the corridor, a large, dark streak stained the tiles. I took my eyes off of it when the two strangers called out to me:

"Psst… Are you coming to relieve us?" asked one of them, whom I recognized: Thierry, the man with the pan.

"Sorry," I whispered, to the chagrin of the other man, whose name I couldn't remember.

He let out a long sigh.

"I can't take it anymore. Besides, I think those scumbags have forgotten that they can still get in through here," he whispered.

"We've only gotten three within, I don't know, two or three hours," Thierry added.

"Two hours and twenty-three minutes," the other man clarified, illuminating his digital watch.

"Where did the body go?" I asked, getting back to the reason for my outing into the hallway.

"Whose, Eric's?"

I nodded.

"Gerald took it away earlier. He didn't say why."

Because he doesn't want everyone to see what he did, I thought.

"Okay, thanks. Good luck," I encouraged them as I walked away.

I followed the dark mark that broke the symmetry of the floor tiles' black and white checkerboard. It stretched all the way to the corner where the hallway turned and entered the school's deserted wing. From there, it continued up to one of the classrooms that lined the wall.

I stopped a few paces from the doorway, where the trail disappeared into even greater darkness.

"Enter," Gerald's voice ordered me.

I shuddered but mechanically did what he said and crossed the threshold. The interior was much darker, its accesses to the courtyard having been barricaded and its windows covered with newspapers. Slowly, my eyes adjusted, and I saw Gerald, who was seated cross-legged on a student desk. Eric's body was lying at his feet.

"I was just thinking about you. I was wondering if you were going to cause me trouble or not."

Here we go, I thought as I leaned against the partition wall across from him.

"What about you? Since you're bringing it up," I risked asking him.

"That all depends on you, my friend."

I remained silent, and a long time passed before Gerald's voice emerged from the darkness again.

"He shouldn't have said that."

"That you killed your daughter and her classmates," I clarified, trying to sound impressive.

"Yeah."

"What happened, exactly?" I asked him, even though I was certain that the truth was unlikely to come out of his mouth.

The room fell silent again, but Gerald finally answered:

"The day everything went to hell, I was working at the office. When I saw clients getting sick and then starting to transform, I rushed home. I picked up my rifle and headed for the school. When I arrived, the healthy teachers had gathered all of the students plus their sick colleagues in one classroom. Right before they started to attack. There weren't a lot of kids, except the ones from the daycare. Most of them had already left, I imagine. Bleuet told me they had started going after the healthy people half an hour after their first symptoms. They had eaten the rest of the teachers. She tried to stop me from going in. I was the only parent who had come, but she did not succeed."

He paused for a moment and swallowed.

"When I walked in... You know. They had all turned into these things, and they pounced on me. I don't know why, but I had already loaded the rifle. I took them all out: the teachers and the children. I don't even know when I killed Sophie."

His voice grew more distressed, letting his feelings show through for the first time. Even in the dark, I knew he was crying.

"When they stopped moving, I turned the bodies over, and I found her. I recognized her clothes, the ones I had helped her put on that very morning, because her face was unrecognizable. I had shot buck-shot into my daughter's head..."

He suppressed a sob, and I sensed movement. He was wiping his face. His story had moved me, but just as I was beginning to see him as a simple, heartbroken father, he added:

"After that, I think I almost forgot about her. I reacted and orga-nized things. The survivors who were arriving were all panicked. I've managed to keep them going until now. They respect me. I need their trust, and I'll do anything to keep it."

He paused deliberately, and I heard him stroke the butt of his gun.

"I know Serge won't say anything about what happened. But the re-al question is you. Are you going to screw up what I've managed to build? I know we're in deep shit right now, but I know I'm going to save them. Again."

I was having a hard time understanding him. Was he telling me he was getting his jollies playing commander-in-chief of the garrison?

I was not much of a psychologist and had long since relegated him to the ranks of complete idiots, but after his explanation, I had the feeling that this apocalypse had completely messed him up, as it had all of us, and that he had created this leader character for himself as a way to cope. Or maybe he was just one of those oversized-ego pieces of garbage who never missed an opportunity to get their hands on some power, no matter how insignificant. I couldn't really pin him down, but I'd made my decision. Surviving the zombies was already a sufficiently tiring concern.

"I won't say anything," I whispered.

"Then everything is perfect," he said simply, getting down from the table. "I can take care of Eric's body now."

I didn't ask him what he was planning to do with it. I stepped away from the wall and headed towards the hallway. He called out to me:

"Hey. Don't forget that you can leave whenever you want. No one is making you stay. We'll take care of Emma if you go."

I nodded, more to myself than to him, and disappeared from the room. Short of breath, I found the long trail of blood. I had barely dared to breathe, not knowing what might have happened during that exchange. He had made it very clear that I was no longer welcome, despite my promise not to say anything. What was the word of a terrified old man worth? Not much, probably. As he had suggested, I needed to leave as soon as possible. It would be better for everybody. I had to take the first opportunity that presented itself. I would certainly be better off alone. Hadn't I been better off since their deaths?

These thoughts carried me back to the cafeteria. I got back on my rug, leaving Emma alone on hers, and held my head in my hands: before I could go, there was a mass problem to be sorted out. A disgusting mass that had surrounded the school. As I considered this terrible dilemma, sleep came over me once again.

***

Gerald's the one who proposed a solution the next morning. He must have spent most of the night awake. Deep, dark circles outlined his reddened eyes, making his expression even more disturbing. Whatever his real motivations, he seemed to have dwelled on his speech for long hours. Seeing him express himself with such determination, it was very easy to believe that he was doing everything he could to take charge of the situation and prevent the survivors from giving in to despair or making stupid decisions. Should I have simply believed him, too, perhaps?

When, still standing on his platform, he had finished laying out his plan, everyone seemed ready to give it a try. Giselle even applauded him warmly, knowing full well that her help would not be required for the operation. The others weren't ecstatic about the idea of what awaited them, but it all fell into place quickly. We had no time to waste: the water resources in the cafeteria were limited, with only a few small bottles that had survived class trips still available.

A group formed under Gerald's leadership, and several men began to move one of the heavy cafeteria tables that had been bunched together in a corner of the room. Together, they had no trouble moving it; they placed it in the center of the room, directly underneath one of the windowpanes that the bright light of the new day was pouring through. They immediately went to get a second table. A shrill squeak was heard as its feet scraped the ground, almost instantly sparking an infernal echo in the courtyard. The men picked it up and went to put it on top of the other one. I came to lend them a hand but felt quite useless as it rose up without my even putting a finger on it.

The stack was unstable, the upper table's legs flirting dangerously with the edges of the tabletop below them. Gerald placed one man at each leg while two others helped Karim to climb up. He easily hoisted himself to the top, where he added a chair that had just been handed to him. Without waiting, he climbed onto it. He was only inches from the ceiling, the glass panel just above him. He moved slightly to make sure his makeshift scaffolding was stable, then asked everybody to step aside. We all did.

He unhooked the metal bat that was attached to his back, surely the one Serge had been utilizing to massacre zombies the day before, and used it to hit the window, which shattered. A shower of glass fell on the young man and spread throughout the cafeteria, forming a strange, shiny, sharp carpet on the floor.

Giselle wasted no time in arriving with a broom, ready to make this light show disappear, as Karim finished removing the jagged pieces that were stuck in the frame. Without warning, he pushed off and propelled himself towards the opening, sending the chair flying. It crashed noisily in front of Giselle, who screamed in fear and pretended to fall, to everyone's complete indifference. All eyes were on the young man who had managed to get out onto the roof: the first part of Gerald's plan was a success.

He came back very quickly with the ladder. Luckily, the zombies hadn't knocked it over in the courtyard. We pushed the tables away, and Karim slid it through the opening. This is where things were going to start getting complicated.

Despite my fear, I had volunteered for the next part of the mission. Karim, Remi, whom I had seen for the first time during Gerald's speech, and Frédéric, the idiot who had run away on the roof yesterday, were also up for it. When I'd raised my hand, I had expected some people to be outraged that the younger guys were not volunteering, but no one had reacted. All I saw was Gerald's approving but still troubling expression.

Remi and Frédéric climbed up one after the other. Emma, who was holding Ms. Bleuet's hand, waved to me as I ascended the ladder after them. I gave her a hint of a somewhat ashamed smile. Trying to forget my pain, I clenched my teeth on the way up.

A dense sea of zombies was waiting for us down in the courtyard. It was swarming with those monsters, who were roaming all over the place in the hopes that a human would suddenly fall into their hands. They knew we were in there, but they had given up on finding an entrance. They were patient. They had all the time in the world.

Karim retrieved the ladder, and we discreetly made our way to the far end of the wing, just above the courtyard gate, which yawned wide open down below. Crouching, we moved forward laboriously, and it took us several minutes to reach our goal. Remi, a brown-haired man in a filthy polo shirt, quickly leaned over the edge of the roof and confirmed what Gerald and Christine had been thinking. The gate had not been ripped off; only the padlock of the small chain that usually kept it closed had given way under the mass of corpses. Karim asked us if we were ready. He then placed the ladder in the gravel along the edge of the roof and, along with Frédéric, lay down beside it. At his signal, Remi and I quickly stood up, screaming.

Instantly, an ocean of eyes washed over us. Dozens of monsters were staring at us eagerly. Their expressions, even though they were dead, left no doubt about the desire they felt for our flesh. No matter how unreachable I was on the roof, my voice trailed off, and I took a step backwards. Remi turned to me, white as a sheet, and with a nod, encouraged me to continue. The zombies bellowed together, stretching out their arms towards us. They were all coming in our direction. The ones wandering at the back of the yard were making an extra effort to try to get closer. All of them were heading towards the two promises of meals that were waving at them from the roof. Their cries were joined by the chattering of their teeth, which clacked together in their pestilential mouths.

I swallowed with difficulty and screamed even louder. Large beads of sweat were running down Remi's forehead. He, too, was struggling with having become, in a matter of seconds, the center of attention for so many predators. Two lambs for dozens of wolves. And yet, we were the ones playing the role of shepherds. Two herdsmen of the apocalypse, leading their flock through a devastated Arcadia. The courtyard's asphalt took the place of delicate pasture grass, and the famished dead embodied the stray sheep.

Almost all the zombies had gathered at the base of the building. We went up to the edge. An unexpected vertigo came over me, and I stared at the horizon to shake off the sight of the mortal tide crashing against the walls. Waving our arms to get the undead's attention, we slowly walked along the ledge to the far end of the building, which extended several feet beyond the edge of the gate. The zombies followed us and started to exit the schoolyard.

That area gradually emptied as the creatures gathered in the small courtyard that really marked the entrance to the school's premises. Some even exited that courtyard and started walking along the wing on the outside of the school grounds. We had to keep up our act for as long as the dead continued taking an interest in us. When the schoolyard was almost entirely deserted, Remi waved his hand to our two accomplices, who were still lying on the ground.

Karim grabbed the ladder, tipped it over the side, and swung his leg over the edge of the roof. He descended at full speed, closely followed by a sweat-soaked Frédéric. Remi and I tried to make as much noise as possible, screaming at the top of our lungs, as the two men down below ran to the gate. With a shrill squeak, they closed the two sides. The noise had attracted the attention of the nearest zombies, who were already heading their way. Karim took a heavy chain from his bag and wrapped it around the central bars. Frédéric was holding several pad-locks in his hand and bouncing in fear behind Karim. Miraculously, he managed to get them through the metal rings before the first dead hurled themselves against the entrance.

Alerted by the noise their peers were making, other zombies lost in-terest in us and smashed against the gate, too. But before it could give way for good, torn out of the ground, Karim and Frédéric appeared alongside us and added their voices to ours. The decibel level rose, and the living dead, attracted by our shouting, abandoned the gate. For the time being.

But we weren't done playing the role of zombie bait.

One by one, we withdrew from our dissonant choir until Remi was all alone, wriggling around in front of the dead. My throat was dry, and I did not protest when Karim asked us to follow him. Frédéric pulled the ladder up and held it under his arm. We crossed the length of the wing again, nervous when the gravel creaked a little too loudly under our feet. When we passed in front of the cafeteria's broken glass panel, Karim briefly poked his head through it to announce that, for the moment, everything was going as planned. I could hear some cheering. I did not see Emma.

We continued on our way, reaching the other wing as Remi's screams echoed through the schoolyard. He was singing *The Show Must Go On* and appeared to be dancing by himself on the edge of his roof. The audience was going wild.

Legs aching, we came to a halt when the wall of the covered playground, which was about six feet higher than the roof, was standing in front of us. This was where we would initiate our descent into Hell.

Frédéric was beginning to regret his decision. He had wanted to make up for his mistake the day before by volunteering, but the mere idea of having to go down when it was his turn paralyzed him. The young man mumbled something incomprehensible, then cursed, and finally, set up the ladder.

Several stragglers were still roaming around in the schoolyard. Some of them were already heading towards us. Karim was the first to descend the rungs of the ladder, and by the time I joined him, he had already shattered the skull of one of the monsters. Others were drawn by the noise. Five zombies were coming in our direction with slow but determined steps. Frédéric arrived in turn. The rollerblading pads and thick wool sweater he had put on made him look particularly ridiculous.

We ran inside the covered playground, out of sight of the mass of zombies admiring Remi's show. We moved apart from each other and waited for the latecomers to arrive and get their tickets stamped by us.

It was cool under the high ceiling, and the short wait gave me a chance to catch my breath, which I was already out of. The playground was wide open to the courtyard, a simple, covered extension of the play area.

Two of the zombies were dragging themselves towards us as the other three barged in at the corner of the covered playground. We had to prevent them from attacking as a group, at all costs. They were only manageable one-on-one; as a group, they became almost invincible.

With just a few words, we were in agreement. We rushed at the first three to arrive; seeing us approaching, they groaned with joy. Carefully maneuvering a few feet away from their infected bodies, we urged them to separate. Each of us had an opponent. No one had to be jealous.

An enormous woman was standing in front of me. Her fat, muck-covered thighs – which were protruding from a torn, soiled, flowery dress – rubbed against each other as she dragged herself painfully towards me. Her bloated belly, swollen with post-mortem gas, resembled a huge, strange cup-and-ball topped by an incongruous protuberance: her ugly, decomposed face. When she lunged at me and parried my hammer blow with a sudden flick of her hand, I wished I'd had to face the scrawny guy who had set his sights on Karim. I narrowly escaped her greasy, powerful grip by hurling myself to the ground. Not wasting any time, I propelled myself away from her as, not being able to bend down, she let herself fall on top of me. The fresh scab that had started to cover my palm tore off, and I groaned as a pool of rotten flesh, liquefied organs, and undigested human remains spread around me. The fat woman's prominent abdomen had exploded with a foul blast. But the creature continued to crawl towards me, her face bathed in her own viscera. I was getting up to finish her off when Karim's boot crushed her skull, adding new ingredients to the soup that covered the ground.

We spun around immediately. Frédéric hadn't finished with his opponent. He kept backing away, getting dangerously close to the other two zombies. He narrowly dodged their attack and had the clarity of mind not to scream. He waved wildly at us. He had been forced into a corner of the building. We ran, but the zombies got there first: the poor man was flattened to the ground under two monsters.

Karim threw himself on the vile heap of limbs flailing in all directions, leaving it to me to get rid of the third corpse, a teenager with a white and red cap – mostly red now – on his head. He was a pathetic opponent compared to the enormous woman, whose stench had pervaded the playground, and he collapsed at the first blow from the hammer.

Karim had beheaded Frédéric's two attackers; Frédéric was curled up in a ball on the ground. He was crying his eyes out and had dropped his weapon. Karim was holding onto his tightly, fully prepared in case his buddy suddenly attacked him. A few seconds passed, and Frédéric sat up.

"Did they bite you?" Karim asked him, not beating around the bush.

The young man, looking distressed, compulsively began to scrutinize every square inch of his skin. Eventually, he calmed down and, in a trembling voice, told us:

"I don't think so. Holy shit, guys, they didn't get me. They didn't get me."

Karim stood back up and held out his hand to him.

"Still on the attack? We have to get going."

Frédéric seized his hand. Once on his feet, he stood there for a moment, turning his head violently in one direction and then the other. He looked possessed. Suddenly, he ran towards the door with the push bar through which I had entered the courtyard the day before. Karim tried to catch him but arrived too late. Copious amounts of blood splashed onto the door, which had been left wide open by Frédéric's sudden exit. A corpse had grabbed him in the middle of his run and had sunk his teeth into his throat. The young man was convulsing as his heart spurted its last quarts of blood through his torn carotid artery.

Karim smashed the creature's skull and cursed as he kicked Frédéric's body. He didn't give him a chance to get up, striking him hard with the machete. I put a hand on the young man's shoulder; he was breathing heavily.

"We can do it together," I told him.

I didn't like playing the hero, but I couldn't pass up such a great opportunity to get away from the school. The hardest part, however, was yet to come.

His face was streaming with sweat. Drops were rolling down his forehead and cutting furrows in the blood that covered it. He turned to me, a glint of excitement in his eyes.

"Yeah, let's go take out the trash."

He pushed the corpses away and closed the door behind us, cutting us off permanently from any retreat.

"Okay, I'll go up towards the village. You go down on the other side," he added.

I said nothing but appreciated this division of labor. We quickly exchanged some encouragement, circled around the building, and dashed to the road that ran alongside the small courtyard where the zombies had clustered.

Remi saw us and shouted:

"Way to go, guys!"

He fell silent, and it was our turn to reveal ourselves.

The dead spotted us immediately and began to move towards us. Karim had placed himself higher up on the road and was attracting some of them in his direction. But a larger pack was choosing to come towards me. Were they doing this with the idea of being able to bite into a bigger piece of meat, or were they just letting themselves be guided by the slope that was leading them directly to me?

Remi had disappeared from the roof, leaving the two groups of the dead to focus exclusively on their bait of choice. Here, right at their fingertips. I knew that the success of this ploy hinged on our ability to let the zombies get close enough, but not too close. A nice carrot on the end of a stick. Always there, but never bitten. However, I very quickly started to run. I didn't care as long as they followed me. From a distance.

Our little game lasted for several long minutes, and the school ended up disappearing from view. I had moved deeper into the residential area, continuing to lead the horde. They were furious to see me perpetually getting further away. Their urge to devour me was palpable. My skin was burning, as if thousands of canine teeth were trying to pierce my skin. The sun was beating hard on my head, but I couldn't afford to stop to take a drink. I had to stay vigilant enough to spot any zombies coming from elsewhere. But I wasn't vigilant enough; I cried out in rage when the street I had taken ended in a cul-de-sac. Looking behind me, I saw the stupid blue, white, and red sign that marked the dead end. Devoid of all logic, the sign had been turned around, and it seemed to be mocking my fate. The horde had already appeared at the entrance to the narrow street, blocking any retreat.

Fucking *déjà vu.*

CHAPTER 12
THE CHERUB'S TEARS

Dumbass, what were you thinking? That you were out for a stroll? I thought as the zombies flooded the alley in one giant, violent wave. Squeezed up against each other, they instantly blocked the exit. I ran to the end of the dead end, where a Renaissance-style mansion stood. Its imposing white walls and slate roof contrasted with the villas around it, huddled behind thick hedges that made them inaccessible. This beautiful home, meanwhile, was protected by a tall, sturdy, wrought iron fence that appeared to encircle completely. An even more impressive gate marked the beginning of a short gravel driveway that ended at the steps to the building's threshold. The barrier, a blue as dark as the slate roof, was topped with blunt spikes that shot up towards the sky at regular intervals. This was an ideal shelter. All I had to do was get inside.

By chance, there was a large trash container disfiguring the end of the cul-de-sac, right where the enclosure met the simple, shabby, green fence of the house next door. I wasted no time and climbed up onto the lid of the garbage can; from there, my heart pounding, I grabbed two iron spikes to hoist myself to the top of the barrier. I waited up there for a few seconds, hesitating to jump, but the first zombies, who were crashing into the gate, presented some irrefutable arguments.

Severe pain shot through my ankle as I landed between two clumps of parched flowers. I moaned and attempted to get up. My heart decided otherwise and started pounding faster and faster, like a bouncing ball locked in my rib cage. Golden flecks suddenly blurred my field of vision.

Behind me, the monsters were sliding their emaciated limbs between the bars and spitting in frustration. I tried to move, my back arched and my breath sputtering, but I collapsed. Unable to combat my body's surrender, I saw the world darken, then disappear.

***

When I opened my eyes, everything was just as dark. But it wasn't the same darkness: it was nighttime. The moon was trying to give some color to this extinct world but only managed to paint it in a wide assortment of greys. I lifted my head. Bits of gravel had lodged in my cheek without piercing my skin. I brushed them away, feeling under my fingertips the imprint they had left, and got to my knees. A huge, pale form was towering before me: the mansion. I stared at its spectral whiteness for a few seconds, then turned around. The zombies were still there. The lunar rays seemed to be avoiding them, and all I could make out was a dark, moving mass that spread all along the fence. My awakening had roused them from their torpor, too.

Had I spent the entire day collapsed on the ground in this house's yard? I found it hard to believe that not a single zombie had come to take advantage of the free buffet. The place must have been truly impenetrable.

I felt rested. My old, rusty machine had suddenly broken down, but the pit stop seemed to have done the trick. With cotton mouth and a dry throat, I drank in gulps, almost completely emptying the only bottle I had brought with me. The sun had assaulted my body all day long, and the top of my head, where the onset of baldness was beginning to appear, was on fire.

A light but warm breeze brought the flower beds to life as I climbed the high steps that led to the building's front door. I wondered what kind of weirdo had had such a structure erected in a small village in Provence.

I inspected the solid oak door and found it locked. I knocked and stuck my ear to the hard, smooth wood: not a sound. The mansion seemed empty, abandoned of all life.

I went back down the steps and walked around the house, checking the windows on the first floor. They were all closed and had burglar-proof glass that my hammer only managed to scratch. There was evidently no way to get in. My feet brought me back around front, to the base of the garage door. Instinctively, I bent down and tried to lift it. It slid silently on its rails.

The large space was devoid of any vehicles. Obviously, the owners had been away when the zombie festivities began. It was surprisingly tidy for a garage, but the owners of such a place certainly would not be without the services of one or two servants.

I quickly inspected the shelves, unable to clearly see what was there, then walked over to the large white rectangle that stood out at the back of the garage. I was thinking again about the dead-end sign, and how it had seemed to be mocking me, when my hand rested on the bunch of keys that was, miraculously, hanging from the lock. I unlocked the door that led inside and, one fist clenched around the handle of my hammer, entered the house.

"Is someone there?" I shouted to make sure my voice carried throughout the structure.

I waited for several minutes, motionless and holding my breath. Nothing broke the silence that weighed heavily inside the house. The place was deserted.

I groped forward in the darkness. I ignored the first closed door on my left and continued to explore. My eyes were starting to get used to the absence of light. I then emerged into a large room, in the center of which stood some enormous, dark shapes. I walked along the walls, one hand pressed against the extensively embossed wallpaper, avoiding the sideboards and other tables that blocked my way. All of a sudden, my fingers brushed a soft, delicate material. A thick velvet curtain hung beside me. I opened it, and the moonlight could finally penetrate the space: a living room adorned with large armchairs and multiple sofas. I drew the curtains on the other windows and got a clearer view of my surroundings. The place was richly decorated, and objects that would make any antique dealer green with envy were lined up on exceptionally elegant pieces of furniture. A plaster cherub stood in front of me, smiling at me and pointing to the large candelabra beside it.

In a drawer of the dresser on which the little statue was positioned, I found an old metal lighter. I smiled back at the cherub and lit the candles that adorned the candelabra. The room lit up with a multitude of colors. All this ostentation was a bit much for me, but I nevertheless took a few seconds to appreciate the delicacy of the décor. All these trivialities from the past put my mind at ease.

Despite it all, I quickly came back to reality and started checking out the rest of the house, candelabra in hand. It cast misshapen shadows on the walls; I jumped more than once, convinced a zombie had just popped up under my nose. But the place was empty.

Pretty quickly, I found the room I was interested in: a large, fully equipped kitchen, the modernity of which was surprising given the owners' attachment to the authentic. I rummaged through all the cupboards, eager to get my hands on some calorie-rich treasure. The pots and pans, porcelain dinnerware, and household appliances were countless, but there wasn't a trace of food. The house was definitely the second home of wealthy Parisians who only came down to the countryside to enjoy the sun for a few days per year. I cursed them for not having chosen the month of June to pay a visit to the south of France and imagined them transformed into zombies in their thousand-square-foot apartment with a view of the Sacré Coeur Basilica.

My throat still arid, I suppressed the urge to finish my meager supply of water. I was overcome with disappointment. I thought I had found the perfect place to settle down for a while, but the thought of having to go out to stock up on necessities and face the horde made it far less appealing. I sighed and continued my tour.

The rest of the ground floor was not much more interesting, with its gigantic dining room, dens, and library. This burglar's paradise turned out to be of little interest to a survivor like me. So, I put all my hopes on the upper floor, but my search there was equally fruitless. My only consolation was that there were plenty of comfortable beds in the just as many bedrooms upstairs. I could rest quietly there, even though I doubted I would get a good night's sleep, what with the stifling heat in all the rooms.

My feet dragged me back down to the ground floor. The candles had lost their poise and height and were slumping pitifully around the exquisite metal of the candelabra.

For lack of anything else to do, I decided to set myself up in the living room and observe the zombies, like I'd been able to do at home. When I walked past the kitchen again, the light from the candles, which was genuinely starting to dim, furtively illuminated a trap door that had escaped my notice during my first inspection. How could I have missed it? My face broke into a broad smile at the thought of what was probably awaiting me beyond the little wooden door. These people hadn't left any supplies, but surely they had forgotten one small bottle in the wine cellar.

I ran to borrow some new candles from the cherub and then retraced my steps. Ready to sink into the bowels of the mansion, I opened the hatch, revealing a flight of rough, dusty stairs. A musty, damp smell instantly invaded my nostrils. Candelabra in hand, I walked down the steps, dodging the cobwebs hanging from the ceiling like a character in a poor parody of the adventure films that aired on public television every week. The short staircase led to a magnificent, vaulted basement. I couldn't believe my eyes.

Not only was there an extraordinary display of bottles running along the entire length of the cellar, but on one of the sections of the wall, there were suspended metal shelves that were abundantly stocked. Dozens of packs of water were lined up on the shelves, and there were even more canned goods stored there. I roared with laughter at the unexpected but formidable outcome of this demonic day.

I put the candelabra down on the old, rotted table that divided the cellar in two and attempted a quick inventory of my discovery. The cans were blank, without labels, which led me to understand that every meal would be a lottery. Good thing I liked living dangerously!

The bottles of wine, on the other hand, proudly displayed their vintages and grape varietals under a thick layer of dust. There seemed to be nothing but great wines. I grabbed a bottle and dusted it off, revealing its name: Château Latour 1989. I figured it would do the trick, and I went back upstairs, a tin can in my other hand. I was finally going to be able to pick up where the zombies had interrupted me several days earlier and have a nice, quiet drink.

In the kitchen, I emptied the contents of the can – a cassoulet that was far richer in beans than duck – into a dish and armed myself with the largest stemmed glass I could find. A corkscrew completed my gear. I brought my booty back to the living room and settled in, pushing the most comfortable-looking chair closer to one of the windows. I collapsed into the plush seat and crossed my legs. My life as Lord of the Apocalypse was beginning. It could perhaps last for several weeks here.

I dipped my fingers into the cold stew and tossed a full handful of beans smothered in grease into my mouth. I marveled at how delicious my taste buds found them, no matter how unappetizing they were.

I chewed as I watched the grey mass of zombies behind the metal railings, and then I uncorked the bottle with the skill of a master. I filled my glass, pretended to be a connoisseur admiring the color of the wine, and downed it in one go. *Not bad*, I thought, pouring myself another glass. I sank my teeth into a duck leg and stuck my fatty fingers to the glass again. I emptied it in a few sips. The bottle had already taken a hit. Not wasting a second, I went to look for more ammunition in the cellar. I was going to need it.

I returned to my chair, several new friends under my arm. I was finally going to be able to forget the fear that had gripped me for far too long now. Without bothering with the glass, I bid farewell to Château Latour, which disappeared for good inside me. The alcohol was starting to take effect, and a strong sensation of heat was radiating from my stomach. My mind was calm. I was finally having clear thoughts. It wouldn't last, and the morning would be another nightmare populated with zombies against a hangover backdrop, but I didn't care in the slightest.

I uncorked the second bottle and had the same fate in store for it. I was indulging in a luxurious buzz and gulping down the *grands crus* like an alcoholic bum does cheap wine. No one was going to come and reproach me for it. I was at home here.

By the third bottle, images began to assail me. I tried to dilute them in more wine, but they kept coming back. The alcohol had made me forget the present, but the past was flooding in. I tried to push these visions out of my drunken mind, but I couldn't. In a fit of anger, I threw the bottle against the wall. It left a huge red stain on the wallpaper and crashed onto the floor. I stood up suddenly from the chair and collapsed as the room started to spin. I couldn't fight it off.

"Hey Dad, you coming?" she asks me, a playful smile on her lips. "Uncle David promised to give me a ride on his motorbike."

Her mother looks at me furiously, already knowing what my answer will be.

"Sorry, sweetie. I'm waiting for an important phone call. But I'm sure it'll be fun. It's not every day that David invites us over to eat at his place."

"Yeah, but it's better if you come," she answers in a voice that hardly masks her exasperation.

I ruffle her hair, and she shies away, complaining that I'm messing it up. Her mother leaves the room. I catch up with her.

"Wait. You know I'm sorry."

She stares at me with her beautiful green eyes, her face impassive.

"He's a really important buyer. I can't miss this call."

She doesn't even try to argue. She is also tired of our numerous discussions and arguments.

I grasp her arm gently. She lets it happen, then turns away.

"We're going, sweetie," she says, not paying any attention to me.

Her silence hurts me. My daughter walks past me and puts on her shoes.

"We're taking your car," my wife adds before leaving.

Standing in the wide-open doorway, I watch her back out, and then they leave: my two loves.

A sharp pain in my head brought me back to the present: I had hit the base of a sideboard.

Forgetting about the bump that was starting to form, I let the anger wash over me. I got up and, with an aggressive swipe of my hand, sent flying all the knick-knacks from the nearest table. They crashed to the ground and shattered into thousands of small pieces. I was screaming in rage and uttering incoherent words. The uproar I was causing woke the zombies. They added their moans to the background noise of my madness. The urge to go open the door for them crossed my mind as other memories, which I had done my best to forget, forced their way into my consciousness.

I wobbled across the living room as if possessed by a drunken demon. I didn't want to see those images anymore and closed my eyes. My eyelids hurt. I had bit my lip, and in my mouth, the taste of blood mingled with that of the wine.

I wanted to forget everything about that damned day, but the images continued to invade my thoughts. My own demons were chasing from my mind the ones in flesh and blood waiting for me outside. Why force myself to relive these moments? I wanted to remain who I was. Patrick, the eternal loner. I had been happy for years like that. Why couldn't I continue to live in this charade of happiness? I had a bourgeois house all to myself! Why not let me enjoy it? I cursed the cowardice that had pushed me to get drunk so easily. Drink to forget: what bullshit.

The flames dance before my eyes. I burn everything that belongs to them. The empty bottles pile up, and I cry out in despair all night long. I am in a trance.

I insult a God I do not believe in. I am enraged at this degenerate world that has punished me for no reason. I let hate take over. I want to jump into the embers and be done with it all. I leave it at that. I am a coward.

I don't go to their funeral. They don't blame me, and then they criticize me for it. David tries to put the pieces back together. Not for long. I am alone. I put up with it. I am happy. Well, I think I am.

The taste of vomit pulled me from the memories' grip, and I sprayed the dresser the plaster cherub was standing on. The smell of undigested wine and gastric juices invaded the room. The little angel kept on smiling. I suddenly found him extremely idiotic.

"So, now you're fucking with me?" I muttered, finding it difficult to line up several words coherently.

"You'll see, you little brat."

I rummaged through the dresser drawer and pulled out several old papers. I took out the small lighter to ignite them. I wanted to burn it all down again. But my accomplice was out of gas and was spitting harmless sparks. Angrily, I sent it crashing into the cherub, which it disfigured by tearing off his upper lip and part of his nose. I fell to the ground and started to cry. Why couldn't they leave me the hell alone?

My thoughts were muddled and intersecting each other indiscriminately. I was mad at the whole world. I had always asked for just one thing: to be allowed to live. In peace. Nothing else. And yet, this crazy world kept refusing that to me.

My pitiful existence made no sense. I was aware of that. I was a selfish bastard who thought he'd find happiness within himself. Even before their death. They had never refused to let me live. They had forbidden me to do so locked in the confined universe of myself. I cried bitterly, hating the real culprit for the first time.

All this madness hitting the Earth was not a punishment they were inflicting on me. How could I have believed such a thing? I was nothing. I was contemptible. Insignificant people did not receive the slightest punishment. They were there, present but useless. I was one witness among others to the destruction of the world, ready to continue playing the parasite: safe in my mansion, taking full advantage of my supplies.

So, I made a promise to myself, not sure I would remember it again the next morning. My mind then began to quiet down, and I managed to articulate a few words:

"Sorry, lil' dude."

The cherub remained silent, and without waiting for his answer, I passed out.

***

My cheek was soaking in a reddish, foul-smelly substance. I had vomited again in my sleep. I sat up and discovered, to my dismay, the state of the room in the light of day. A good number of the decorations were broken on the floor, a table was knocked over, and even a curtain was torn. I knew the zombies weren't to blame. The shame I felt was nothing compared to the vise that was squeezing my skull. I hadn't had a hangover like this in years. I wanted to stay there, stinking and terrifying, and doze for a few hours, but I remembered the resolution I had made: to return to the school.

I had found a perfect refuge to wait and see if things would settle down eventually, but I no longer had the desire to do so. What was the point of staying locked up here? The apocalypse had dramatically reduced the list of human activities, boiling it down to one essential hobby: surviving. But why survive alone in an unfamiliar home? I had to learn how to live, as I had done during those days spent with Emma. For the first time in years, I missed someone. How could I have been so blind? Unable to do anything about it, I had become attached to her.

My head feeling heavy, I stood up and dragged myself to the downstairs bathroom. I searched under the sink and dug up a towel, which I gently cleaned my face with. I smelled like a dirty, sick person, and that bothered me. I sprayed myself with perfume to mask it, a very French thing to do. Its scent was also unpleasant to me, although far less so than my body's.

Then I went upstairs where, after long minutes spent going through the contents of the bedroom dressers and wardrobes, I finally ferreted out some clothes in my size. I swapped my ripped and stained pants for thick, immaculate jeans. A simple black T-shirt completed my new outfit. There was little chance of my launching a fashion line, especially in the middle of a zombie apocalypse. I couldn't bring myself to leave my motorcycle jacket behind and stuffed it in my bag.

I approached the large window, which looked out onto the cul-de-sac. The zombies were still there. Some had dispersed, having gone in another direction long ago, ready to form a new horde as they shuffled on. But the majority of my flock was still waiting for me. Unperturbed, they clung to the last image they had of me, to motivate themselves, to keep moving their rotten carcasses. Did they really remember me, or were they continuing to attack the barrier simply out of habit? I had no idea. The problem remained the same for me: they were still there.

I crossed the upstairs from one end to the other and went into a room I had briefly visited the day before: a perfectly organized nursery, where a delicate smell of clean linen wafted despite the time that had elapsed since the owners' last visit. A French door opened onto a small balcony, from the height of which I once again noticed how stifling the heat was. The night before, I hadn't paid attention to the house's surroundings, obsessed as I had been with the possibility of finding shelter here. A large field of wheat stretched out behind the mansion, separated from the property's yard by the iron fence, which was just as imposing there as at the front of the building. I caught a glimpse of a single zombie roaming around out there, the ears of wheat tickling his knees delicately.

Cheered up by the discovery of this escape route, I went back down to the cellar, where I piled as many supplies as possible into my bag.

Bottles of water were the first to find homes there, followed closely by a few cans, the memory of the stew still fresh in my mind. Once the bag was full, I went to say goodbye to the cherub, once again apologizing to him. I thanked him and then walked out the back door, which I was careful not to lock behind me. The deserted, dying yard greeted me silently. I crossed it slowly and then climbed the fence, not without some difficulty. I dropped down smoothly on the other side. My ankle had swollen again, but the pain was bearable.

The zombie I'd spotted from the second floor hadn't missed one bit of my escape and was heading towards me. He was strangely mute, and his head was bobbling in a bizarre way. He came closer. Most of his throat had been devoured, and the few muscles that remained were struggling to support the weight of his skull. I lost interest in him and went in the opposite direction: theoretically, towards the school.

I crossed the field, wondering if I had ever met its owner, and stroked the tops of the ears with my left hand. The wheat quickly turned into grass, which then gave way to an expanse of asphalt. The small road lined with oak trees that I had arrived on brought me back to the outskirts of the residential area and then began a more sustained climb. My load was slowing me down, but I did my best to keep up a good pace. Behind me, I could no longer see the zombie with the slit throat.

At the top of an even steeper hill, I finally saw the school building. I was on the road I had watched with Christine, the one the horde had arrived on. The place was quiet. I was relieved to see that our strategy seemed to have worked.

My strides lengthened, and I reached the building. A small beige van was parked along the wall where the window had given way under the weight of the zombies. Its side mirror had been torn off in the maneuver and was lying on the asphalt, useless. The vehicle, marooned a few inches from the school windows, covered the breach, preventing intrusion by new creatures. I walked around it and stuck my face against one of the building's still intact windows, trying to see what was going on inside between two sheets of newspaper that were stuck to it: shadows with dragging gaits still haunted this part of the school. I hoped the barricade hadn't given way.

I turned around and climbed onto the hood of the van and then up on its cabin; the ledge of the roof was within easy reach. I lifted my bag off my shoulders and pushed it on top of the building. I was getting ready to pull myself up when an outstretched hand appeared over the concrete wall:

"Hello again," I heard Karim's voice say.

CHAPTER 13
DODGING THE BULLET

The young man pulled me up to him with a grip that was surprisingly strong for his stature.

"I didn't see you coming. I was watching the road on the other side. Damn, am I glad to see you," he told me, not letting go of my hand.

"Me too, Karim," I answered him in all honesty. "I didn't think the two of us were going to get out of that."

"Yeah, it's amazing. I was on the run for hours before I lost them. It was close. I thought I was a goner."

Karim finally released my fingers and nodded towards the bag:

"Did you do your shopping at the same time? You didn't have that much stuff when you left."

I looked down at the object of his interest and smiled at him:

"I found Ali Baba's cave. What I took isn't even close to all of it."

The young man's eyes lit up, and he held out his fist to me.

"Fist bump, Patrick. You've saved the day."

Surprised, I followed suit.

He punched my fist softly.

"We have to go tell Gerald about this," he added.

Some of my good mood went out the window when he mentioned their leader's name, but I quickly wiped his face from my mind. Karim had picked up my bag and slipped his arms through the straps.

"You coming? They're gonna give you a hero's welcome!" he exclaimed cheerfully.

The other survivors had surely reacted enthusiastically upon his own return, and he seemed excited to relive that moment of fleeting glory.

I followed him for a few yards over to the ladder, happy to be able to go down it stress-free: the last time, it had led me straight into the lion's den. But, as my feet landed in the courtyard, I was startled by a hoarse, throaty growl coming from a window a little further away.

"We haven't been able to get rid of them all yet," Karim explained to me. "I cornered them when I parked the van."

This young man was incredible. Not only had he risked his life to draw the zombies away from the school, but he had come back with a solution to seal off the breach. I couldn't help but thank him.

"For the van? Sure, but you're the one who brought food and water," he said, smiling.

He headed towards the end of the courtyard, where the door to the bathroom awaited us. The room was still just as putrid, and we walked through it quickly. The smell in the hallway was even worse. The bacteria were continuing to work their fingers – and other extremities – to the bone, spreading rot among the pile of corpses that loomed a few paces away.

The revolting scent emanating from it made me gag. You didn't have to be a hypochondriac to feel instantly contaminated. Death was loitering in the hallway, leaving behind its multitudes of disease and infection.

Holding our breath, we ran to the cafeteria. That room stank almost as much despite the timid breath of fresh air coming through the glass panel Karim had broken.

As we entered, all eyes turned towards us, but mine met Gerald's first. Most of the survivors were gathered around him. Was he in the middle of giving out new orders? If he was surprised to see me, he hid it well and said in his deep voice:

"Patrick, I'm so glad you came back."

It was time for another scene. I remained silent, and as the survivors began to whisper among themselves, he strode over to me, one hand outstretched in my direction. I took it limply and let him shake my hand for a moment.

"That's not the way we greet a hero," he said, moving aside so everybody could see me.

Some applause broke out, and several people from the group came to greet me warmly.

Not knowing how to react, I just nodded in agreement. I was the center of attention for a few minutes, then everyone gathered around Gerald, who was resuming his speech. Had I almost gotten my ass handed to me just for that?

"Mr. Patrick!" she cried, running in my direction.

No, it was for that.

Emma threw herself into my arms. I lifted her tenderly and placed a kiss on her cheek.

"You're prickly! And you smell all weird," she told me with the frankness characteristic of her age.

I guffawed, unable to control myself. Gerald glared at me then continued to dictate his instructions. I didn't care; it felt so good to laugh.

"I thought you weren't coming back," she whispered to me when I finally calmed down.

"I wasn't about to abandon you," I replied, smiling through my thick beard and trying to mask the shame her words had caused me.

Yes, I had wanted to abandon her.

"Giselle said you had left," she continued.

"That's not the first time she's been wrong," intervened a voice I didn't immediately recognize.

Christine had come up behind me, and she gave me a friendly smile when I turned around.

"I'm happy to see you again, Patrick. I really thought something bad had happened to you."

"I'm happy to be in one piece," I joked.

Emma made a face, and I laughed again, accompanied by Christine.

"How did it go yesterday?" I asked her.

"We played the quiet game all day. Didn't we, Emma?" she said, stroking the little girl's arm. "We stayed in the cafeteria. We didn't want to mess up the plan by making noise. We waited, hoping you'd come back. Then, Karim arrived with the van. He managed to get here with the engine turned off a good part of the way. Can you believe it? Anyway, the zombies were gone. I think Gerald wants to mount an expedition to go look for food today, but..."

The cheers that rang out behind us interrupted Christine. There was excitement around Gerald, whom Karim had just started talking to. Motivated by his speech, the survivors dispersed around the room and returned to the center armed with their weapons. They looked as ridiculous as when we'd first met, but now I knew what they were capable of. Almost everybody, around twenty people, had gathered.

Gerald, who had grabbed his machete while talking to Karim, was now walking towards us.

"Is it far?" he asked me, rubbing his chin.

Met with my stupefaction, he kept going.

"Where you found the food."

"No, not really," I answered, taken aback by his request. "You want to go there now?"

He shook his head and turned away from me:

"Come on, guys, follow me!" he shouted at the mock army standing behind him.

He took one step towards the exit and then addressed me again, in a menacing tone:

"We're gonna need you."

He ignored me yet again and led his troops outside. We moved aside to let them pass.

"What an asshole," I remarked, remembering far too late that I was still holding Emma.

She chuckled, and Christine smiled at me, confirming that she thought the same thing. The little one was getting heavy, so I put her down and looked around. A few women, an elderly man I had never noticed before, and a young boy were still there. Giselle, sitting in the corner, was giving me the evil eye.

"Patrick!" Karim called suddenly, standing in the doorway. "You coming?"

Gerald had obviously briefed him well. I sighed and crouched down next to Emma:

"I'll be back."

Christine stepped forward and took her hand.

"It's okay, go ahead," she said.

I got up and joined the young man who was holding the door open.

"What's happening?" I asked him, even though he already had his machete in hand.

"We're gonna go beat the crap out of some zombies. Gerald wants us to clean out the wing they've invaded," he replied in an almost innocuous tone.

I couldn't believe it. I had barely gotten back, and that bastard wanted to send me to the front again. I almost had the urge to get killed over there just to piss him off. How would he find the mansion without my directions? Perhaps seeing me gone for good was more important to him. He had been able to hide his surprise when he saw me arrive with Karim, but I was sure he hadn't counted on ever seeing me again. He had played it well, prompting me to sail off into the sunset, but he had forgotten one piece of the equation: my protégée and my own insanity that had convinced me to come back. Now, I had to be wary of him. He probably wouldn't do me any favors even if I did keep quiet. I followed Karim.

In the courtyard, along the row of trees running through its center, Gerald had already lined up his men. They seemed ready to tackle the dead. I took a spot at the end of the row and waited. The man with the gun briefly reviewed his troops, like a general about to embark on a historic battle. He then motioned to Karim, who approached the cursed wing the zombies were crammed into. He was going to shake the hive.

He turned to us and then, deeming us ready, gave a monumental kick to one of the classroom doors, which flew open. The impact was so hard that it bounced against the interior partition and closed again. Cautiously, Karim turned the knob and pushed the door back gently. A first corpse appeared almost immediately, but no sooner had he stepped out of the doorway than he collapsed like an old pile of dirty rags, his skull split open by a machete. The young man zealously stepped over the threshold and howled. There was no doubt now: the swarm was awake. Our friend ran back to join us.

The zombies' grunting intensified, and a terrible racket filled the building's interior. Enraged, the creatures were searching for where the noise was coming from. The smartest, or just the closest, were heading our way. They eventually emerged from the classroom. Their dry, monstrous faces seemed to light up when they saw the human shish kabob lined up in front of them. One by one, they threw themselves at us.

As the monsters approached, the row that Gerald had carefully put into place broke apart. Faced with the reality of the danger, some of the survivors looked like they were about to have a breakdown. But others, mainly those who'd dealt with the group of zombies when I'd first arrived, were ready to fight to the finish. One of them, with a motorcycle helmet securely on his head, rushed at the first creature and smashed his jaw with a metal bar. The zombie didn't stop and, jaw hanging in the air, tried to bite the stranger on the head but only managed to crush his bloody upper gum against the visor, leaving a disgusting mark. The man pushed the corpse away, and Karim, who had also joined the hand-to-hand fighting, cut off the top of the creature's skull.

The battle was taking shape, and the fights were increasing in number. Even Gerald was taking part in the fray. Having only one way out, the zombies were arriving in dribs and drabs, deprived of the strength in numbers. We were taking part in true carnage. The walking cadavers were being eliminated as if on an assembly line. Several members of the group stayed behind us, paralyzed by the appearance of the dead, but those who were fighting were doing so without restraint. Even Thierry, still equipped with his completely banged up frying pans, was accumulating victims.

I had only slaughtered one zombie so far, a teenage girl with strange blue locks of hair who offered no resistance when my hammer sank into her bulging forehead. During the fighting, without realizing it, I had gotten closer to Gerald and was just a few steps behind him. He had just eliminated another opponent, and a new one was already taking his place. This one was a real circus freak, a mountain of muscles. The steroids hadn't prevented him from transforming. His huge, necrotic arms hung limply at his sides as if he had lost the use of them. He was chattering his teeth like a lunatic. He suddenly accelerated and hurled his more than six-foot frame at Gerald, who was facing him. Gerald raised his machete, ready to plunge it into his throat, but suddenly, he dodged his attacker's charge.

In a fraction of a second, I found myself underneath the creature. Unable to move his arms, he was shaking his head all around and trying to seize me by the throat. Miraculously, I had managed to place my arm under his chin, preventing his disgusting face from approaching mine to give me a deadly kiss. The impact had knocked the wind out of me, and I was struggling to keep the creature at bay. His weight was preventing me from breathing normally, and I was pinned to the ground. The colossus was pushing with his legs in the hope of reaching me. I tried to scream but couldn't.

When the sound finally emerged from my throat, the zombie had ceased moving. With his neck slashed several inches deep by Karim's machete, and his skull smashed by the man in the motorcycle helmet's metal bar, he lay dead, once and for all, on top of me. My two rescuers rolled the heavy carcass to the side.

Karim extended his hand and helped me to my feet. But, without thanking him and still gasping for air, I walked over to Gerald, who was watching the zombies continuing to come out. The punch knocked him to the ground.

With gritted teeth and rubbing his cheek, he sprang to his feet:

"What's the matter with you? Are you out of your mind?" he spat.

I couldn't contain myself any longer.

"You must be kidding me, you scumbag! You got out of the way on purpose!"

I could feel the anger growing inside me, and I was ready to hit him again. My fingers were sore, and I was worried that I had cracked a knuckle, but I was having trouble controlling myself.

"What?" he said, feigning ignorance. "You've really got a problem, Gramps."

I lunged at him again. This time, I was brandishing my hammer. Two pairs of powerful hands grabbed my arms.

"Dammit, calm down, Patrick!" Karim shouted, holding me back, assisted by the man in the motorcycle helmet.

The other survivors were watching us, as the last living dead seemed to have left the classrooms and been eliminated.

"Seriously, what's come over you?" the young man added.

I tried to regain my composure.

"The zombie. He avoided him deliberately."

"What?"

"That big bastard you pulled off me," I said, pointing to the monster's almost decapitated body. "Gerald avoided him to let him attack me. He could have killed him. He let it charge at me. Intentionally."

I emphasized each of the syllables of that last word while staring at Gerald, who was holding his jaw.

"You're really sick," he said, approaching.

He touched my chest with the tip of his finger and added:

"He was faster than I thought, and I had to move aside. And if you think I'm going to apologize because you were behind me, you can go fuck yourself."

If Karim had let go of me, I would certainly have tried to hit him again, but he was gripping me tightly.

"Seriously, why would he do that?" interjected the other man who was holding me back.

He released my arm and took off his helmet: it was Serge, the other witness to the sergeant's murder.

"Oh, son of a bitch, I can't believe this," I said, rolling my eyes. "You know very well why."

At the same time, a troop of zombie latecomers exited the building. The survivors watching the scene were surprised by this unexpected eruption of the dead. Gerald yelled, and they reorganized themselves. Karim and Serge, who had put his helmet back on, rushed towards the monsters. New corpses joined the ones already covering the ground.

Gerald suddenly grabbed his rifle, ready to use it.

"Guys, with me!" he shouted at the more seasoned men, the ones who had killed the most victims.

They joined him and entered the school wing to exterminate the last zombies, leaving me alone in the yard with the others. They were looking sideways at me. In a matter of minutes, I had gone from being a hero to being a crazy old man. I felt betrayed, and I was quite incapable of getting things back to the way they were. This incident called into question my choice to stay at the school. Any desire I'd had to do so had vanished. So, to avoid letting that sordid darkness capture my thoughts, I did what I did best: take action. I gripped the feet of the nearest corpse and began to move it.

"We need to burn them," I said to the small group that was still staring at me strangely.

I dragged the body under the covered playground. No one had moved. Were these sheep waiting for their Gerald to give them instructions?

I was amazed at how quickly the human brain could reprogram itself: follow one person one day, follow another the next; all without ever making a decision yourself. They approached the apocalypse and their survival the same way as their lives: as a preset sequence of tasks to be completed. Only on demand.

I ignored them and grasped the neck of the T-shirt on the corpse of a young teenage girl; a dirty pair of headphones protruded from it. I pulled her towards me. The garment rode up, revealing a grey, lacerated stomach. I dropped her next to the first body and started the operation over again. As I was taking care of my fourth cadaver, the others decided to help me. One of them emptied his stomach against a tree after moving a stiff only a few inches. Even so, our chore progressed quickly, and the vile carpet of the dead that had adorned the courtyard transformed into a towering, smelly heap.

Karim reappeared in the doorway. An even thicker layer of blood covered his face. He waved to us and shouted:

"We're going to get the last ones out! Start collecting the ones in the hallway!"

My back aching from going back and forth so many times, I followed my companions, who were complying. The number of rotting carcasses waiting for us inside was much greater. The joints in my elbow would retain a painful memory of this massacre.

First, we removed the barricade of desks, which came unstuck from the bodies with a sucking sound. I felt like I was removing a spoiled cake from the pan: the pile of corpses had fit perfectly, and now a perfectly straight wall of crushed faces and other shattered limbs stood in front of us. Disregarding the reality, we dismantled the pieces of this appalling work of art one by one. The trail of blood that Eric's body had left on the floor was quickly forgotten and replaced by a veritable highway of redness that started from the barricade, changed direction into the bathroom, and stretched as far as the playground.

The mound located there was impressive. Even the most fearsome death squads would have been jealous of it. Except that this pile of bodies was not born from a degenerate ideology but from a simple necessity: to survive.

Gerald's group also brought its contributions – that is, its corpses – to the heap, clearing a large number of remains from the area the zombies had invaded. During the entire operation, no one spoke to me. Not even Christine, who had come to help but who, far too emotional, was keeping a low profile amid her grief.

When the hallway was finally emptied of its last cadaver, I quietly climbed onto the roof, pushed by the desire to be alone so I could think calmly. We were well into the afternoon, but the heat was still grueling. The sunlight reflecting off the white gravel blinded me.

One hand over my eyes, I dragged myself to the lawn chairs I had sat on with Christine and dropped into one, to the sound of an ominous crack. It held, and I relaxed all my muscles, glad to be able to take a break.

I reviewed the events of the day and wondered if I really had made the right decision. I never thought Gerald would attempt something so direct. Despite my promise not to say anything, that bastard wanted to see me dead. Now it would be him or me. I wouldn't give him such a nice opportunity again. Convincing people had never been my strong suit, but I had to do something.

The creaking of the gravel suddenly pulled me from my thoughts. I turned around aggressively, convinced that Gerald had come to finish the job. It was Serge.

He came over and sat down next to me in the other chair.

"You shouldn't have done that," he began. "It wasn't the right thing to do."

I wanted to insult him, tell him how pathetic he was, but I remained calm. After all, it took some courage for him to stand up to me after witnessing my anger in the courtyard.

"Why didn't you say anything?"

"Say what? That it's Gerald's fault Eric is dead? Because it wouldn't do any good. Just now, that was a fucking accident."

"No. He wanted to kill me," I blurted out sharply.

Serge looked at me for a moment, his mouth half open:

"I know this mess has shaken us up. We're all tired."

"Shit, that has nothing to do with it. He threatened me to get me to leave the school, and now he's trying to knock me off."

"What do you mean, threatened?" he asked, surprised.

I told him briefly about my encounter with Gerald after Eric's murder. Serge listened to me attentively and then mulled it over.

"I don't know. I don't think he was threatening you physically. He just wants to protect the group. That's all."

"He wants to protect his own ass, especially." Faced with such an outburst of idiocy, I had lost my temper.

"Without him, we would all be dead!"

"Without Karim and me, too!"

"That's exactly why I came to see you. I know you're a good guy. I just wanted to tell you that you shouldn't have done it. That's all. We have other things to do than fight with each other."

With that, he stood up and walked away. I watched him disappear behind the roof ledge as he descended the ladder. Was he really convinced that Gerald was innocent? Was I the one who was wrong? No, I couldn't be that paranoid. Gerald's intentions were the only certainty I could hang on to. I tried to think of what I could tell the others to show them how dangerous he was, but even my best imaginary speeches weren't that convincing. Even Serge, who had witnessed Gerald's madness, had not been swayed by my arguments. So, what would the people who were sure he was their savior, their self-proclaimed protector, say? I saw no way out that was to my advantage. They had no reason to believe an old farmer over their leader.

I made an arc with my toe, carving a small groove in the gravel. What to do? I suddenly thought of all the food that was waiting in the cellar of my unexpected refuge. I knew what to do: join in Gerald's game without ever letting my guard down.

I leaned on the armrests and stood up, exhausted. Coming down from the roof, I prepared myself to step into character and suppress my emotions. I entered the building. Gerald was where I expected to find him: lying in his spot on the platform in the cafeteria.

Almost all the survivors had gathered there to rest after lugging around so many bodies.

Strangely, he didn't notice me right away, and I was almost on top of him when he whirled around. I thought I saw a glimmer of dread and surprise in his eyes before the blackness returned to his pupils.

"What do you want?" he asked me with animosity.

"I came to apologize."

Looking astonished, he sat up. I added:

"Fear took over my senses. I'm sorry."

I extended a hand to him, which he looked at for a moment before taking it. I gave him a long, firm handshake, making sure everyone witnessed it. I looked him deep in the eyes and said:

"I think it's time to go get some supplies."

CHAPTER 14
MATHEMATICAL REALITY

Everything went off without a hitch. Along the way, we encountered only a few zombies, who offered only minor resistance. We even ran into the creature with the gutted throat who had followed me into the wheat field. He finished his wanderings on the roadside: beheaded, once and for all.

Fearing the horde might still be stationed in front of the house, we went to the back of the structure and entered the property by scaling the metal barrier. My companions had been dazzled by the presence and singularity of the mansion, but the sight of the stores in the cellar left them speechless. They thanked me sincerely, and even Gerald's attitude towards me seemed more human.

Eight survivors had let me guide them to the building. We divided the packs of water and canned goods amongst ourselves, but we couldn't carry it all in one trip. Bags full and arms straining from the six quarts of water each of us was lugging, we struggled to return to the school. Worn out, I passed my turn while some others left to collect the last of the provisions. Gerald also stayed behind. He helped the other survivors collect all the flammable items they could locate in the school.

I found Emma playing with a twelve-year-old boy, the only other child. Giselle was watching them. Reassured to see her having fun, I climbed back up to the roof as the small group, led by Karim, disappeared behind a mound of dirt. Since I had met him, that young man had never stopped doing his utmost. Undetectable under his almost sickly appearance, he had incredible energy.

Several hours later, mine still hadn't returned. I felt like an old rechargeable battery that was draining faster and faster and taking longer and longer to recharge. I was out of juice.

Karim's group had long since returned, but I had not left my observation post, sitting on a white chair on the roof. I had kept a can of food and was devouring its contents – cold, unappealing ravioli – as the sun began to disappear over the horizon. The heat was gradually dispersing, finally allowing the coolness to emerge from its hiding place. I closed my eyes, savoring this first invigorating night, when the sound of footsteps echoed through the courtyard. By the light of the moon, which was displaying its perfect roundness in a starry sky such as I had never seen before, I could make out a small group heading towards the covered playground. I wasn't able to count the participants in this dark procession, but I understood that they had come to pay one last homage to the dead.

During our expedition, the survivors who had stayed at the school had taken care of the corpses of the children and teachers, which had been piled up outside for the first few days, by adding their decaying carcasses to the putrid heap that rose ominously in the covered playground.

After a long silence, voices finally rose up. I couldn't make out the words but recognized Christine's sing-song accent. I imagined her dedicating a final eulogy to those who had been her students and her colleagues. The courtyard quickly fell silent again, but it was soon illuminated by tall, powerful flames. The putrid black mass of cadavers had suddenly lit up like the sun. The bones began to crackle to the rhythm of the spluttering fire, and the smell of roasting pig filled the smoky air.

I was worried that it might attract zombies but finally convinced myself that it was a risk that had to be taken. They could have chosen a worse time to burn the bodies. The darkness of the night masked the smoke, and the thick walls of the courtyard the harsh, brilliant light that emanated from the blaze. This glowing bonfire, consuming the flesh of so many people, operated shamefully, cut off from the world. Only the scent of the charred bodies could guide the zombies to us. But we had no reason to think they were still using their noses. At least, I hoped they weren't.

My eyes immersed in the flames that were insatiably continuing their feast, I wondered how long it would be before my body joined such a heap. An ordinary corpse among so many sacrificed ones. With the supplies we had brought back, I figured we had enough to last a long time before we had to risk facing the outside world again. But my rational and contradictory mind was starting to crunch the numbers. The calculation was completed quickly. I realized that what was a huge stock for one man ultimately didn't mean much for a group the size of ours: we had enough for a week, at most. Would this madness never end?

⁕⁕⁕

Two weeks later.

The situation quickly got worse. We organized several expeditions to loot nearby homes for provisions, but not all of them were successful. In spite of it all, we managed to last another week after the food from the great Renaissance mansion was already a distant, digested memory. Each day, the explorers – including myself, far too often to my liking – had to venture further and further away. The number of zombies in the streets kept growing and adding to the omnipresent threat of the corpses of the owners of the houses that we invaded. It was rare that they were empty. Danger was everywhere.

The group suffered two more casualties: two men in their thirties, who had taken part in the majority of the excursions, were killed in two of them. One had been trapped in the middle of the street trying to buy time for his comrades. At any rate, that's what the survivors told us. On the other hand, I witnessed the death of the second man, stupidly bitten by a zombie mother.

We had set our sights on a modest house in the village. Finding the front door unlocked, we knew straight away that we would soon have company. We were therefore extra cautious and entered carefully. It all happened quickly when we discovered the disemboweled body of a boy around ten years old, the inside of his ribcage emptied of all organs, like an empty shell. The man was unable to tear himself away from this vision of horror – as I myself had been when faced with the body of Arnaud, Emma's brother – and did not react in time when the party who was guilty of this bloodshed, the child's own mother, bit his forearm. She had been hidden behind the kitchen counter and had sprung out like a jack-in-the-box. Despite her astonishing speed, her macabre presence on this Earth was soon over. We slaughtered her. As well as our friend. It was not a pretty sight.

Confronted with such a situation, Gerald decided to have us do something big. I had been keeping my distance from him for the past two weeks, but I'd kept my eye on him. He hadn't tried anything new. Had he gotten used to the idea of my presence?

Tired of seeing far too precious lives lost for far too often disappointing results, he wanted to cram all the danger into one single mission. It was worth the risk, much more so than these suicide expeditions we'd been condemned to. Go through the village, traveling one or two miles, and pillage the only mini-market in town: that was his plan.

Serge suggested that we use the van Karim had brought back to get there, but he hadn't taken into account the dozens of crashed vehicles littering the main streets. I had seen very few of them thus far, but Karim swore that the biggest roads were all impassable. How many people had transformed while they were driving? In the end, the first zombies I had encountered had been quite lucky to be born in the middle of a traffic jam. They very well could have, like probably thousands of others, started their careers as assholes from beyond the grave embedded in a tree, trapped in a crumpled web of metal. Serge insisted, arguing that we could move the cars one by one – surely, for the most part, they still worked – but the idea of getting hung up along the way and making so much noise removed all doubt: we would have to go on foot. We left at dawn, the majority of us on an empty stomach.

Gerald led the march, followed by Karim and Serge, who never left his side. Remi, Thierry, three other people, and I completed the group. Gerald had tasked those who were staying behind with reinforcing the school's gate and covering it to block any view of the courtyard from the outside. It had been several minutes since we'd left the comfort of the school grounds. We walked in silence, not exchanging a single word. Gerald and Karim had agreed on the best route, and we let ourselves be led. We all knew we would have to face zombies. The real question was: when?

We went up the road that led to the center of the village, skirting the fences of the houses that surrounded the school. There was something truly unsettling about seeing the streets so deserted and quiet. Our propensity to think of ourselves as the masters of the world had turned into mumbling resignation. Only the zombies continued to cry out. Their glory was nothing monumental, and they would never build anything, but their omnipotence was sublime. Within weeks, they had completely changed the world. Our noisy, reassuring hustle and bustle had become a terrifying silence.

Ready to defend ourselves, we listened for the slightest sound, inevitably a harbinger of danger. The street split in two. To the right, there was a small parking lot where now useless vehicles lay dormant. We entered the lane on the left, which threaded its way between two blocks of row houses. Confirming what Karim had said, a car was lying motionless in the middle of the road. Only its left headlight was broken. The driver must not have been going fast when he crossed the street and crashed into the building's facade. We made our way discreetly towards the damaged automobile. The creature behind the wheel spotted us and started to moan. Locked in by his seat belt, he was writhing around, trying to break free from its diabolical embrace. I smiled, imagining how many of them must have been in a similar situation near my house, next to the blackened ruins of what was left of it.

We went around the vehicle one after the other, trying to ignore the zombie's mournful complaints. He was moving his upper body around like a lunatic and rhythmically banging on the cracked-open window. We jumped when the vehicle's horn honked loudly and powerfully. The monster, pounding hard on the steering wheel, had found the perfect way to invite his friends over. The sound rang out again. Karim didn't waste a second: he smashed the car window with a machete and cut off the troublemaker's head, which rolled between his legs and ended up nestled between the pedals. We immediately fled. Gerald, who was still at the head of the group, ran off at full speed. Inwardly, I was selfishly hoping that his haste would lead him straight into the zombies' dirty, emaciated hands. But this was not the case.

I very quickly found myself at the back of the pack as the others pressed ahead. I tried to keep up the pace, convinced they wouldn't wait for me. However, Thierry turned around and slowed down, letting me catch up to him.

After a short, nerve-wracking run, we got to the small county road that ran through the heart of the village and went by Emma's house.

The others had already crossed it and entered the vineyard that bordered it. They had stopped, crouched behind a row of grapevines. We quickly joined them.

"Son of a bitch, that was close," said Karim.

"We'll chat later," Gerald cut him off. "We shouldn't dawdle here."

He looked at me then turned his head.

"Come on, let's go."

Did that bastard regret bringing me on this mission?

We crossed the field, hunched over, and came out into a small, wooded area. They clearly had no intention of lingering on the roads. There was no path, but they didn't care. We plunged between the broom plants and phillyrea bushes. Karim had taken the lead and was already weaving through the oak trees that inhabited the surrounding area. We walked single file for a long distance. Despite the thirst that was tormenting me, I tried to delay the inevitable moment when I would empty my last bottle of water. Fortunately, the shade from the trees made the heat bearable. Suddenly, the group stopped. In front of us, the forest was ending and opening onto vines again. About two hundred yards away stood the mini-market, built on the edge of a roundabout that led directly to its small parking lot. We were not the only ones interested in it. A pack of zombies was standing in front of the building. They were repeatedly striking the metal security shutters, which had been lowered. I walked up to join Karim and Gerald, who were discussing the situation.

"Do you think there are any survivors inside?" the younger man asked.

"Yeah. I'm sure of it."

Gerald let out a long sigh while everybody stared at him. This news seemed to annoy him deeply.

"I hope they aren't going to be a pain in the ass," he added.

"We have to give it a try," said Thierry, who had finally exchanged his frying pans for a crowbar he'd found during an expedition.

"Okay. The plan is simple. We get rid of the zombies and try to get inside."

"What if they stop us?" Karim asked.

"I don't think they'll be able to. There are, what? A dozen zombies out front? There must not be very many people inside, and they are most likely not well-armed."

"We can bring them back with us," suggested Serge.

Gerald looked up at him and, after a short moment, answered:

"Eventually."

"What do you mean by that?" I asked him

"First, we'll just see if there is anyone, okay?" he said to bring the conversation to an end.

He grabbed his rifle and made sure it was loaded. He looked us over with a cold expression.

"Are you ready? Good. Go!"

He turned around and ran towards the store. The others followed him without hesitation, their weapons at the ready. Their courage impressed me. Despite my repeated encounters with the zombies, they were far from becoming commonplace in my daily life. I continued to fear every confrontation. These guys were charging headlong into danger. Had they taken a liking to this life, where everyone could play the hero? I wiped a big bead of sweat from my forehead and set off after them.

They had hidden behind a car parked at the edge of the lot. The zombies hadn't spotted us yet.

"On three, we rush 'em. Kill one and then move back. Don't let them surround you. Understood?" whispered Gerald.

They all nodded. I remained still, crouched down on the outside of the group. Gerald slowly counted to three. We stood up and advanced on the zombies. We didn't have time to surprise them; another pack, who had just emerged from behind the building, had seen us. The dead moaned in unison and dragged themselves in our direction. Now there were about twenty of them.

"Crap! What do we do?" Remi shrieked. "There's too many of them."

"If we do nothing, we'll die of hunger and thirst. We need this place!" Gerald yelled.

He rushed towards the group that had stopped hammering on the entrance to the mini-market, immediately followed by Karim and Serge. I put my hand on Remi's shoulder:

"*The show must go on*, remember?" I said, trying to reassure him.

He snickered, squared his shoulders, and tightened his grip on his metal bat. Gerald was right. We had no choice. It was our turn to hurl ourselves, trembling, into the battle. I quickly did the math. There were three times as many zombies as us. So, I just had to eliminate three of them.

Beside me, Remi swung his weapon at a woman whose hair must have been blond before it got covered in the blood of one of her victims. Her neck snapped, and she collapsed to the ground. Remi then turned his attention to his next adversary, a fat, bald man in a white tank top.

"Finish her!" I shouted at him as the female zombie, her head completely twisted around, started crawling towards him.

I threw myself at the monster in the tank top and smashed his skull with a blow from my hammer. His body collapsed without any resistance.

"Thanks, Pat," Remi said to me.

I did not answer: a new adversary was already taking the place of those who had fallen in combat. One down. Two to go.

Total chaos surrounded us. Aside from Remi, the others had gotten deep into the fray. The survivors' cries of rage were added to the zombies' deafening moans. With each howl, a fatal blow was dealt to the monsters. Refusing to let myself be controlled by fear, I imitated my colleagues and rushed forward, bellowing at my next victim. The hammer raised above my head, I was about to strike his skull when the living dead tripped over his sagging pants and crashed to the ground. Carried forward by the momentum from my attack, I found myself in the arms of another creature. I could hear his teeth chattering inches from my ear. His deathly breath crept into my nostrils, and my brain was beset with disgusting neurological associations. I pushed him away with a punch to his sternum. Then, the claws of the zombie I had just missed, who was crawling on the ground behind me, closed around my calf. He opened his mouth to bite me.

Remi was faster and married his head to the asphalt in the parking lot for eternity. Without stopping, he shoved me aside for my own protection, sending me rolling across the tar. The other zombie, the one whose aroma continued to panic my senses, had just suffered a similar fate. I stood up and thanked Remi in turn.

"The show must go on," he replied, chuckling.

I let out a laugh, and together, we launched ourselves on our next target.

Several minutes later, the parking lot was covered with corpses as putrid as they were dead, truly dead. None of us had been hurt. It was a real miracle. We were all covered in blood. This ensemble of human remains had become one of our most common outfits. We regrouped in front of the mini-market's lowered security shutter. Karim, his head pressed to the metal, peered inside through the gaps.

"It's dead in there," he said.

Gerald checked, too, then turned to Thierry, who seemed drained.

"See if you can move it."

The short man's crowbar was finally going to be used for its intended purpose. He slipped the tool under the metal shutter and levered it. The heavy structure remained motionless. Several of us joined in, trying to dislodge it from its tracks, but the result was the same. It had been designed to do this, after all: to resist.

We walked around the building, and another opportunity presented itself: at the top of a small concrete staircase, a back door was waiting for us. Thierry inserted his crowbar and began to force it.

"Ho ho," said a voice above us.

We all looked up, surprised. A young man in his twenties, with a bow in his hand, was pointing an arrow in our direction.

"It would be best if you were to leave, guys," he added, aiming at each of us successively.

"We need food," one of the men replied.

"Get lost!" he screamed.

We stepped back several feet to get a better view of the stranger. He sounded serious. I didn't like this.

"Are you all alone, kid?" Gerald asked him in his monotonous voice.

"What's it to you?"

"Because I'm not," he purred, loading his rifle. "So, you will kindly let us in. We'll take what we need, and we'll leave. Deal?"

The young man laughed and released his arm, as if he had listened to reason:

"Hey, guys!" he called out.

Four teenagers appeared beside him. He must have been the oldest. They were all armed, and two of them were threatening us with sling-shots – not the kinds that were cobbled together with a branch and a rubber band, but real weapons, like the ones carnies let little rascals win at village fairs.

"Okay, let's all calm down," tried Thierry, who was interrupted by a hand gesture from Gerald.

"Guys, I swear to you, you don't want it to come to this," he told them, pointing his gun at the head kid. "We're not kidding around."

No sooner had he finished his sentence than a marble shattered the window of the car parked just behind him, passing inches from his left arm. I held my breath, convinced that he was going to respond by shooting the young man, but he didn't do anything.

"The next one's for your face," warned our adversaries' leader.

Long seconds ticked by. Time seemed to be standing still. I felt like I was taking part in a scene from one of those old westerns. Gerald was holding our enemies at bay, ready to fire. Suddenly, he lowered his gun.

"Let's go, men," he said simply.

Karim wanted to protest, but he silenced him. Gerald was beside himself. We walked away as chuckling arose from the roof of the store. We were about to leave the parking lot when the voice was heard again:

"And thanks for the zombies, friends."

The laughter increased. Gerald had taken the lead, and he hastened forward, trying to put as much distance as possible between him and this humiliation. What was he going to say? That he came back with nothing because of a bunch of kids? Karim and Serge caught up with him. I stayed further back with the others, Remi right behind me.

"What fucking bad luck," he said, heaving a sigh.

"Do you think they really would have targeted us?" asked Thierry.

I didn't know, but I was sure it must have taken a huge effort for Gerald not to pick off the boss of the mini-market gang. That unexpected restraint had probably saved our lives.

"Yeah," Remi replied. "Those bastards weren't messing around. It's good that we left."

"Except that we're going to die of thirst," added the man who was bringing up the rear. "I hope they all get eaten."

The threesome up front had slowed down, and we caught up to them. Gerald remained silent, leaving it to Karim to speak:

"We're going to try a few houses along the way, so as not to come back empty-handed. Okay with you?"

I nodded, well aware that we didn't have much of a choice. The level of our reserves was drastically low. We were in dire need of water.

And the sky still refused to open up. A glass of rainwater would have given me such great pleasure.

We returned to the woods we had arrived through. Its almost cool temperature soothed me again. Our disappointment had sapped the morale from all of us, and being less vigilant, we did not notice the arrival of the zombies whose frail, dry bodies were wandering among the trunks of the oak trees. There were a dozen of them, scattered down a long line of death.

Karim was the first to spot them, and he put his hand on Gerald's shoulder to stop him. The latter raised his head and, without warning, charged at the dead, screaming like a madman. I was transported back to that scene in the hallway, when the sergeant had perished, except this time, Gerald was throwing himself into the midst of the zombies. Stunned, Karim did not react and, like the rest of us, watched Gerald cut down the first living dead in the line. His machete danced over his head before plunging into the necrotic flesh. He showed no mercy and, enraged, got rid of each monster. He stood still for a few seconds in the middle of the carnage, then came back to us.

"That's good, I feel better now," he said simply, wiping away the black blood running down his cheek. "We can go."

Remi looked bewildered, and he couldn't take his eyes off Gerald, who had started walking again.

"You okay?" I asked him.

"Seriously, did you see that?" he replied, looking at me wide-eyed.

"Yeah. It's not the first time."

"What do you mean?"

"Nothing, forget it. He was just pissed off. I'd love to let off steam on a zombie, too," I lied.

"Not me. I'm starving to death."

We continued for several minutes through the woods, silent, images of Gerald's madness going through everybody's minds. Then, Karim stopped, his finger pointed at an isolated building down below.

"Gerald, wanna try this house?"

"Yeah," he answered, not getting any deeper into the question.

Without exchanging a word, we all went in that direction. The place seemed deserted, but the many trees that surrounded the building could conceal a lot of dangers. The insatiable, fragrant kind. We moved closer as quietly as possible, the cracking of twigs under our feet echoing off the walls. Karim glanced quickly over his shoulder.

The front door was on the other side. We walked around the house. The yard was poorly maintained, and a lot of unnecessary crap was piled up in the tall grass. A real dump. When we arrived at the front of the house, Karim turned to us:

"Wait here. Not a sound," he said hastily before running off.

As he disappeared around the opposite corner, we exchanged astonished glances: what had gotten into him? I went over to the door and took a seat on the small bench adorning the entrance. The wood, with its peeling paint, creaked under my weight. Thierry sat down with me. The others remained standing. A few minutes passed, and Gerald was starting to get impatient.

"What the hell is he doing, seriously?" he complained.

One of the men was about to go looking for Karim when we heard screams. It wasn't the zombies, but a thin, almost shrill voice.

We ran towards the source of the noise: Karim was pushing a young boy in front of him. One of the kids from the mini-market.

CHAPTER 15
BIRDS OF ILL OMEN

"This is not okay!" she yelled at Gerald, out of her mind. "What is this bullshit?"

Christine, whom everyone knew to be a calm and collected person, was really furious. If her students had seen her like this, their jaws probably would have unhinged in surprise. Fortunately, Emma was not present.

"What are you gonna do? Imprison him and keep him hostage?" she added, screaming.

Gerald remained silent and continued to move down the school's corridor. Behind him, Karim was pushing the young boy.

He couldn't have been more than fourteen years old, a simple middle school student. His face was all red, his eyes bloodshot. He hadn't stopped crying and whining since his capture. At first, he had sworn that we would regret this, that we would pay dearly for it; then, he had given in and begged us not to kill him. At one point, exasperated by his moaning, Gerald had threatened to punch him in the face. It had worked. Not for long, though.

When the survivors in charge of keeping watch had opened the door to the playground for us, we'd bumped into Christine, who had come to welcome us. She had immediately recognized her former student. Her fury had erupted when she'd realized he was our prisoner.

She knocked Gerald with her shoulder and approached Karim and the boy.

"Let him go," she ordered.

Karim shook his head and replied:

"No. He'll try to escape again."

"Do you hear yourself? This is not war! What's the matter with you? You're acting like terrorists!"

Karim tried to pass, but she stretched out her arms to block the corridor. She glared at me, seeing that I was keeping quiet.

"Let me through," Karim told her.

"Let him go."

Gerald suddenly turned around and headed towards Christine. Something about his approach struck me the wrong way, and I jostled Serge and Remi out of the way so I could get closer to the action. My hand automatically closed around the handle of my hammer.

"We've had just about enough of you, Mother Theresa! We risk our skins to bring back food, and this is how you thank us? Without this little shit and his friends, we would have enough to chow down! So, if you want to live, you're going to shut up."

Christine, who was still facing Karim, turned around vehemently and slapped Gerald with the back of her hand.

"This is a child," she cried as, reflexively, Gerald also raised his hand.

I slipped between Karim and the wall and pulled Christine towards me. She pushed me away.

"Let go of me!"

She grabbed the young boy's arm and tried to pull him with her, but Karim had a tight hold on him.

"Stop, you bastard! Ms. Bleuet is right. I'm only thirteen!"

"Let him go," insisted Christine, who was on the verge of hurling herself at Karim.

"Let him go," I repeated in turn to Karim. "He won't get far."

The young man looked at me then turned to Gerald, who was biting his thumbnail, a purplish mark on his cheek.

The boy took the opportunity to extricate himself and punched Karim in the chest. Despite the attacker's young age, the blow left him gasping for air, and the teenager got completely free from his grip. He then pushed Christine and tried to run down the hall. Gerald seized him by the collar and slammed him up against the wall.

"You're gonna stop busting my balls, you little brat," he said threateningly.

The boy started to cry again.

"Let me go. I want to go back to my brother. I won't tell them you're living at the school."

"Your brother?" asked Gerald, whose voice had resumed its usual tone.

The youngster let out a sob and looked up at Christine, who was standing behind Gerald. She was seething with anger.

"Yes, he's the one who told me to follow you. He doesn't care about me..."

"Your brother is at the store?" Christine asked him, surprised.

"Yes, with the others," answered the boy. "They won't let you in."

"I don't understand," she added.

"I told you, they prevented us from entering. Your protégé's little friends threatened us. They were armed," Gerald explained to her.

She was silent for a moment, visibly unsettled.

She sighed.

"Mistreating Mathieu isn't going to get you anywhere. Why did they threaten you?"

"Damn it, it's the apocalypse, Ms. Bleuet," the one named Mathieu replied, as if the answer were self-evident.

She let out another long sigh.

"So, now what do we do?" she asked Gerald.

"We go back tomorrow, and we reason with those kids."

Christine seemed reassured, but I knew Gerald had something completely different in mind.

"You're not going to hurt me?" the boy asked, wiping his nose on his wrist.

"Not if you keep quiet," Gerald replied.

Christine glared at him and rectified:

"Of course not. Come with me."

She took the teenager's arm, forcing Gerald to release him, and brought him with her towards the entrance to the cafeteria. They disappeared inside.

"Pain in the ass," Gerald muttered, looking irritated. "Karim, don't let him out of your sight. We need him."

He turned to me and added:

"You get along well with the teacher, don't you? Try to get it into her skull that without that brat, we're all going to die."

I clenched my teeth and remained silent. No matter how much I agreed with him, I didn't like the turn this whole business was taking at all.

"Well, they must be starving to death in there. Let's go," said Gerald, heading to the cafeteria, as well.

We went in and set out everything we had collected along the way. Several bottles of water and quite a few boxes of cookies. Enough to last until tomorrow. The survivors gathered around us, and Gerald, helped by Serge, began to distribute the food. I kept a small bottle of mineral water and a box of cookies and looked around for Emma. She was sitting on her teacher's rug and chatting with her. Mathieu was with them.

I walked over.

Emma saw me coming and gave me a big smile.

"Mr. Patrick, this is my neighbor," she said, pointing to the teenager.

I sat down and extended my hand to the young boy as if this were the first time we'd met.

"Mathieu, I'm Patrick."

He looked at me oddly, then shook my hand briefly.

"Your boss isn't going to do anything to me?" he finally said, glancing towards the center of the room.

"No, no," Christine reassured him again. "Like he said, tomorrow we'll take you back to the mini-market. I'm sure it's just a misunderstanding."

The boy let out a sigh of relief.

"But they won't let you in anyway. Victor said it was just for us. That we had to defend our reserves."

"Is Victor alive, too?" Emma asked interestedly, surprised that so many people she knew could still be living.

She had come to terms with losing everyone in her life, but now some were reappearing. I was happy for her. Each new familiar face should make this world a little less spooky, even if it also meant remembering those she would never see again.

"Yeah, he's the boss over there. What about Arnaud? Is he dead?" he asked abruptly.

The little girl's face froze. Her eyes stared off into space.

"Oh, sorry," the boy corrected himself, having just recognized his lack of tact. "Sorry, Emma."

"He's dead," she replied dryly, as if she were angrier with her brother for abandoning her than with Mathieu for his question.

Feeling the anxiety mounting in me, I intervened, clearing my throat and saying in a shaky tone of voice:

"Who wants a cookie?"

They turned to me. Emma's face had regained its expressiveness. It was now displaying her childish curiosity.

"Are those the ones with nougat?" she asked me, visibly excited.

I looked for the reference on the box and then changed my mind.

"We'll see," I said, opening it.

Despite the absence of nougat, the disappointment was quickly forgotten, and the little one accepted the cookie I handed her with a big smile. I gave one each to Christine and Mathieu, who thanked me. The box ran out too quickly for our taste, but this chocolatey interlude had delighted Emma. She stood up as she finished the last cookie:

"Mr. Patrick, come see what I did earlier."

She took my hand and led me across the room to where Giselle was sitting with the young boy. She pointed to the wall in front of her.

"Romain came up with the idea. Isn't it beautiful?"

She and her friend had had fun drawing directly on the wall using large color markers that were still lying on the floor. I easily differentiated the little girl's drawings, which were less confident than her elder's but also much livelier. Across the white paint on the wall ran a whole menagerie of misshapen, colorful animals. I even thought I recognized a unicorn. These joyful, pudgy creatures, with their legs reduced to simple lines, were facing the terrifying zombies that Romain had drawn. He had limited himself to reflecting reality, using the red felt-tip pen mercilessly. One of the figures standing in front of the living dead, however, seemed to be faring better than the others thanks to its submachine gun.

"It's very nice," I said to the little girl, patting her on the head. "Is that a unicorn you drew there?"

"Yes," she replied happily. "She's going to go kill all the zombies with her horn."

That last sentence saddened me. This entire herd of magical animals was ultimately just a fairytale army that had to face the same evil as us. Like Romain, she had not freed herself from reality.

***

I woke up with a start, my body covered in sweat. In my nightmare, the zombies had made short work of Emma's gentle creatures. Everything had turned red, the rainbow of colors the little one had used completely gone

I straightened up and looked around. It was still dark, but a bit of harsh light was already slipping through the glass panels in the cafeteria ceiling. The sun was just coming up.

I stretched my numb muscles and confirmed that Mathieu was still there. He was sleeping several feet away from me, his back against the wall. Between the two of us, Emma slumbered peacefully, her small body rising and falling to the regular rhythm of her breathing. A movement caught my attention. Gerald had just sat up and was putting on his shoes, thick ranger boots made of black leather. He stayed like that for a moment on the edge of his platform, then stood up. He took a few steps and crouched down next to Karim, whom he shook gently. He then approached Serge and Remi, whom he also pulled from the arms of Morpheus. Soon, commotion swept over the room, and the survivors awoke one by one. Mathieu was one of the first. Clearly frightened, he kept glancing around him, his eyes resting regularly on Gerald.

Knowing what Gerald had in mind, I got ready, too. I didn't even have the luxury of changing clothes. I put on my shoes and checked that my weapon was there. I was prepared to face a new day.

Christine had also stood up and was trying to reassure Mathieu. There was a metal bar protruding from the bag she was carrying on her back. She seemed determined to accompany us.

Emma suddenly turned over on her rug and opened her eyes.

I smiled at her:

"Did you sleep well?"

"What is all this noise?" she complained in a small voice.

"We're going to go look for food."

She rubbed her eyes and made a pouty face:

"You're leaving again?"

"If we want to eat tonight, I have to," I told her. "Everything will be fine. We'll see each other again in just a couple of hours. Giselle is going to take care of you."

"I don't like her," she confessed, looking sidelong at the old woman, who was dozing in her corner. "She smells bad, and she's mean."

I let out a laugh.

"She always says I should be afraid of you. That you're mean."

Surprised, I quickly pushed these words aside and threw myself at Emma, tickling her:

"Very mean!"

She flailed about, laughing.

"Stop it, Mr. Patrick!" she begged me, giggling.

I withdrew my hands. She smiled at me, then her face became serious again.

"She scares me. Sometimes, she talks to herself, and she calls me Celine!"

"Celine?"

"She says that's her favorite granddaughter."

Troubled, I looked in Giselle's direction. So, the old shrew was losing her mind. It didn't really surprise me.

"Don't pay any attention to her. As for me, I'll be back very soon. And I won't have to leave as often after this."

"Really?" she said impulsively.

"Really," I answered sincerely.

Karim came up to us and greeted me with a handshake.

"You ready? The others are eager to get going."

"I'm ready," said Christine, slipping between us.

"Uh, Gerald said..." stammered Karim.

"What did he say?" she asked curtly.

"Nothing. Come on, then. Let's go."

I crouched next to Emma and kissed her on the forehead:

"See you later, okay?"

"Is Ms. Bleuet leaving, too?"

"Looks that way."

She sighed.

"It's gonna be even worse today."

"I'll be back soon. I promise."

I got up, gave her one last wave, and joined the group. It consisted of the same people as for the first expedition, with three differences: Christine and Mathieu were accompanying us, while Thierry had decided to stay behind. The schoolteacher, with her hand on the young man's shoulder, made it clear that she was responsible for him. Gerald made no comment and gave the order for everyone to head out.

The sun had gotten a little higher, and its first rays were illuminating a day that promised to be sweltering yet again. Overnight, the temperature hadn't decreased, and I was almost happy to leave the scorching enclosure of the cafeteria. The mission incumbent on us pleased me much less: how were we going to reason with these kids? I hoped Christine's presence would help us find common ground, rather than a battlefield. I had no desire to end up pierced by an arrow shot by an apocalyptic Robin Hood wannabe.

We gradually got further away from the school. Christine stayed close to Mathieu. Karim and Serge were on full alert, ready to catch him if he tried to escape. They never took their eyes off him. As usual, Gerald led the way, taking exactly the same route we had followed the day before. We passed the zombie with the car horn again. This time, only the whirring of the wings of the flies busying themselves in the dead man's rotting carcass broke the silence of the passenger compartment. We crossed the county road. Gerald smashed the skull of an isolated zombie in the vineyard, then we entered the underbrush. We were progressing at a steady pace, and the pressure was building in the group. We all knew that things could go downhill very quickly.

Beads of sweat were running down Serge's bony neck in front of me. His back was soaked, and a large oval mark had already appeared on his T-shirt. It couldn't have been later than eight o'clock in the morning, and yet it was already almost an early afternoon temperature. Like the day before, Gerald stopped at the edge of the woods. Despite the lack of wind, the foul stench of the rotting zombies in front of the store reached us. Crows were feeding on the carrion. One of them had what appeared to be a nasty piece of intestine in its beak.

"You let me do the talking, okay?" Gerald said, looking at each of us in turn. "They're armed, so stay on your guard."

With those words, he grabbed his rifle, made sure it was loaded, and slung the strap over his left shoulder. He grabbed Mathieu roughly by the collar and placed him in front of him.

"Come on, let's go."

Christine protested, trying to catch hold of the young boy, but Karim intervened. Gerald was already hurtling down the slight slope that led to the vineyard. The rest of the group followed. I put a hand on the teacher's shoulder.

"It's going to be fine," I tried to reassure her.

She looked at me with her green eyes. Her face bore the marks of fatigue and dehydration. Her features were drawn. Her dry skin accentuated the lines that ran across her sweaty forehead. She blinked, gave me a small smile, and started moving after the others. I followed her.

As we approached, the birds flew away, their beating wings circulating the stale air that hung over the area. The odor was unbearable. However, Gerald stood up straight in the middle of the bodies, about ten yards from the entrance to the mini-market. Serge and Karim flanked him, one step behind. The others were scattered around. Some watched the surroundings, ready to alert us to the arrival of zombies. Christine wanted to join her former student, but Karim prevented her from passing. I stayed back, at the far end of the parking lot. I knew our own survival was at stake, but I didn't want to be part of this sham of a medieval siege. The role of the emissary who wanted to be king fell to Gerald. I was only there to help bring back the spoils.

Gerald, who was holding Mathieu firmly against him, cleared his throat and made his presence known with a short, loud shout. I thought I could make out some movement behind the store's security shutter, but several seconds passed in complete silence. In the distance, the crows cawed, impatiently waiting to resume their feast.

A figure was finally silhouetted on the roof of the mini-market. The sun was shining from behind his back.

"Son of a bitch, Mat, what the hell have you done?" he blurted out, ignoring the rest of us.

The boy wanted to answer, but Gerald pressed a hand over his mouth.

"I'm the one you're talking to, my good man," he said to Mathieu's brother.

"Release my bro first."

"I'll let him go. On one condition. And you know very well what that is."

The young man let out a snicker and walked over to the edge of the roof. He had his bow in his hand, a quiver on his back.

"I already told you. This is our food. We were here first."

"Victor!" cried Christine. "I'm sure we can share. There's enough food for everybody."

"Ms. Bleuet," he said before starting to laugh. "I didn't even recognize you. You've gotten old, haven't you?"

Christine did not know how to reply to that, and Gerald resumed:

"Victor, is that it? Don't make us use force. She's right."

"What force? Yeah, there are more of you. So what? You won't be able to get in. You can just sit there and wait. The zombies will come and take care of you."

"Dammit, I have your brother!" Gerald said angrily.

"Yeah, like I'm gonna trade my food for him? All that moron had to do was not get caught. You can keep him. I don't give a shit. You'll end up getting sick of him, and he'll come back."

"How can you say that?" Christine asked, offended.

"Oh, shut up, you old hag," he replied. "Don't you get it? We're not in the schoolyard anymore."

He waved his hand, and his two buddies, still equipped with their slingshots, positioned themselves on either side of him.

"Now, get lost!"

He grabbed an arrow and drew the bowstring.

It was Gerald's turn to laugh.

"You don't quite understand…"

His fingers wrapped around the handle of his machete, and he placed the weapon under Mathieu's throat. The boy began to cry and plead with his brother.

"Last chance," added Gerald.

Christine tried to intervene, but this time, Karim didn't just stop her. He pushed her violently to the ground. I ran my ass over there.

"Dammit, stop this bullshit!" I shouted.

I looked at the others, who were doing nothing other than watching the scene.

"This is going too far."

"Shut up, Grandpa!" yelled Victor, obviously losing patience. To Gerald, he shouted, "Let go of my brother and get the hell out of here, asshole!"

"Finally, you want him back," Gerald said in his deep voice as I helped Christine to her feet.

Overwhelmed by the events, she slumped against the hood of a car, her heart pounding. I wanted to get closer to Gerald, but Karim blocked my way.

"Fuck you!" I protested, at the end of my rope.

"Sorry, Pat," he said. "We need this food."

Behind him, Gerald continued his show, his weapon still pressed against Mathieu's neck. The boy's body was shaking from his sobs.

"So, you want your brother back?"

"Buzz off!" yelled the archer.

"You want him?" Gerald bellowed even louder.

"Get out of here!"

Gerald did not answer immediately, and a deep silence suddenly invaded the parking lot. Zombie cries could be heard in the distance. They were coming.

"Very well," Gerald whispered.

He swept his eyes over his adversaries and, with a sharp, powerful motion, slit Mathieu's throat, which was instantly covered with a thick, red coat. With a kick, he sent the boy crashing to the asphalt. The teenager tried to crawl away, but his life was bubbling out of the gash in his neck. Christine screamed, but her cries were covered by Victor's.

"Motherfucker!" he howled, releasing his bowstring.

The arrow flew, grazed Gerald's shoulder, and went through Serge's throat, driven in at the level of the glottis and coming out in the middle of his neck, where his sweat was now tinged red. Eyes wide, he turned to us. Blood was already coming out of his mouth.

Gerald reacted instantly and, his rifle pointed in front of him, added a sudden, deafening bang to the surrounding chaos. The body of a teenager fell from the roof, his chest torn open from buckshot.

The survivors from our group started to disperse and take cover. I wanted to do the same and dragged Christine by the arm, but she resisted, as if frozen by the horror that was taking shape before her tired eyes.

"Come on," I shouted at her, panicked.

She then let out a sort of sickly hiccup. A marble had hit her full in the face, turning the inside of her right eye socket into disgusting mush. She collapsed, and her body convulsed on the ground. A second marble hit the hood of the car. I sheltered behind the vehicle, cradling my head in my hands.

The teacher's feet were sticking out, shaking with her last spasms.

Another shot rang out. Gerald, bent over, suddenly appeared behind the car. He had a crazed look in his eye. Instinctively, I threw myself on top of him. I was going to kill him. He kicked me hard in the jaw, and I crashed to the ground, the metallic taste of blood in my mouth. He straightened up, leaned on the roof of the car, and shot again in the direction of the mini-market.

Still on the ground, I grabbed his ankle; he kicked me again, almost knocking me out. My mind was racing. I wanted to find the strength to eliminate this parasite, but my vision was blurred. I was starting to snap out of it when Gerald pushed me back against the asphalt and fled. I saw his feet moving away. Others were following him.

My tongue was bathed in my own blood, and I spat out a thick clot of it. Two hands grabbed me under the armpits and helped me sit up: Remi.

"Don't stay here, Patrick," he told me, terrorized.

I turned my aching head towards the roof. It was deserted. Had Gerald shot them all?

Remi insisted:

"Come on, dude!"

The zombies' howling had intensified. Judging by their volume, the battle seemed to have attracted a significant number of them. I stood up and followed Remi, who was zigzagging between the stiffs that littered the parking lot. I didn't stop to see which human ones had just been added during this madness. In the distance, I thought I saw Gerald disappearing hastily into the small forest. There was no doubt: I was going to kill him. Serge was dead, but the others would no longer need his testimony to believe me. That piece of garbage had finally shown his true colors. He would pay dearly for it. He was not only responsible for the casualties from the battle, but for the deaths of each one of us. He had just condemned us all.

In the middle of the vineyard, as we made our way towards the woods, I felt tears run down my cheeks: an even darker thought had invaded my mind. What on Earth was I going to tell Emma?

But, without any respite, a shrill hiss brought me back to reality again.

In front of me, Remi collapsed, an arrow stuck in his thigh, just above the knee. The projectile had skewered his leg. I went to help him and was trying to pick him up when another arrow sank into the ground beside us. Remi moaned as he got to his feet but, leaning against me, he held on. His wound was bleeding profusely. With every step, he left a reddish mark on the ground.

A succulent olfactory trail for the approaching zombies.

CHAPTER 16
THE CIRCLE OF JUSTICE

Remi was getting heavier and heavier. Despite his efforts, his full weight was falling on my left shoulder. With one hand, he was compressing the wound and holding the tip of the arrow in place. He was dragging his wounded leg painfully. We had only taken a few steps in the undergrowth adjacent to the small vineyard when he stopped and leaned against an oak tree. I took the opportunity to try to catch my breath. Behind us, more and more zombies were gathering in the store's parking lot. Some were circling the building, eager to get their hands on what was there, but others were already heading in our direction. They were as slow as us.

"You have to take it out of me," Remi said weakly.

My eyes immediately fell to the black carbon arrow going through my friend's leg.

"You sure?" I asked him, having a hard time hiding my doubts.

"I'm gonna lose all my blood if we don't remove it."

He wiped his face and added:

"The point is straight in. You should be able to take it out easily."

The projectile, the end of which was protruding from Remi's blood-soaked jeans, seemed to be staring at me mockingly.

"Okay," I said, crouching down beside him. "Stretch out your leg. This is going to hurt."

He did as I'd asked. His leg was shaking violently. Feeling uncomfortable, I took hold of the arrow, placing my hand as close to the wound as possible, but not touching it.

"Okay, you ready? One…"

I pulled sharply, and the arrow slipped easily out of Remi's flesh. Feeling it leave his muscles, he dropped to the ground. He was white as a sheet. A large quantity of blood was flowing through the two gaping holes.

"Tourniquet," he managed to mumble through his purplish lips.

I took off my T-shirt and hurriedly tied it around his leg. I tightened it as much as the fabric allowed, hoping to reduce the bleeding, and ignored the fleeting vision that crossed my mind of the thousands of germs that were all over the soiled material: I had nothing else at hand. It was a matter of life and death. The garment was quickly saturated with blood. How could Remi have been losing so much from such small holes?

He was close to passing out, and his eyelids kept closing. I felt like he was about to leave me. I didn't give him the chance and shook him gently.

"We gotta go. Lean on me," I told him, passing his arm around the back of my neck.

He opened his eyes and nodded slightly. I helped him stand up. He was still just as heavy, but without the arrow, he had regained better mobility and was moving faster, letting out a small cry of pain with each step. But we still weren't fast enough. The zombies had already crossed a good part of the field. Remi's blood was guiding them straight to us.

"Come on, man. We have to get out of here," I urged him on.

He groaned and tried to pick up the pace. We ended up adopting a steady rhythm, similar to that of the living dead who were still at a worrisome distance.

After several minutes, we were both panting profusely. Our tortured lungs protested, but we continued on. Stopping meant certain death. At least for Remi. I almost expected him to say, "Leave me, I'm just holding you back," but the reality was quite different. He was clinging to life and was not resigned to giving up. Yet, his pale face, covered in thick sweat, looked like a condemned man's.

"I'm not dead yet," he said, seeing that I was watching him.

I laughed, even though the situation didn't really call for it, and firmed up my grip around my companion's waist.

"We're going to make it," I huffed as we approached the edge of the woods. "Another half mile, and we'll be back at the school."

We finally left the cover of the trees.

"It's so nice out," murmured Remi, whose pallor was even more terrifying in broad daylight.

I was far from finding it so pleasant. The sun was shining brutally on the white skin of my uncovered stomach. On the other hand, Remi's cold, bloodless skin found some consolation in those rays. We had almost gotten to the end of the field when, at the corner of the house bordering the vineyard, several zombies appeared, strolling along the county road.

"Get down," I whispered to Remi.

We attempted to hide behind a row of grapevines, but Remi screamed in pain when his knee buckled under his weight. All their heads turned to us as one. Through the foliage, I could see more and more feet dragging themselves towards us.

"Quick," I said to Remi, but there wasn't the slightest reaction.

He had lost consciousness.

I abruptly stood up, revealing myself to the zombies' dead eyes, and raced to the small road. They had not yet entered the field or spotted Remi's collapsed body. I crossed the expanse of tar and tried to draw their attention to me. There were even more of them than I'd thought.

Around thirty, maybe. Impossible to face them alone. I had to lure them and get them away from Remi. As fast as possible.

I was about to take off running down the road when a corpse, emerging from the underbrush about fifty yards away, messed up my entire plan. I had completely forgotten about the ones who were following us. He hadn't noticed me, but he was walking steadily towards my passed-out friend.

"Hey, ugly!" I shouted, waving my arms to get his attention. In vain.

The creature was advancing with one goal: to feast on Remi's flesh. I cursed and, as the group on the road had gotten closer, faced my first opponent: a huge beanpole wearing shorts. Despite his height, I slaughtered him with a precise hammer blow right in the face. His skull cracked open, and he fell to the ground. I was getting good at this little game.

Not wasting any time, I dodged a second monster and rushed towards the field. Seeing me slip through its fingers, the pack moaned in unison and spread out, closing off access to the row of vines where my companion had blacked out.

New zombies had left the woods and were all flocking towards Remi, the promise of a meal as tasty as it was docile. Seeing no solution, I plucked up my courage and quickly moved up a line of grapevines parallel to the one where Remi was. We were only separated by two rows. The zombies' skinny, sickly upper bodies swayed in rhythm with their uncertain steps, headed in his direction. With the road horde just behind me, I tried to climb over the vines right away. My feet got tangled in the strands the grapes were growing on, and I sprawled out full length in the rocky clay, scratching a large portion of my bare stomach. Faced with the urgency of the situation, I forgot about my own injuries and jumped over the second row of vines. I landed in front of Remi at the same time as the first zombie coming from the forest. Realizing that I was there to ruin his feast, he let out a terrifying cry that only ended when my weapon sank into the thickness of his forehead.

Panicked, I shook my comrade, but I got no reaction. A second monster was already arriving. I eliminated him and then tried to pick up Remi.

"Wake up!" I yelled as large numbers of the road zombies converged on us, just a few strides away.

"Come on, Remi," I insisted, smacking him.

I grabbed his arms and started pulling him. His jeans rubbed against the dirt and turned over clumps of clay in their wake. Around ten zombies had come out of the woods, and the two groups were cornering us in a pincer attack in this terrifying corridor of wood and heart-shaped leaves. They were almost to us. In the hopes of getting to the adjacent row, which the living dead had not yet infiltrated, I slipped Remi's arms under the row of plants and then hurriedly jumped over the wall of vegetation, adding more scratches to my protruding belly. I immediately seized my companion's hands and tried to get him under the first wire that was stretched between the vines.

His body slid, his head emerged, and then he stopped. The zombies were on top of him, gripping his blood-covered legs. The swarming mass lunged at his lower limbs and began to devour him alive. The ones who were not getting their share of the feast tried to climb through the plants to get to me, but being far too clumsy, they got stuck. I let out a scream of rage at the sound of the creatures chewing, and I let go of Remi. He was gone.

I was hoping inwardly that he had already succumbed to his wounds when he abruptly opened his eyes and exclaimed:

"Help me, Patrick!"

He gesticulated in a last burst of energy, then joined the ranks of our enemies. He began to move with a liveliness and strength that were surprising for someone who had lost so much blood. His teeth chattered in the air. Since his new peers had lost interest in his flesh, he managed to free his devoured limbs and started to crawl in my direction. I stepped back, unable to take my eyes off the horror that Remi had become: his legs had been picked cleaned, and only a few scraps of muscle were still clinging to them. He was dragging behind him two skeletal, bloody limbs. A real monstrosity.

I wanted to finish him off, but several zombies toppled over into our row and joined us.

"Sorry," I whispered as I fled to the county road.

Panicked and exhausted, my mind couldn't organize the thoughts spinning through it. Everything around me was baffling. My instincts took control and were guiding me on my mad rush to the school while gruesome images whirled around in my head. I saw Mathieu's slit throat again, the clots of blood gushing out of it; the arrow piercing Serge's neck; Ms. Bleuet's green eye exploding, her body convulsing, a schoolteacher abandoning the last of her students; and finally, Remi, transformed into an abomination.

How could we have come to this through the fault of one man? I saw Gerald's face and then his feet – his damned black ranger boots – fleeing as far from the battlefield as possible. Anger swept over me, and I started to scream as I ran faster and faster.

My legs were crying out in pain, my heart was racing like a wild beast on the loose, and my lungs were burning from the stifling air they were circulating at an infernal pace, but I didn't stop.

The road was clear. It wouldn't be for long. I had left them behind, but I knew the zombies were dragging themselves along after me and would soon reach the school. One of them, deprived of his legs, would take longer.

The school building soon appeared. I dashed to the covered playground and drummed on the metal door. There were certainly other creatures in the area, but I screamed, adding to the din from my fists.

"Open up!"

The door was suddenly cracked open. Raymond, the old man of the group, was standing behind it. Without saying a word to him, I entered and burst into the courtyard, my anger pushing me all the way to the cafeteria. Yelling echoed in the hallway as I went into the building. It was coming from the cafeteria. I crossed the threshold and was assailed by a whole bunch of voices, mingling hysteria and rage. A small group had formed in the middle of the room, shaken up by a heated debate.

Gerald was being vehemently taken to task by some survivors of the mini-market attack. One man, in his forties with a crew cut, who had also hidden as soon as things turned into a massacre, was facing them and protecting Gerald in the absence of Karim, whom I did not see anywhere. Had his recklessness gotten the better of him?

Those who had stayed at the school and did not witness the carnage added their voices to the confusion. I couldn't make out what they were saying, and I didn't care; I only had one desire.

Gerald, too busy trying to justify himself in the prevailing hubbub, did not see me skirt the group. With my sweaty forehead, bare chest, and an ever-thicker beard covering the lower part of my face, I must have looked like a real psychotic when I rushed at him, my hammer ready to judge his actions. A powerful hand grabbed my forearm, and I found myself pinned to the ground by Gerald's protector.

The survivors became agitated, and Gerald stepped backwards when he saw me.

I struggled to try to free myself from the man's grip, but he was strong. Too strong.

"Let me go, scumbag!" I shouted at him, thrashing about like crazy.

Without replying, he tightened his grip around my wrist. I let out a cry of pain and dropped my weapon, which my adversary immediately deprived me of.

"Leave him alone," Thierry intervened, pushing him aside.

The others insisted, demanding that he release me. He complied under the pressure. I got up, ready to fight anyone who came between Gerald and me.

"Don't move," a strangely hoarse voice yelled.

Gerald had me in his sight. He didn't seem to be kidding, either.

"You haven't killed enough people today, you piece of shit!" I spat.

In response, he pointed the barrel of his gun at my head.

The survivors fell silent and watched the scene, hypnotized.

"Yeah, you haven't had your fill, that's for sure," I told him. "But you're not going to get away with it like this."

Confirming my words, Thierry and a young woman with brown hair stepped forward, placing themselves between Gerald and me.

"Give me your weapon," Thierry ordered him curtly.

"And if I don't?" he replied, not taking his eyes off me.

"Are you going to kill all of us?" I said to him over my saviors' shoulders.

"Shut up, Patrick," retorted Thierry. "Hand over your gun!" he yelled, revealing unexpected courage for his small size.

Seeing the situation completely getting away from him, Gerald took another step back and lowered his weapon.

"Go on, give it to him," said the young woman who had intervened, in a thoughtful voice. "Let's talk."

Thierry stepped forward and grabbed the end of the shotgun. Gerald withdrew his finger from the trigger and let himself be disarmed in silence.

I violently pushed aside the young brunette who was standing in front of me and thrust my fist towards Gerald. He dodged the attack and elbowed me in the back, knocking me to the ground once again.

"There's no talking with him," he complained.

Hearing him try to pass for the victim gave me the strength to stand up, but his bodyguard immobilized me again.

"Dammit, Patrick, stop!" cried Thierry, who was holding the gun.

The young woman behind him was rubbing her shoulder.

But how could I stop while the faces of Mathieu, Serge, Remi, and Christine, dead and rigid, kept parading through my mind? Were they all so blind that they couldn't see who Gerald really was?

Emma suddenly appeared behind the other survivors. Giselle was standing by her side. She tried to stop the little girl as she weaved between the survivors' legs, but she did not succeed. I ceased my struggling and watched her come, looking sad.

"What's going on?" she asked, tears in her eyes. "Why are you all screaming like that? Mr. Patrick?"

My rage level was so high that, despite the girl's presence, I couldn't control my words and replied in a bitter voice:

"He killed your teacher," I said, pointing at Gerald.

She stared at me as if she didn't understand.

"She's dead!" I screamed.

I pulled out of my guard's grip and hit Gerald with all my strength in his lower abdomen. The guy who was built like a tank stepped in and threw me against the wall, knocking all the air out of my lungs. I dropped to the ground, my vision faltering. I could still make out the small silhouette of Emma running away, though. What had I done?

There were enough monsters in this world. Why did I have to prove to be so terrifying right in front of her? My anger had completely dissipated. I stood up painfully and dragged myself to the other end of the cafeteria. The survivors moved aside, letting me pass, as the colossus held back an enraged Gerald. He was yelling insults at me, but I couldn't hear them. I had to explain myself. Emma had taken refuge on her rug. Curled up in a ball, she was crying. Seeing me approach, Giselle tried to block my way.

"Get lost," I whispered.

Shocked, she let out a gasp of surprise. I walked around her without paying attention and joined the little one. I crouched down and placed my hand on her body, which was shaking from her sobs. She jumped away like a frightened animal.

"It's me, Emma."

"You scare me," she replied, crying.

Her words broke my heart, and my eyes got misty.

"I'm sorry," I told her in a weak voice. "I am truly sorry. I didn't want… you to see me like that. I was mad."

She said nothing and kept crying. Had I killed the last person she could trust: me? I cursed the impulsive old bastard hiding inside me. I sat down on the rug and continued, notwithstanding the multitude of emotions inundating me.

"Gerald did some bad things, and I was really angry with him. I promise you it won't happen again."

"You'll still be angry," she said.

I tried to reply but couldn't find the words. She was right. It was all just a facade. Deep down inside me, the desire to get rid of Gerald was still burning feverishly. How could the other survivors allow this situation?

"He's going to go to jail," she added, straightening up.

She rubbed her eyes and, without waiting for my response, continued:

"He killed the teacher; he has to go to jail. He's not like the zombies. They don't do it on purpose."

"I don't think there are any more prisons, Emma," I answered, not knowing what to say.

"Then, he's going to kill other people," she concluded, staring at me with her wet eyes.

"I promise you that will not happen. He won't hurt anyone else."

"You have to put him with the zombies, then," she said gravely.

Her words took me by surprise, and I imagined him being devoured by Remi, the young man hoisting himself up to Gerald's carotid artery inch by inch, dragging his bony legs.

"Maybe so."

Someone cleared their throat at my back. Thierry was standing behind me. He had slung the rifle over his shoulder.

"Patrick, can you come with me? I want to know what happened over there."

"Okay," I replied, standing up.

I turned back around to the little one and added:

"I'm really sorry for what just happened. Do you forgive me?"

She gave me a small smile and nodded. I repressed a sudden urge to take her in my arms and followed Thierry. A semblance of calm had returned to the room, which Gerald had evidently left.

"We asked him to isolate himself with Roland," Thierry told me, answering my questions. "We will hear his side of the story later."

"His side of the story," I said with a sneer. "What are you going to do? Listen to the different parties and render a judgment?"

"Exactly. But for now, we are not judging anyone."

"You already have your guilty party, in any case."

"We'll see," he replied, obviously taking the matter very seriously.

The idea of a trial seemed stupid and inappropriate to me, but I was relieved to see that Gerald wasn't going to get off easily. His barbarism was going to be revealed for all to see. The survivors would not be willing to go on living with him at their side. Everything was going to work out. No doubt about it.

We joined the other survivors, who were talking among themselves, still shaken by the commotion of the last few minutes. Some of the ones who had taken part in the attack were already recounting the events. Thierry cleared his throat:

"Now that everyone has calmed down, we're going to try to clear things up. Please sit in a circle."

Without a word, we did as he asked and found ourselves in this strange arrangement in the center of the cafeteria. Thierry, who had taken a spot next to me, turned to the man to his left:

"Stéphane, would you like to start?" he asked him in a calm voice.

"Uh, yeah," he stammered.

I had gone on several expeditions with him. He was always there to help. An exceptionally shy guy who didn't stand out. In the panic during the attack, I had quickly lost sight of him.

All the same, he recounted the events at the mini-market in great detail. When he got to the moment when Gerald slit Mathieu's throat, Thierry cut him off and asked him to repeat that.

He confirmed what he'd said, and I nodded in agreement when Thierry turned to me, his eyes wide. Stéphane continued with Serge's death, then stopped. He had fled at that point.

It was my turn next. I tried to contain my emotions and described Christine's death with surgical coldness, how Gerald had shot another young man with his rifle, and then, Remi's tragic fate. Everybody held their breath as I exposed these horrors. They were terrified.

Some were crying.

"It's not possible," said the young brunette between sobs. "It's not possible," she repeated.

"I think we've heard enough," stated Thierry, standing up. "I'll go get Gerald now."

"We don't need to hear from him," exclaimed the young woman. "He killed those boys, and the others are dead because of him! We must banish him!"

The word I'd been wanting to hear had finally been said, and inwardly, I was savoring what was happening.

"We live in a country of laws," replied Thierry.

"You're kidding, right?" intervened Stéphane. "There are no more countries. Everyone is dead."

"We're going to listen to him anyway," Thierry added curtly. "And you're going to let him speak. Once we have heard him out, we'll vote on the best thing to do. Okay?"

The survivors nodded.

"We're wasting our time…" Stéphane sighed.

Thierry exited the circle and left the room. A heavy silence hung over the cafeteria for a long minute.

"He's a monster," said the young woman, very disturbed by the story that had just been told.

"He wanted food, like the rest of us," Giselle, who had joined the group, chimed in.

"I'd rather starve to death than kill children," the short brunette snapped at her.

Then, the door opened. Thierry entered the room, followed by Gerald and the guy named Roland. The survivors at the other end of the circle moved back several feet, leaving an open space for the newcomers to sit down, at a safe distance.

I avoided meeting Gerald's gaze for fear of stoking my anger again. I had to control myself and let him dig his own grave. The others would make the right decision. I would soon be rid of him. Thierry motioned to the two men to sit down.

They hesitated.

"What is this, a trial?" Gerald scoffed.

No one responded to the affront, and he finally joined us on the ground. Roland did the same.

Thierry took his seat again and began:

"We have listened to Stéphane and Patrick, and now…"

"And what did they tell you? That I killed the kid? That I'm a monster?" Gerald interrupted. "It's true, but it was the only way to get the food. Aren't you starving to death? Because I am. And I'm not gonna let a gang of snot-nosed kids decide my fate."

"But you can decide other people's fate?" the outraged young woman said emotionally. "You're a murderer!"

"Yeah, and you'll all be dead from hunger soon, if you don't accept reality."

"Killing the kid sure helped us," said Stéphane, clenching his fist.

"Okay, so that got screwed up. But I gave it a shot. I did what no one else had the balls to do."

"Nobody wanted to kill that kid. You're out of your mind. They would have ended up letting us in."

"You believe that? You still haven't understood that those kids were signing our death warrant? They've figured out how this works. It's every man for himself."

I watched them exchange their arguments and felt the tension building up again. Thierry was trying to regain control of the conversation but couldn't. Giselle added her hoarse voice to the confusion:

"He's right. He did all that for us!"

The members of the circle had risen, and once again, Roland was trying to protect Gerald, who was exchanging insults with the young brunette, calling her a cowardly and useless bitch.

My anger was feeding off this chaos and beckoning me to partake in the madness, but the memory of Emma's scared face helped me to contain it. I urged Thierry with my eyes to get him to intervene, but the little man was quite overwhelmed.

All of a sudden, Giselle slapped the young brunette who, with no hesitation, hit her back. The old woman let out a moan, and the discussion turned into a free-for-all. Roland punched Stéphane right in the face, sending him to the floor. Thierry was yelling at them to stop, but his screams were covered by the din.

"Stop!" a young, powerful voice suddenly cried out.

Everybody stopped and turned towards the entrance. Karim was standing in the doorway with several full, white plastic bags in his hands.

"It's fine. They left. We have food."

CHAPTER 17
TEARS OF RELIEF

That's not possible, I thought, my eyes scouring the protruding contours of the sacks of food Karim was carrying. They were full. The others, equally surprised, remained silent, some of them frozen in comical wrestling positions.

Gerald was the first to pull himself together. He walked towards Karim:

"The kids took off?"

"Yeah, they're gone."

"And the coast is clear?"

I piped up, not leaving time for the young man to continue his report.

"It's not possible. The supermarket was surrounded. They had no reason to leave. It's not possible."

It didn't make sense. Could Karim have gone to loot a house in the village to stall for time for Gerald?

Well-sheltered, with everything they needed, those young people could have survived for months inside the store. But lo and behold, they abandoned their refuge in the presence of a horde of zombies. Something wasn't quite right.

"Plus, you ran away like everyone else," I added. "How could you have known?"

The tension in the room was thick, and I was obviously not the only one doubting Karim's story.

"I didn't run away. When I took off, I hid further down on the road that leads to the village. I could see everything that was happening. I saw you helping Remi. Did he get hit by an arrow?"

He turned away from the angry look on my face, but he kept going:

"Five minutes later, they came out the back door with a couple of bicycles and skedaddled, with all the zombies in hot pursuit. They were really scared we would come back. There were only two of them left! It's all ours now."

"And they're going to die, too!" cried the young brunette, dropping to her knees.

"You won't whine so much when you have something to eat tonight," Gerald told her sourly.

Thierry wanted to say something, but my voice covered his:

"And you came back without a hitch?" I asked Karim.

"Well, here I am," he replied, slapping his chest with both hands.

Then he understood where I was coming from and added:

"I killed a few, but I had to avoid the horde. They're probably in front of the school by now."

"What?!" cried Thierry and Gerald at the same time.

"You guys attracted quite a few while you were fleeing," explained Karim.

"How many?" Gerald asked.

"A good twenty, I'd say."

"Okay, we'll get rid of them and go stock up."

"What the hell is the matter with you?" the young woman bellowed, still kneeling on the ground.

She was crying her eyes out, her nerves frayed.

"This guy is a murderer. He needs to be kicked out," she added in a sharp voice.

"Without me, you would be dead!" Gerald replied vehemently.

The survivors exchanged glances, ready to fight each other again. In a calm voice, Thierry said:

"We're going to vote. Right now."

In one fell swoop, all my hopes of getting rid of Gerald disappeared. It was unreal. The outcome of the vote was a foregone conclusion. Gerald did not seem reassured, however, and was rubbing his beard. Karim put a hand on his shoulder and nodded his head at him.

"Sit down," ordered Thierry. "Everybody."

Some survivors did so without a word. Giselle and Roland were standing next to Gerald and Karim, who refused to obey. The young man rummaged through his bags and gave bottles of water and a couple packets of cookies to those who had sat down. This vote was a farce. For starters, just like an African tyrant, the main defendant was buying off his starving subjects. My companions were not going to vote with their hearts but with their stomachs. And Gerald had just figured that out.

He was now smiling broadly as the survivors pounced on the provisions being distributed.

"Okay," said Thierry in a serious, almost theatrical voice. "Gerald, for having killed two children..."

The man cleared his throat and continued:

"And for having caused the deaths of several of us, you are subject to being banned from our group. We are therefore going to vote on whether we can forgive such acts and accept your presence among us."

"Very well," answered the relevant party.

"Good. Who votes for Gerald to be banned from the group?"

The young brunette immediately raised her hand, as did I. Gerald looked me in the eye, and I stared back threateningly. I watched out of the corner of my eye for other movements. Three other hands joined us, and then everything became still. Even Thierry's arms had remained submissively crossed over his chest.

"Okay, that's five. Who votes for Gerald to stay with us?"

Karim, Giselle, and Roland quickly raised their hands, followed by many of the survivors. Some did so discreetly, their elbows still bent, ashamed of their choice.

"Thirteen," Thierry counted.

"Okay, get your weapons and your bags, and let's go," Gerald said, not wasting a second.

The survivors did as he said, leaving to retrieve their equipment. I stood still, the young brunette behind me. She was crying, her face buried in her delicate fingers. I took one step towards Thierry to try to reason with him, but I stopped in the middle of the room when he turned to Gerald and gave him back his gun. The only firearm in the group had just found its way back into its owner's hands. It would spread death again, of that I was sure.

I no longer knew what to do. Everything would have been simpler if I had just managed to eliminate him. I would have taken his place at the trial, but we would have been rid of him. I certainly could have convinced the survivors of the correctness of my actions. Each fewer monster in this crazy world was a step towards normalcy. They would have understood that. Now I was scared, and not just for myself. To get revenge, was he capable of going after Emma?

I had seen quite well that, child or not, whatever stood in his way ended up dead, definitively. He wouldn't hesitate.

Subconsciously, my steps had guided me towards the little one, who was observing the commotion around us. The survivors were getting ready, excited by the treasure waiting for them – a whole mini-market, just for them – and were moving around, back and forth, in the room. My mind muddled, I sat down next to Emma silently. My knees creaked loudly and then became quiet as I stretched my legs out on the ground.

"Mr. Patrick?" the girl asked me in a crystalline voice.

"Yes?" I replied, staring straight in front of me, my brain overrun with various thoughts.

"You're not going to throw him to the zombies, then?"

"Nope. We're not going to do anything. People are cowards, you know."

She fell silent, and for a few seconds, I tried to sort out the ideas in my head.

Then, she sat down on my lap and placed a hand on my cheek.

"Does this mean the bad guys always win?"

I looked at her pretty, oval face.

"Not always, but often."

"The zombies are going to win, then. We're going to die anyway. Everybody dies."

I stroked her face in turn.

"No, you're not going to die. I'll protect you."

"Papa and Mama used to say that, too."

I didn't know how to respond to that and just brushed her skin with my dirty fingertips.

"We're going to starve to death, Mr. Patrick. I'm so hungry."

Her expression broke down, and she burst into tears as she threw herself against me. For the second time that day, she broke my heart. Her sadness was so great, it overwhelmed me. Her tears rolled down my neck and snaked between the thick hairs of my beard. With her head buried in the crook of my shoulder, she tugged at the collar of my T-shirt, her hands clenched.

Her crying echoed throughout the room, and some of the survivors had ceased their hustle and bustle and were looking at us. Giselle took a few steps in our direction, but I shook my head, making her understand that she was not welcome.

"I can't take it anymore," Emma whimpered in my ear.

By way of response, I stroked her hair and hugged her. I couldn't leave her in this state. Was she, too, starting to understand that a life like this was not worth living? I couldn't accept that such a radiant child could give up. I realized that I had deserted her the past few days, going on more and more excursions outside the school grounds and only seeing her again briefly before collapsing from fatigue. With her having nothing to do, stuck here, I should have understood that the confinement and loneliness would eventually hurt her morale. Even in the middle of the apocalypse, there was nothing comforting about an ivory tower.

"It's going to be fine, sweetie…"

This last word came out of my mouth completely naturally and shocked me far more than it surprised Emma. Her tears stopped, and she pulled her wet face away from my neck. She stared at me with her misty eyes.

"We're all going to go pick up some food. After that, I promise, we'll never leave each other again. I'll really take care of you. You won't be alone anymore," I added, my tone of voice betraying the emotions that were flooding me.

"You promise? For the last time?"

"I swear. And tonight, you won't be hungry anymore. All I want now is for you to be happy."

She smiled at me and kissed me on the cheek, just under my eye. A tear slid down almost exactly where she had deposited her kiss. I wiped my eyes and squeezed her against me before reluctantly releasing her. I had to go.

I was still in shock from the deaths of my fellow survivors, but my pragmatism was gaining the upper hand. They were deceased. That couldn't be changed. I would never forgive Gerald for his madness, but once again, I had to keep a low profile. The school was the safest place for the little one, and if we managed to solve the food problem, I could finally spend more time with her. Who knew what we could rebuild together from this garden-variety village school. Was a future still possible?

Gerald was a murderer, a psychotic bastard, but I would have to follow him once more. He was nothing but a means to achieve my ends, a simple tool. I would protect the girl at all costs. He could play leader, make unacceptable decisions, and be suspicious of me; I would stay in the shadows, keeping Emma happy.

I stood up, ready to face the trek to the store again. We would not come back empty-handed this time. I retrieved my bag, which I had left in the middle of the room during the altercations, and quietly joined the group of survivors who were waiting for the signal to leave.

I sensed that Gerald was watching me and inwardly relishing seeing me yield to his oppression. The last survivors arrived. Some had donned many layers of clothing and looked more determined than ever.

Gerald was heading for the door when Thierry called out to him:

"Gerald! I was just thinking. Wouldn't it be better if we all just moved to the mini-market? It would be easier."

A few murmurs ran through the crowd, and then the man with the shotgun replied in a confident voice:

"It's too small and too exposed. The zombies could corner us there in two seconds. It's better here, with the courtyard and everything."

Thierry nodded, convinced, and Gerald added:

"Okay, then, here we go. Be ready. And be on the lookout for zombies."

The group set off, leaving only Giselle, Raymond, Romain, and Emma in the room. I returned the little girl's wave and smiled at her before disappearing into the corridor.

I was having a hard time comprehending that, that very morning, my companions had perished atrociously because of the man who was now leading almost all of us to our salvation. If it hadn't been for Emma, either Gerald or I, one of the two of us, also would have died. I was convinced of it.

In the covered playground, Gerald gave final instructions, and we left the school grounds. As Karim had predicted, the zombie pack had followed us here. The majority of them had ventured into the little courtyard and were wandering around aimlessly; others, closer, were trying to go around the building to find an entrance. Remi didn't seem to be among them. The unfortunate man must have been dragging himself several hundred yards further.

When they saw us, the stiffs let out their characteristic moan. I had heard it so much that I easily understood its meaning. They were uttering a single word: "Eat!"

Gerald ordered the survivors to disperse in order to force the zombies to separate. The more experienced people obeyed without hesitation, their weapons ready to enter the fray. Others stayed back, trembling with fear under their many clothes, their faces streaming with sweat.

I took up a position as far away from Gerald as possible and watched my first enemy approach: a really banged-up young woman. The creature was in a sorry state, and a festering stump sat enthroned where her right arm should have been. She extended towards me the scrawny remains of her limb, a simple mass of ligaments and necrotic flesh. Her filthy, grey face was covered in bruises that had stopped bleeding long ago. Her clothes were in tatters, and her torn blouse revealed a breast that moved repulsively to the rhythm of her jerky footsteps. When the monster was within two yards, I could make out shards of glass sunk into the wounds on her face.

"You should have worn your seatbelt," I scolded her, brandishing my hammer.

The blow hit her on the top of her head, and an expression of relief seemed to pass over her emaciated face as her body collapsed, lifeless.

I got rid of a second adversary, trying not to think about his personal story, and ended the battle. In seconds, the pack had been reduced to nothing: a new pile of corpses to burn.

"Come on, let's not waste time!" shouted Gerald, taking off down the road towards the village without giving us a chance to catch our breath.

We quickly started after him. Out of the blue, Karim passed me, riding a bicycle. He slowed down when he reached Gerald at the head of the line, spoke with him for a brief moment, then moved ahead of the group. He continued to sweep our group's surroundings, swallowing the tar with a few pedal strokes, confirming that no danger was lurking and then coming back to us. Not once did he have to warn us of the presence of zombies, and we safely made it back to the small forest that led to the store. Our procession was moving slowly. A lead weight was heavy on our shoulders as the sun continued to accomplish its deadly plan to completely dry up our world. The heat was so bad that every drop of sweat beading on my forehead seemed to evaporate instantly. When we got within sight of the mini-market, the group heaved a collective sigh of relief. But it wasn't over yet.

Despite what Karim had said, about thirty living dead were lurking around the building. I managed to catch his eye and gave him a questioning look. He just shrugged. He got back on his bike, which he had pushed through the woods, and suddenly set off down the slope of the vineyard. He shot like an arrow between two rows of vines, crossed the field, and in seconds, climbed the small hill that led to the store's parking lot. He began to slalom deftly between the dead, getting them to follow him. He exited the lot and rode to the small roundabout a few yards away. The zombies had regrouped and were dragging themselves in his direction. They pushed and shoved each other, driven by the urge to catch this strange human made of flesh and metal who was taunting them. Karim let them get within a few feet of him, and then he moved off again, leading them away from us.

Next, Gerald signaled to us, and we entered the vineyard one after another, with the selfish hope that all the monsters had set off in pursuit of Karim. In groups, the living dead were formidable, but an isolated zombie, inopportunely concealed, was just as deadly.

I was dreading the moment when my eyes would meet the empty, dead ones of Christine's corpse again. Nothing, though, could have prepared me for the horror that awaited us on the asphalt. Upon seeing the disemboweled and almost entirely devoured remains of our cohorts, several survivors whimpered. Some began to cry. I hoped that one of them would have the courage to hurl himself at Gerald, too, but they all stood still, unable to take their eyes off the disgusting sight.

Christine's rib cage had been torn open and emptied of all its organs, and her lower limbs had suffered the same fate as Remi's. Only her face seemed to have been of no interest to the dead. The hair that fell over her forehead didn't mask the bloody mush that had replaced her right eye, however. Serge's corpse was leaning back on the hubcap of the car he had collapsed against, both hands – or at least what was left of them – eternally stiffened around the arrow that had pierced his throat. As for Mathieu, he had said his final farewell to this world. All that remained of his body was a bloody pile of clothes; even his bones appeared to have been devoured by the horde.

Gerald must have been delighted. The sight of the young boy with his throat cut certainly would have stirred up his opponents' wrath.

With my stomach tied up in a knot, I tried to control my resentment towards him. As he observed the carnage with his cold, indifferent expression, the man with the gun finally approached the back door, closely followed by his new lapdog of a bodyguard. Gradually, the survivors followed him, not taking their eyes off the cadavers. This was about when, normally, someone would come and cover each body with a sheet. But we didn't have anything like that with us. Only the scorching rays of the sun enveloped them, cruelly, accelerating their decomposition.

When I turned the corner of the building, among the last to have managed to tear their gaze from our former companions rotting in the parking lot, the survivors had already flooded into the mini-market through the service door. Had the youngsters left it unlocked when they left, or had it been Karim?

I wasn't looking to find out right away, so I stepped into the coolness of the back of the store. This secondary entrance led directly into a small office, which must have been used by the store's manager. His computer screen had been smashed and almost torn off its stand. Papers and documents, which had probably been well organized before the zombies arrived, were strewn about and covered the floor. Surely the work of the teenagers who, dying of boredom, had indulged in one of the favorite activities of that age: destruction.

On the other side of the office, another door led to locker rooms and a break room for the staff. No survivors had lingered in the entryway; all of them had gone through the double-leaf doors that led to the back of the store. They were busy at the shelves, drunk with happiness, like a swarm of bees in a lavender field. They didn't know which way to turn and filled their bags ecstatically.

One of them had violently ripped open a bag of chips and was jamming the contents into his mouth, not caring how disgusting he looked.

Soon, the place was echoing with the sound of survivors chewing and filling their tired, empty stomachs. I was doing the same, devouring peanuts by the handful. I couldn't have cared less about the choking hazard. Thirst quickly drove me to the beverage aisle, where several survivors had gathered. I was surprised to see that the dozens of packages of water and other liquids that were piled up there had not been deliberately destroyed by the kids before their escape. They had really gone and left all the provisions intact for us. Probably not out of altruism. Had they been so scared as to leave the premises that quickly?

I grabbed a bottle of mineral water and took a long sip, washing down the salty taste from the peanuts. Reflexively, I looked at the label and discovered that it was just ordinary, supermarket-brand water. All of a sudden, I saw Karim's head stick out above the display. I joined him in the next aisle, where he was loading his bag with canned goods.

"You lost 'em?" I asked, not managing to mask my animosity towards him.

"Yeah. I did a U-turn through a block of houses up the road, and they didn't see me leave. They're going to be looking for me for quite a while, I think," he replied proudly, still collecting new supplies.

"And the kids, they really left, just like that?"

He turned to face me and stared at me determinedly.

"Yes, like I told you. What do you think I did? That I came back? That I killed them? Maybe that's what I would have done if they hadn't left," he said defiantly.

"How did you get in?"

He sighed.

"When they bugged out, I went up onto the roof. I hoisted myself up by the gutter. I propped the back door open when I left again."

"Okay," I told him, not entirely convinced.

He turned away, grabbed a new can, then added:

"I'm sorry about Christine, by the way."

"Yeah, me too," I mumbled as I walked away, after grabbing a bunch of canned peas and carrots.

I hoped the little one liked those. Especially cold.

I continued my shopping, and my bag quickly grew heavy. It wasn't long before the straps were killing my shoulders, but I was ready to endure this pain to soothe the one that had been assaulting my hungry stomach for the past few days.

I suddenly noticed a small white door at the end of the pharmacy aisle, where a few survivors had decided to stop. They were raiding it like junkies looking for anything to get one last fix. One for the road.

Intrigued, I walked past them and put one hand on the doorknob, which was painted the same color as the walls, and the other on my weapon. I had learned to be suspicious at all times. I pressed down, and the door opened without making a sound. The interior was darker than the rest of the shop, lit only by a small window covered with a metal grate that let in just a few rays of sunshine. The room was filled with shelves that were overflowing with household products. They were doomed to wait centuries in this position, gradually getting covered with their ultimate enemy: that devious dust they would never be done with.

I was about to go back out when I noticed a colorful box in the back of the room. I went over to it and lifted it up to eye level. Through a thin sheet of plastic, a blue unicorn with a rainbow-colored mane was staring at me with doleful eyes that had been crudely painted on in a Chinese factory. It looked like it was squinting, and I chuckled at the sight of such a creature. I had no idea what children saw in dreadful toys like this, but I was sure Emma would like it.

I was smiling stupidly at my discovery when, all of a sudden, the door slammed behind me.

Not knowing what was going on, I found myself violently pressed against one of the shelves, a cold metal band against my neck. Gerald was standing in front of me and pressing his machete's blade to my throat.

"Okay, listen to me, you giant piece of shit," he said to me, looking deep into my eyes with his murderous ones. "I'm not going to take you out now, because that would fuck things up even more, but you're gonna beat it and fast, or I swear, I'll kill you."

He paused for a few seconds and sneered before adding, as he blew his foul breath into my face:

"I won't fail. Not like last time, in the courtyard."

I dropped the box with the toy and wanted to lift the hand holding my weapon, but Gerald pressed the blade even harder against my skin. I felt blood beginning to flow and lowered my hammer.

"I'll give you until tomorrow, asshole," he added.

He withdrew his machete and backed up defensively towards the door. He opened it behind his back with one hand and stepped out, one finger of his left hand raised to his mouth. He closed the door, and I heard him chatting with another survivor just outside.

"There's nothing in there, just some cleaning stuff."

I dropped to the ground, one hand pressed to my nicked throat. I had forgotten about the box and crushed it under all my weight. Flattened by my posterior, the unicorn probably could have dreamed up more magical places to be. Gerald couldn't have been more crystal clear with me, and the anger I'd been feeling towards him turned into terror again. That motherfucker wasn't kidding around. But unwittingly, he had resolved a dilemma that had been gnawing at me. I had truly considered staying at the school, looking after Emma and being there for her, even if it meant doing it under Gerald's threatening and disturbing watch. That was no longer a valid option. I had to leave as soon as possible. But this time, I wouldn't be alone. It was time for Emma and me to leave the school.

I stood back up and picked up the package containing the unicorn. Its neck was broken, and its eyes seemed to have forgotten their squint and were glaring at me in anger. I put it back on the shelf. I would find toys that were less ugly after we left. Tomorrow.

CHAPTER 18
NOCTURNAL MONSTERS

The cafeteria was bathed in darkness. The survivors were sleeping soundly despite the loud snoring from some of them. Outside, it was a beautiful night. Beyond the glass ceiling panels, the clear, cloudless sky displayed its collection of bright constellations. I sat up quietly and peered into the dark. It felt like time was standing still. Emma was dozing beside me, lying on her side. I put a hand on her shoulder and shook her gently. I leaned down to her ear and whispered:

"Emma, it's time to go."

She opened her eyelids and remained silent. In the dark, her eyes shone with determination and excitement.

After getting back from the mini-market a few hours earlier, I had unpacked only part of my bag, and we had enjoyed an invigorating meal together. Between bites, I had explained to her that the bad guys wanted me gone, and she'd immediately replied that she wanted to come with me. Relieved by her reaction, I had asked her to pack her things as discreetly as possible.

The bad guys didn't need to know what we were up to.

I stood up in the dark and put my arms through the straps of my backpack. It was heavy with several days' worth of provisions. A reassuring but crushing weight. Noiselessly, the little one copied me. Like me, she was crumbling under her load, but she did not complain. She had insisted on carrying her share of our food, but secretly, once she had fallen asleep, I had relieved her of a few canned goods.

I looked over at the platform where Gerald was sleeping, perfectly still. A few steps, a well-placed hammer blow, and I could be done with that piece of garbage, but I knew that such a cold-blooded murder wouldn't bring any good. We were going to go our separate ways once and for all. This world would end up picking him off, as it would all of us. I wouldn't be there to enjoy that show, but it didn't matter.

I took Emma by the hand, and we weaved our way through the snoozing survivors on their rugs on the floor. I pushed open one of the door flaps and graciously welcomed the hinges' silence.

I let the girl walk into the hallway first. She only took a few steps, clearly concerned about the total darkness of the corridor. She slipped her hand into mine again, and we headed blindly towards the facilities.

My left hand resting on the wall, I let my fingers guide us to the bathroom door. When they brushed against its frame, we turned left. Within a few seconds, after holding our breath through the stench from the toilets, we reached the tranquility of the schoolyard.

The air was mild and pleasant. The dark silhouettes of the trees in the courtyard stood out against the deep grey of the sky. Hand in hand, we crossed the outdoor play area and entered the covered playground.

"You're not too scared? You're okay?" I asked Emma, whose clenched fingers were gripping my thumb.

She hadn't gone outside for several weeks, and leaving the ostensible safety of the school had to be scary for her.

"No, I'm fine," she replied, trying to sound brave.

I knew that fleeing at night was not the best solution. The monsters lurking in the dark were very real, but the survivors certainly wouldn't have let me leave with Emma in broad daylight, and there was no way I was going to abandon her again. My plan was simple: run away without being seen, walk a few hundred yards, and hide in a house for the rest of the night.

I imagined our journey would continue like that, from refuge to refuge, all the way to the heart of the Alps. Perhaps we could take shelter there in an isolated chalet. It seemed like the perfect place to me: not a lot of people before the epidemic, and rough terrain that would keep the zombies at bay. The food issue would still need to be resolved, but I had many long days left to find a solution before the Alpine peaks stood before us in all their majesty.

Determined, I was putting my hand on the push bar of the playground's emergency exit door when a voice rang out behind us.

"Patrick, wait."

It was Karim.

"I'm sorry, but I can't let you take Emma. This is suicide."

The little girl tightened her grip around my hand and hid behind my legs.

"I don't care what Gerald said to you; she's coming with me."

Karim was not denying that he was acting on Gerald's order. His arm, a simple black ribbon from what I could see, moved in the direction of his weapon. I stayed still. I knew very well that if it went that far, he would take the upper hand in seconds. I had already had that bitter experience.

"Let her decide for herself," I told him.

"No. Emma stays here."

I sighed and released the girl's hand.

"Listen to him, Emma. I'm sorry."

The little one took a step back, horrified by my words. I crouched down and added, in a whisper only she could hear:

"Run past him. I'll take care of everything."

She threw her bag onto the ground and ran towards the school building. As she passed Karim, the young man turned to grab her. At the same instant, I launched myself at him and struck a blow on the back of his head with the handle of my hammer. The impact sent him to the ground. He tried to get back up, but my second attack rendered

him unconscious. Emma, who had stopped in the middle of the courtyard, quickly came back over to me.

"Did you kill him, Mr. Patrick?" she asked me worriedly.

"No, he's just knocked out," I replied, hoping deep down that Karim
wouldn't have any lasting after-effects.

I helped the little girl put her backpack on again, and we moved towards the exit. Calm had returned to the courtyard, and it looked like
no one else was going to emerge from the darkness to hold us back.

"Are you ready?" I asked her.

"Yes!" she exclaimed, her courage having returned.

I pushed the door open, and we disappeared into the night as it
closed behind our backs. Despite the stillness outside, I didn't hear the
door open again and the sound of Karim's body collapsing in the crack,
well and truly unconscious this time. Even less did I see the monster
with the devoured legs dragging himself in Karim's direction, followed
closely by his friends.

***

A light wind had started up and was stirring the trees along the
road. Its uneven breeze was giving life to their branches. They were
moving peacefully above us as the moonlight cast their sinister shadows on the asphalt. At each movement, we jumped, terrorized by the
idea of seeing a zombie suddenly pounce on us. We walked in single
file down the middle of the road, leaving empty space on either side. I
was leading the way, with the little one so close behind me that she had
run into me when I'd come to a sudden stop a few minutes earlier,
thinking I had heard something approaching. Nothing had appeared,
and we had continued on our way. For all that, Emma hadn't bolted
off; she was still following me silently.

We listened for the slightest noise, convinced that each shadow would transform into a moaning zombie, but only the chirping of the crickets, true cicadas of the night, broke the silence.

Our steps had led us near the residential area where the large Renaissance house was located. I hesitated for a moment trying to find it, but in the darkness, I only had a vague idea of where we were. The landscape was painted a dark grey, and I couldn't see more than a few yards away. Maybe we had already passed it. Better to keep pressing ahead. A little further. I didn't intend to tempt fate for too long, however, and even though Emma wasn't complaining, I didn't want her to run out of energy.

The road suddenly split in two. A private asphalt driveway climbed the steep hill on our right, while the street we were on kept winding its way among the trees. I slowed down and then stopped. The little one came over to my side. The moon lit up the pale walls of a large villa built on the hillside, among the dark silhouettes of the oak and pine trees that surrounded it. The place seemed perfect to me for spending the night. I crouched down and whispered:

"We'll go see if we can sleep here, okay?" I said to Emma, who answered with a simple nod, afraid of making any noise.

We left the main road and climbed the steep path that brought us to the front of the house. The driveway led to a gravel-covered courtyard along which the building extended. In addition to its ground floor, the villa had two other levels. A car was parked in front of a closed garage door. Its presence did not reassure me. The place was probably not deserted. Were there zombies waiting for us there, locked inside? I began to question my decision, but sore legs and fatigue convinced me to forge ahead. We might as well try our luck here.

I took Emma's hand, and we walked across the courtyard. The thick layer of gravel covering it creaked under our feet, and the villa's high facade sent a disturbing echo back to us. A narrow staircase led to the first floor, where the entrance had to be. I moved between the two brick walls bordering the steps, hammer in hand. The girl was right behind me, watching our backs.

The stairs led to a large wooden deck. The smell of varnish hung in the air, as if the slats had been repainted a few days before the crisis. The homeowners would never get to enjoy the beauty of the freshly stained, shiny wood. Wicker loungers and chairs were the only occupants. They were soaking up the freshness of the night.

Unsurprisingly, a large door was located just across from the steps. I moved forward and tried to open it. It was locked. Perhaps the house was deserted, after all? Not having any desire to rouse the whole neighborhood by breaking it down, let alone to dislocate my shoulder, which was far more likely, I went over to the sliding glass doors that were in line with the door. One of them was half open. The question of how to get in had just been answered, but the one about what was waiting for us inside was more pressing than ever.

The moon's rays only illuminated part of the interior; they demarcated a grey rectangle that ended at the top of the cushions of a sofa that was turned towards the terrace. The back of the room was plunged into total darkness. I removed my bag from my shoulders and pulled a flashlight out of one of its side pockets. I hadn't used it yet for fear that, outdoors, this comforting source of light would become a beacon indicating our presence to the zombies. But entering this building without using it would have been madness.

"Stay behind me," I whispered to Emma, who had also put her bag down outside, against the terrace door.

She was holding a small knife.

I turned on the flashlight and swept the interior. The beam quickly covered the many pieces of furniture that decorated it, revealing an overcrowded living room. There was nobody there. I slid the glass door open more and crossed the threshold. As soon as I pointed the flashlight in a new direction, the heavy, ominous darkness reasserted itself and let my imagination birth legions of monsters patiently lurking in the pitch blackness.

We walked around the sofa and the coffee table in front of it and made our way to a terrifyingly dark frame: the beginning of a hallway that sank deeper into the bowels of the villa. My hands started to shake. I felt like I had gone back in time to childhood, when the dark was still the scariest thing, when creatures hidden in the shadows were just imaginary. Times had changed. Anything my brain was coming up with now could materialize at any given moment. The knuckles of my fingers were crying out in pain around the handle of my hammer, which I was holding in my other hand.

The darkness prevailing in the hall dissipated as the beam of light finally slipped between its walls. Emma, also terrified, was clutching the back of my pants. We both let out a yelp when the sound of breaking dishes rattled the sides of the corridor. Embarrassed at having displayed such bravery, I tried to take matters into my own hands and moved at a snail's pace towards the origin of the crash. All the doors along the hallway seemed to be closed except for one: the first on my right, less than three feet away. I placed my hand on Emma's chest, making her understand not to move, and launched myself through the opening, flashlight pointed in and my hammer ready to go. Right away, the light landed on the troublemaker's back: an old woman in a floral dress, who immediately turned around and leaped in my direction, screaming. Surprised by her speed, I moved aside sharply, almost knocking Emma over. The woman crashed into the wall, her head penetrating the insulation with a thunderous noise. Pointing the flashlight at this ostrich from hell, I smashed the base of her neck and then the back of her skull. Her body went still and slumped against the partition, her head still sunk into the wall.

My heart racing, I listened for any suspicious noise, any sign that more zombies were coming, but all I heard was the incessant pounding of my ticker echoing against my eardrums.

"Do you hear anything?" I asked Emma, who immediately pricked up her ears.

She had a serious expression on her face for several seconds then shook her head, a slight smile on her lips. Somewhat reassured, I once again lit up the interior of the kitchen, the floor of which was littered with debris from the smashed plates. Obviously, this had not been the zombie's first household gaffe. I motioned for Emma to follow me, and we entered the room. Bits of china clinked under our feet, once again violating the sepulchral silence that hung over the house.

On the table, the beam from my flashlight discovered an open book of crosswords. The half-filled puzzle was covered with dry, creased petals that had fallen from a bouquet of dead flowers adorning the center of the table. Aside from the tiled floor, which was covered with thousands of fragments, the room was in perfect order. However, all the upper shelves hanging above the sink and ceramic glass stovetop appeared to have been emptied of their contents. We weren't the first to have stopped by here. Had the old woman, still so nimble and quick, transformed recently, and had her companions just left? I would never know.

I sighed and left the kitchen.

"Let's go try to find a bedroom, okay?" I said to Emma, eager to leave the tension behind in favor of some semblance of safety.

We walked past the other doors in the hallway without stopping and arrived at a large staircase with banisters painted an ominous grey. I blazed the trail again, taking a bite out of each step with the slowness of an anorexic in a pie-eating competition. Nevertheless, I eventually reached the top of it, emerging into a corridor that was much less dark than the one on the floor below. A large window at the end of it enthusiastically let in the moon's rays. It was completely silent.

I didn't linger over the layout of the other rooms and put my hand on the knob of the first door I came to. It creaked as it opened into the darkness, but its sonorous betrayal did not summon the sharp claws of any zombies. The large bedroom revealing itself to us was unoccupied. We hastened inside, and I closed the door again. I quickly inspected the interior of the closet and checked under the bed as a precaution. Nothing. Reassured by the absence of danger, I ran downstairs and bolted back up with our bags, which had been patiently waiting for me where we'd left them.

I was out of breath when I burst into the bedroom, but I started moving the heavy chest of drawers by its entrance anyway. The dresser scraped loudly against the floor and tore thick splinters of wood from the doorframe as it landed forcefully against it. Arranged this way, it was a paltry barrier that probably wouldn't withstand pushing from several zombies, but if they tried to move it, we would be woken up for sure.

"Welcome to your new abode, my lady," I said to Emma in a deep, dramatic voice as I bowed before her.

The girl couldn't help but laugh, and she sank onto the bed. The thick mattress sagged under her weight as she slipped under the sheet. Two small thwacks made me jump when her shoes hit the floor at my feet. I quickly lined them up, keeping them close by, and walked over to the bedroom's single, large window. I opened it wide, letting the balmy, clean air fill the space. The night was still very calm, and only the songs of the nocturnal insects continued to break the silence.

"Mr. Patrick, do you want a drink?" Emma asked me, handing me her little bottle from the bed, which she had knelt on.

I accepted and took a sip, savoring the sensation of the water flowing down my throat.

"Thank you," I said, smiling.

She retrieved her bottle and placed it on the square nightstand to the left of the bed, pushing aside a frame that stood there. Her gaze lingered for a few seconds on the old couple smiling at her, then she turned the photo around, a sad look on her face.

She stared at me with a questioning look in her tired eyes.

"You can go to sleep, don't worry," I told her. "Do you have every-thing you need?"

She yawned in response then nodded her head slightly. I sat down next to her and kissed her on the forehead.

"Good night, then. Do you mind sharing your bed with an old gen-tleman whose clothes are as filthy as mine?"

She made a funny face and laughed as she kissed me on the cheek. Then, she let her head drop onto the pillow, where she fell asleep almost immediately.

I returned to the window and stared into the darkness. The moon bathed the deserted courtyard below in a pale glow. Further away, the starlight struggled to penetrate the branches of the massive pine trees surrounding the house. Maybe zombies were creeping between their trunks, pushing on their blood-engorged legs to climb up to us.

I preferred not to think about it. For the time being.

On the other hand, I kept seeing Karim's body lying on the ground. I sincerely hoped I hadn't hurt him seriously. But deep down, I was reveling in the image of Gerald's face when he found out I had left with Emma. I stifled a snigger so as not to disturb the little one, whose breathing had already adopted the rhythm of sleep.

I thought again about my idea of fleeing to the Alps; it was really starting to take shape in my head. Was it just a dream or a real possi-bility? I didn't know for sure, but we couldn't move forward without a goal in mind. We could cover maybe six or seven miles a day. In a matter of weeks, we would be safe, protected by the vastness of the mountains.

My mind drifted off freely, alternating between happy scenarios and tragedies, when suddenly, a violent urge to urinate took hold of my lower abdomen and brought me back to reality.

"Fuckin' old man," I grumbled through my teeth, imagining my prostate finding this hilariously funny.

Unable to hold it, I unzipped my pants and let a long stream shoot out the window. I was chuckling at the thought of a zombie passing by below when a voice startled me. I almost splashed my fingers.

"Hey! You're peeing out the window!" Emma cried before collapsing in a fit of laughter.

"Don't look," I replied, taken aback and embarrassed.

The girl's laughter filled the room, and I joined in as I finished my business. For a few seconds, we didn't give a damn about the ruckus we were making and just enjoyed the moment. Kneeling on the bed, Emma amused herself by imitating me, and I couldn't contain a fit of the giggles that ended up coming over her, too. After a few minutes, with my neurons electrified by this moment of joy and my eyes still moist, I joined her on the bed.

Our fatigue soon took over, and we fell asleep at last, a smile on each of our faces.

***

The din resonating from downstairs pulled me from my slumber. I instinctively turned my head towards the door. My neck protested at the sharp movement, but it was also reassured to see that the dresser holding it closed had not moved. The noises had also woken Emma, who was rubbing her eyes next to me.

"Did you sleep well?" I asked her, forgetting the brouhaha underneath us for a few seconds: one last moment of normalcy before diving back into this crazy world.

She nodded and looked at the door.

"Get ready quickly. We're leaving," I told her as the sound of breaking dishes was heard again: they were in the kitchen.

We put on our backpacks at the same time, ready to go in the blink of an eye. I didn't know what was down there, but the racket was such that we surely had more than one visitor. I realized then that I had left the terrace door open the night before when I'd gone to get our bags, panicked by what might have been hiding in the dark. *You idiot*, I thought to myself. We had no time to lose; if a large number of creatures were to gather outside our room, we would be cornered. The window was much too high for us to jump; the door was our only way out.

"I'll go first. Stay right behind me," I said to Emma with feigned composure.

Squatting down, I placed my back against the chest of drawers and took a deep breath. I pushed with my legs, and it moved aside with a thunderous sound. I exited the room, hammer in hand, on the lookout for an opponent. It was clear. I started down the stairs, followed closely by Emma.

When we got to the hallway on the first floor, two zombies had already stormed it and were heading towards us. Behind them, a third emerged from the kitchen with a final crunch of dishes. Instinctively, I opened the door across from me, right at the foot of the stairs. By chance, the study we discovered was empty; its only occupants were dozens of dusty books carefully arranged on shelves that appeared to cover every wall in the room. We went inside. I slammed the door shut and locked it. Seconds later, the zombies started pounding on it, moaning. No matter: we were about to bid farewell to this house.

I helped Emma through the study's window, which I had already extricated myself from, landing on a narrow section of the wooden deck that extended the length of the house, above the courtyard. I grabbed her by the waist and set her down beside me. I glanced quickly over the railing. Several zombies were dragging themselves around in the yard below. They were looking for access. We were lucky that not all of them had managed to climb the steps that led to the terrace while we were sleeping. My mistake could have cost us our lives.

I pulled Emma after me. We moved along the villa's main facade for a few seconds, passing in front of the kitchen window, then arrived at the tiled stairs that led down to the courtyard. All of a sudden, a zombie popped out in front of us. A kick to the abdomen sent him rolling down the staircase. I didn't wait for his tumbling performance to end and started down the steps after him. I thanked him for his acrobatics act, though, and I split open his head with the hammer as I passed by.

The commotion had excited the zombies in the courtyard, who were now heading our way. I counted four of them. They were all coming from the same direction, dragging bodies that their necrotic muscles were struggling more and more to get moving. We took cover behind the car and let them converge on us. They were gradually clearing the way. When they reached the left side of the car, almost all at the same time, we went around it to the right. We ran down the driveway that led to the main road, under their astonished eyes; their meal was getting away.

Moving around in broad daylight wasn't as comforting as I'd thought it would be. While the night had had fun with our imaginations during our last trek, our daytime peregrinations left no room for fantasies and divulged the harsh reality to us without artifice. These weren't hypothetical monsters waiting for us in the dark; dozens of zombies were wandering all around us. Those slow, tottering figures had become an inescapable sight in the landscape. Wherever I turned, there was always one to remind me that nowhere was safe for us.

Luckily, they had not yet regrouped to form a devastating horde, and much to the chagrin of our hearts and lungs, which were being put to the test, we managed to get away. Little by little, the zombie presence diminished, and our surroundings thinned out.

The day had only just begun, and we were already drenched in sweat. I smelled terrible; huge halos surrounded my armpits, and my T-shirt clung unpleasantly to my back.

We went around a wrecked vehicle that looked like it had rolled over several times before ending up on its roof in the middle of the road, coming out of a curve. I didn't know how much distance we could cover without exhausting ourselves and taking too many risks, but I was already thinking about our next safe haven. As long as we remained mobile and vigilant, isolated zombies weren't a big threat, but their constant presence was already starting to erode my courage. Emma was not feeling much safer and was scanning the area in an almost constant side-to-side motion with her head. She was going to get a stiff neck if she kept doing that.

I concentrated more on the road, which opened up straight ahead of us and twisted between the clumps of oak trees whose chiseled shadows covered the pavement.

As I was just starting to catch my breath, I wiped away the sweat that was streaming down my forehead and constantly getting in my eyes. My heart lurched when a screech, accompanied by a loud grinding noise, came from behind us. I turned around.

CHAPTER 19
THE FORK OF DESPAIR

A young man on a bicycle had stopped short, just past the over-turned car. His skid had left a long, black tire track on the road, and he was looking at us in amazement. We remained silent for a moment, watching each other with suspicion and surprise. Like us, he was carrying a bulky bag, and an easily accessible metal bar was protruding from his gear. He couldn't have been more than twenty years old. All of a sudden, I saw the revolver hanging on his belt. All he would have had to do to take everything we had was draw his gun and make a few threats, but he didn't move. He just stood there, in the middle of the road.

Emma seemed rather delighted to see a new face – she hadn't completely lost faith in Humanity, like I had – and protested when I told her to keep walking. I didn't want to stay there all day, especially since several zombies were clumsily descending the wooded hill bordering the road. The stranger had spotted them, too, and gave them a sinister look before taking an interest again in the two of us, but we had turned our backs to him.

I expected him to call out to us, thus putting an end to Emma's whining about wanting to talk to him, but he didn't say anything. Before going around the next curve in the road, I turned around briefly: he was still there, motionless, watching us walk away as the zombies got closer and closer to him. *Weird guy*, I thought, prepared to see him come chasing after us when he was done with the stiffs. But once again, he didn't do anything.

"Why not?" Emma whimpered, dragging her feet. "He seemed nice!"

"We don't know him. Maybe he was going to steal our stuff."

"No. He looked like a nice guy."

"Maybe, but we don't know what he wanted."

"Does that mean we're never going to talk to anyone ever again?" she asked with a sigh.

"No. Of course not. But we can't trust just anyone. We have to be careful."

"I still would have liked to talk to him."

She sighed again and added, with a glimmer in her eyes:

"He looked like Arnaud."

The image of her brother's skull, ravaged by my blows, struck me. I couldn't recall the boy's features; the only thing etched in my memory was the bloody mess I'd made of his face.

"Yes, that's true," I confirmed, in spite of it all, trying to make her forget her disappointment.

"If we see him again, will we talk to him?" she asked, delighted with my response.

"I don't know. Maybe."

Some moaning started coming from our left, where a metal guardrail had been knocked down and the concrete blocks that had secured it to the ground fully ripped out. Two wide ruts were carved into the grass and plunged down the roadside, a steep slope covered with trees. The zombies' cries, long and plaintive, were echoing strangely. I cautiously moved towards the source of the noise, Emma on my heels.

A motorcoach had rolled down the slope a few yards, very quickly caught by the thick, solid trunks of the oak trees that were growing there. A small yellow sign, showing two schoolchildren holding hands, was attached to the rear of the vehicle.

"That's the middle school bus; it comes by my house in the morning," Emma said. "Arnaud takes it."

"Let's not stay here," I advised her, as putrid hands began to beat rhythmically against the back window of the bus.

The moans grew more intense, and the middle school students, trapped in their metal coffin, got excited and banged harder on the glass. We left, but that didn't stop their uproar. They would never return home and would remain locked in that crumpled pile of metal until the madness that had transformed them into zombies was over. It was, perhaps, their tomb for all eternity.

Emma didn't comment on this new horror but quickened her pace, deep in thought. Was she trying to remember what life had been like before, when the bus still used to drop her brother off at their doorstep and hadn't landed at the bottom of a ravine to lie there in the bright sun?

There was another grinding noise, which pulled Emma from her thoughts.

"Do you think it's the boy on the bike?" she asked me, scanning the road behind us.

"Most likely," I replied.

I took her hand and urged her to keep moving ahead.

"Let's go, come on."

There was no sign of the young man, but the sound had left no doubt: he was following us. What could he have wanted from us? I had no intention of waiting around to find out. If we stayed on the road, he wouldn't leave us be, and with his bike, he would catch up to us without any difficulty.

We continued to follow the asphalt strip for several minutes, casting glances behind us periodically; then, the beginning of a dirt trail opened up on the side of the road. I didn't like the idea of rushing blindly onto a path that could be a dead end and get us nowhere, but having this stranger on our heels bothered me more. So, I gestured to the little one, and we hurtled down the first few yards of the trail, with clods of dirt and small stones rolling under our feet. We quickly left behind the cleared trailhead – a large furrow, hollowed out by the water that ran through here whenever it rained, cut the trail in two – and got back under the cover of trees. We already couldn't see the road anymore.

Although battered by runoff, the path seemed to have been used regularly before the arrival of the zombies, and the bushes were careful not to try to invade it, staying wisely to either side. It plunged straight into the forest in a long tunnel of greenery crowned by the slender pine needles and scalloped oak leaves of the trees that overwhelmingly populated the area. Suspicious noises frequently escaped from between the trunks, forcing us to be on our guard as we progressed. Zombies were everywhere. I knew that. But, deep down, more than anything else, I was hoping not to hear the screech of the stranger's tires again.

I picked up the pace.

After a good hundred yards, the verdant tunnel suddenly came to an end and opened out onto an olive grove. The young plants, simple stems topped with a few oval leaves, were basking in the sun amid an ocean of turned earth. I was afraid the trail would stop there, but I saw a gap between the trees on the other side of the expanse of olive saplings. We left the relative coolness of the pines and launched ourselves into the furnace of the field. My body was covered in sweat, and my T-shirt was nothing more than a filthy, soggy piece of cloth at this point. I tried to distract my attention from the hellish heat and to cheer up Emma, whose tongue was hanging out as she walked:

"Last one there is a rotten egg," I told her, rushing awkwardly towards the edge of the woods, my bag bouncing all over the place and whacking my butt cheeks with each stride.

On her tiny legs, Emma was doing her best to keep up, laughing as she stared determinedly at her goal. I slowed down, feigning fatigue, and let her take the lead by three yards. She finally got to where the trail went back into the forest and turned around looking triumphant, a big smile across her lips. At the same moment, right behind her, a corpse jumped out from between the thorny branches of two junipers, which had hidden him until then.

Terrified, I tried to grab my hammer, but my clammy fingers slipped off the handle. Carried by my momentum and unarmed, I plowed head-first into the cadaver as his grubby hands passed a few inches from Emma's hair. Upon impact, the zombie lost his balance, and we both fell to the ground. A sharp pain radiated from my lower back, where a sharp stone had sunk into my skin through my damp T-shirt. But that was the least of my worries: the zombie had climbed on top of me and was trying to bite me.

His rotted mouth almost closed over my shoulder as I was trying to extricate myself. I grabbed him by the throat to push back his inhuman face. My fingers encountered the soft, swollen flesh of his neck and sank between the greyish folds of his skin. I resisted the feeling of disgust that this contact caused within me and held the monster at bay, unable to disentangle myself from him. He had grabbed my clothes and was holding them tightly. Despite the decomposition of his muscles, he was exhibiting incredible strength, and my arms were already starting to shake.

Suddenly, the creature's head jerked bizarrely and fell limp, all life having abandoned it. I rolled the corpse over and discovered a small knife stuck deep in the back of his head.

Emma threw herself down next to me, her hands trembling.

"I did it, Mr. Patrick! I killed one of them!" she exclaimed, her tone oscillating between excitement and emotion.

"Yes, you did it," I confirmed, trying to stand up, my muscles tight from the confrontation.

I was reminded of the pain around my kidneys as a warm liquid slowly covered my skin. Blood had started to flow through my pants, and I could feel it going down my leg.

"You're bleeding!" the little one cried out, staring at the soiled bottom of my T-shirt.

I lifted the garment and twisted my body in vain, trying to get a look at the wound.

"How does it look?" I asked the girl.

She peeked at the injury and turned towards me, pale. It couldn't really be that bad, could it?

"There's a lot of blood, Mr. Patrick," she replied worriedly.

"You'll have to make a bandage for me, Emma. Do you think you can do that?"

Her uncertainty seemed to be growing, but she gave me a small smile as she answered:

"Maybe. Yes."

"Okay, but let's not hang around here."

I didn't like being out in the open, and the encounter with the zombie might have attracted others. I preferred to move a bit further away. I winced as I pressed down on the cut with my right hand and tried to pull Emma's small pocketknife out of the cadaver's skull with the other. She had really driven the blade in there, and I had to strain to extract it from the creature's flesh and broken bones. The knife, thin and sharp, finally came out. I wiped it off quickly and handed it to the little one.

"Here you go, my savior," I said, smiling.

She seemed embarrassed, and her cheekbones flushed softly as she retrieved her weapon. We then resumed our route, trying to put as much distance as possible between us and the scene of the fight. The trail plunged into the forest, bordered by thick, dry vegetation that cast its scent of Corsican scrub into the air.

With each step, my bag rubbed against the hand I was keeping pressed against my back to contain the bleeding. It ended up throbbing, too.

I was mad at myself for putting Emma in that kind of danger. Letting our guard down, even for a few seconds, had become unthinkable.

An innocent game could end in a bloodbath at any moment. And yet...
I had tempted fate, putting both my life and Emma's in danger. I
couldn't afford to do that. Not until we were safe, high up in the Alps. I
was sure we would be out of the zombies' reach there. Not like in these
stifling woods.

As if to corroborate my thoughts, a zombie emerged from between
the trees about fifty yards away. He dragged himself to the middle of
the path and stopped. His body was swaying oddly from side to side,
like a broken pendulum. His upper body turned towards us, and I could
finally see his face – at least, what was left of it. The monster had been
completely disfigured. His head was nothing but a heap of foul, torn
flesh. His eyes seemed to have disappeared under the folds of bloody
skin that covered them. Blind, the corpse stood still for a long minute,
which felt unending to me as the blood continued to flow between my
fingers, then started off again, disappearing into the vegetation.

"Come on," I said to Emma, who had hidden behind me.

I was in a hurry to find some shelter so I could rest. The wound was
probably superficial, but the bleeding was starting to worry me.

Several minutes went by without our passing a single zombie. The
trail, which had seemed interminable, finally opened onto a small
clearing, where it split in two. In the center of the fork, at the foot of a
grand oak tree that reminded me of the one that had graced the yard at
my house before being consumed by flames, stood a small stone building. I smiled when I saw the bright, immaculate orange tiles that
evidenced a recent roof restoration.

"What do you think of this place?" I asked Emma.

"We have to make the bandage for you," she replied, paying no attention to my question. Her eyes were focused on the red stain on my
T-shirt that kept getting bigger.

"Sure thing, doc," I joked, wincing. "Follow me."

I grabbed hold of my hammer. My bloodied hand left a dark mark
on the wood handle as scarlet drops began to trickle down it.

We walked slowly towards the structure. The narrow windows, located around five feet above the ground, gave away its agricultural nature. The roof, which was in perfect condition, contrasted with the worn stones and the dilapidated cement that held them together. The wooden door, installed under a large arch, appeared to be the only entrance. The place was apparently deserted, and we were greeted with total silence when we reached the front of the building.

I placed my ear against the rough, aged wood – probably original – of one of the door flaps, which a closed bolt connected to the other, and listened. Concentrating, I let my gaze get lost in the tall grass growing along the pillars of the arch. A metallic sparkle caught my attention. I bent down and reached for the object that was reflecting the sun's rays: a padlock. It had been visibly forced and was studded with dozens of splinters. I swept my eyes over the area suspiciously, then tried once again to pick up the slightest noise coming from inside. Not a sound slipped out.

I gently pulled on the sliding bolt and disengaged its head from the strike. The door creaked and began to swing open on its own, letting the smell of pine resin fill the air. I took a step back, one hand on Emma's shoulder.

My heart jumped in my chest and the little one screamed in fear when an object violently struck the door flap to my left. A carbon arrow was deeply embedded in it.

How had he managed to find us so quickly? My worry grew, almost rivaling the intensity of the pain radiating from my injury. I felt like I could feel my ticker beating at an alarming pace through it. Seeing the situation slip away from me once more, I turned around slowly, not making any sudden movements, prepared to find out what he wanted from us… but it wasn't him.

"Victor!" Emma cried, recognizing her neighbor. "What are you doing here?"

The boy was aiming at us with his bow, which he had rearmed right away. He seemed bewildered to see the girl but soon recovered an impassive expression.

"Hi, Emma," he said in a cold, worrisome voice.

A young teenager, the second survivor of the attack on the mini-market, was standing beside him and threatening us with his slingshot. He had stretched the elastic towards himself, and his arm was already shaking under the pressure from the rubber band.

How could I have had such bad luck? All this could only go wrong. They had seen me during the assault on the small grocery store, when I confronted Gerald; there was no doubt about that.

Emma started walking in their direction, not understanding why the two young men continued to point their weapons at me.

"I'm happy…"

"Shut up and stay where you are," Victor told her.

The little girl stopped abruptly and turned to me, surprised by the violence of her neighbor's words.

"You were with that other son of a bitch, weren't you?" he asked me in a tone that made clear he already knew the answer.

"Yeah, I recognize him. He got in a fight with that piece of shit Arab," added his sidekick, who looked excited to rip into me.

My confused mind took little interest in his remark. It was all happening too suddenly, and I didn't know what to say. I hadn't done anything to them and had even tried to stop that madness. But what difference could that possibly make to them?

Gerald had killed Mathieu right in front of his brother, and I had been incapable of doing anything to stop him. I, too, was guilty of that tragedy. I had to accept the consequences. But the priority was to protect Emma.

"Well?" insisted Victor, who was already losing patience.

The knuckles on the fingers of his hand that was drawing the bowstring were pale and itching to regain their color. To release the arrow, let the projectile sink into my flesh, and enjoy the blood returning to their vessels. That was definitely their plan.

"Yes, I was there, but I tried…"

"Shut up!" bellowed the young man, his voice cracking from the fierceness of his scream. "You helped them kill my brother, you fucking asshole."

"No…" I tried to defend myself.

"Shut up, I told you," he cut me off, pulling more on the bowstring.

"Mr. Patrick didn't do anything," Emma intervened, a horrified expression on her face now that she understood what was happening.

"Pierre, take care of her. I want her to shut up," Victor said to his friend in the same cold tone he had greeted the girl with.

"Leave her alone!" I yelled when I saw the teenager approaching the little one. "Come here, Emma."

She rushed over to me and hid behind my back.

"Don't get smart with me, fat ass. Throw down your weapon and take off your backpack, or I'll kill you," Victor threatened.

I looked at him incredulously, as if my brain were working in slow motion, but his tone left no doubt. I ended up obeying him. I threw my hammer into the thickets and let my bag slip off my shoulders. I moaned when it grazed my wound.

"Okay. Now, Emma, come here."

"No!" she cried.

"Goddamn it, tell her to get her ass over here," he responded, addressing me.

"Don't hurt her, please," I begged him.

"We're not gonna do anything to her. We don't give a crap about her," said Victor.

Faced with my silence, he added:

"Move it, Emma, or I'll kill your buddy."

"No!" she yelled. "Stop!"

"Listen to him, sweetie," I told her, trying to hold back my tears. "Do what he says."

"But, Mr. Patrick," she whimpered.

"Do it for me, I added, trying to smile. "Everything will be all right."

She started to cry and walked towards the two boys, her head down.

"Hold her, Pierre!" Victor ordered when the little girl got close to his friend.

The teenager obeyed and immobilized Emma, pinning both her arms behind her back.

She struggled in vain.

"Stop it! You promised not to hurt her!"

"If you let this happen, yes," replied Victor with a sneer.

He released the pressure on his weapon and leaned it against a tree next to Pierre.

"Don't move, big guy."

He put his bag down at his feet and pulled out a metallic object, which he slipped between his fingers. He closed his hand and checked that the brass knuckles were in the correct position as he started to come towards me.

I threw myself to my knees:

"I swear to you, I tried to stop them."

He took another step in my direction.

"I didn't want that."

He was only six feet away.

"It was Gerald…"

The impact sent me to the ground, and the metallic taste of blood filled my mouth. My head felt groggy, and a powerful echo was resonating through it. I brought my hand up to the bottom of my face, where Victor had hit me with all his might. The flesh on my cheek had been ripped open, and it was bleeding profusely.

"Stop it!" Emma screamed, her voice cracking.

"Get up, motherfucker, if you don't want us to hit her."

My skull buzzing, I slowly stood up after putting one knee on the ground.

The second blow, which hit my rib cage with a loud crack, landed me flat on my face in the dry grass. It immediately soaked up the blood that was gushing from my cheek's ravaged flesh. My abdomen was on fire. The wind had been knocked out of me, and I lay there, my entire body in pain.

"Get up, you son of a bitch!" yelled the young man, enraged.

I could feel my strength giving out. I tried to straighten up, without success.

"Damn, that was too easy," Victor cursed, taking off his brass knuckles.

He grabbed me by the collar and hit me in the face, right where he had struck me before. The explosion of pain made me scream, and I almost lost consciousness.

"Hey Victor, some are coming," said Pierre worriedly.

Victor let go of me, and I fell back to the ground, still breathless.

"Hold onto the kid," said the young man.

I was unable to see what he was doing, but I heard the steady sound of inert bodies collapsing. It only seemed to last a fraction of a second, and then he came back towards me, laughing.

"You killed my brother, didn't you?" he said, grabbing my collar again.

"Don't hurt her," I murmured in a voice choked with the blood streaming down my throat and filling my mouth.

The response hit me right at eye level, and I felt my brow bone snap from its strength. A reddish thread spilled over my eyelids, the surrounding tissue of which was already swelling.

"No!" Emma wailed, crying.

"Ow! She bit me!" Pierre complained as I heard the little one come running towards me.

A crack sounded, and Emma collapsed in the dirt.

"You wanna get smart with me?" said Victor, his hand still raised towards the girl. "Come here, Pierre."

I groaned when he kicked my lower abdomen.

"You can have some fun, too," he added.

I curled up into a ball to try to protect myself. All my muscles were screaming in pain. Despite my left eye being blinded from the swelling and bleeding, I saw Emma stand up. Doubled over, fists clenched, and her face distorted with horror, she bellowed:

"Stop! Stop!"

She rushed at my attackers, but Victor pushed her aside with a ferocious wave of his hand. I tried to get up, but the blows continued to rain down, pinning me to the ground. The pain was so bad that it started to become surreal. My nerves no longer had the strength to carry all of this excruciating information to my weakened brain. I was going to die like a dog, beaten to death. All because of Gerald. I should have killed him when I'd had the chance. But this remorse was nothing compared to the dismay I felt. What was going to happen to Emma? Were they going to abandon her and leave her all alone? Why had all of this happened?

A powerful voice pulled me from my thoughts and put an end to the kicking.

"Stop!"

Pounded into the grass, my body battered, my only movements were limited to the trembling of my injured muscles. I tried to twist my neck to see where that unfamiliar voice had come from, but I couldn't.

"Get away from him," it added.

"And who are you?" Victor asked contemptuously.

"Get lost, I said."

"You're the one who's going to split on that bike of yours if you don't want any trouble."

The youngster on the bicycle? There was a silence, then Pierre stifled a gasp of surprise.

"I said, get lost," the stranger repeated, enunciating each syllable.

"Damn. That can't be real," said Victor. "Take him out, Pierre."

I saw the teenager, who was standing above me, slip a marble into his slingshot, but a gunshot rang out before he could stretch the elastic. The two boys jumped.

"Throw down your slingshot and get lost!"

I heard the weapon drop beside me, and they fled without wasting any time. They must not have gone more than a few yards before Emma threw herself against me.

"Mr. Patrick," she croaked, crying.

With my mouth full of blood and my jaw all messed up, only a disgusting gurgling sound came out of my throat in response. The world seemed distant and cold to me.

"We're going to make you all better, right?" she added, desperate.

The clicking of a bicycle approached.

"Oh, damn," the young man said fearfully when he saw my condition.

He pulled himself together and added, to the girl:

"What's your name?"

"Emma," replied the little one, sniffling loudly.

"Okay, Emma, we need to get this man to shelter so we can take care of him."

His voice, soft and deep, seemed more and more distant to me, but I could clearly distinguish the moaning that suddenly arose behind my savior.

"They're all we needed," he complained.

Emma huddled against me, her body shaking with sobs.

"Why, Mr. Patrick, why?" she kept repeating, traumatized by what she had just witnessed.

Her whispers were quickly covered by the sound of skulls breaking around us. Several times, the young man cried out in rage before slaying a zombie. This macabre concert, which was engaging my exhausted mind less and less, ended after several minutes. When the stranger on the bike joined us again, in a funereal silence, I finally knew Emma was safe. Then, everything went black.

CHAPTER 20
A GLIMMER AT DUSK

Each time my frayed mind caught a snippet of the conversation between Emma and the young man, their words ended up tirelessly extricating themselves from my grasp and escaping my understanding. What they were saying was reduced to an irritating buzzing that made no sense. I wanted to understand, but my brain had slowed down as my nerves radiated intense pain that was putting my whole body to the test. And I was hot. Sticky, smelly sweat covered my skin, leaving me with an unpleasant feeling. But much worse was the furnace burning inside me. A fever had set in. How long had I been in this condition?

I tried to clear my head, to regain control of my being, crushed under the heavy weight of my suffering, but my thoughts drifted endlessly. Like the words exchanged between the girl and the stranger, they escaped me, disappearing in an incomprehensible whirlwind.

My temperature didn't seem to want to go down. My skull was locked in a fiery vice, squeezed between the torment of my ravaged cheek and cracked browbone and the feverish haze that plunged me into uncontrollable drowsiness. I was in so much pain. This exhausted body, refusing to respond to my orders, was just a big, motionless, and useless thing. Plus, where was I?

The room was immersed in a dusk-like darkness. The dim ambient light was dodging me, refusing to show me what this purgatory I was trapped in looked like. A terrifying blackness covered the swollen flesh that enveloped my left eye. A shy beam of light slipped through the heavy lid of my unharmed, slightly open eye, but all that danced in my limited field of vision were fuzzy shapes. This indistinct ballet found no echo in my thoughts, which continued to wander freely. And then there was that rumbling that still didn't make sense. What were they doing?

Annoyed and affected by a new burst of pain, I let out a groan from my dry throat. Like everything else, the sound seemed distant to me, but my suffering was very real. The voices fell silent, forcing me to strain my ears and concentrate more. It took a huge effort, but for a moment, I was back in the world of the living, and I clearly heard some words spoken with palpable empathy:

"Easy, now. Drink this."

My split lips weakly welcomed the mouth of a bottle, and lukewarm water flooded my mouth. Almost choking on it, I coughed and then returned to the nothingness that refused to set me free.

***

When I regained consciousness, my body was still on fire. Even though my head was immersed in an inferno, the hellish heat of which was attempting to make my every thought evaporate, I began to reconnect with the world. Each breath I drew moved my rib cage, which had been badly bruised by my assailants' blows, and reminded me of the horror of my condition.

Everything around me was still bathed in blackness. But it was no longer because of my weakened state but rather the warm, dark night. My breathing was jerky and punctuated by a hoarse, throaty rattling as I waited in my forced immobility, letting my eye get used to the dusk.

Grey and often indistinct shapes quickly emerged from the blackness. Large stone walls appeared, interspersed with thin bands of a bleak light. And that smell of resin still hovered there. Obviously, we hadn't gone very far. The young man must have simply pulled me inside the small barn.

Were Victor and Pierre really gone, or would they come back to finish what they'd started? In this state, I was not a threat. Rendered useless, things being what they were. A human whose very presence on this contaminated Earth was dependent on a few inches of rock and cement separating him from his predators and on the astonishing intervention by a complete stranger. I was an incompetent, not even able to accomplish the one mission I had sworn to fulfill. Emma was lucky to still be alive, with such a ridiculous guardian angel. At least her new friend had a weapon, a real one. He wasn't a broken-down old man with a hammer who had been taken out by two kids. *Ancient, useless piece of crap*, I thought to myself, letting my gaze sink deeper into the room.

It finally landed on Emma's small form; she was sleeping on the floor. Pressing against one of the building's dusty walls, I made a superhuman effort to sit up. My ribs screamed in pain when the broken ones found themselves crushed under the weight of my torso. Still, I managed to lean against the stone wall, my legs stretched out in front of me and my head wobbly.

"You'd be better off not moving too much."

I turned my head in the direction of the voice; the strain on my cheek wound made me wince in pain. The young man was crouched down a few feet from me, his back against the opposite wall. His eyes shone in the dark.

"You've got some broken ribs. I think so, anyway. It's not a pretty sight."

His words wove their way into my feverish mind, which was rapidly swamped with questions I wanted to ask him. But only one word managed to escape my dry lips, in a deep, unpleasant croak:

"Thanks."

The boy was silent for a moment. Then he got up and came over:

"It was nothing. I couldn't let them do that."

He knelt down beside me and brought the bottle to my mouth again.

"You need to drink some more. Without spitting it all out this time."

I chuckled, contracting the aching muscles in my lower abdomen, and parted my lips. The liquid flowed in slowly, and I swallowed painfully. Then the delicate stream stopped. Drinking did me some good, and I felt like I was coming out of my torpor more. My muscles stopped responding with nothing but shudders of pain and seemed able to obey me again.

The stranger straightened up and took a few steps into the darkness. He turned his back to me and rummaged through what must have been his bag. After finding what he was looking for, he came back to my side and opened his hand in front of me.

"Take these. They should help with your pain. I couldn't get you to swallow them earlier…"

Without a word, I slowly took the pills he was holding out to me. My arms hadn't been spared either; they were covered in bluish bruises, but the pain was bearable. I then grasped the bottle he offered me and drank from it alone, without his help. My body reveled once again in that hydrating liquid and didn't even try to reject the tablets sliding down my throat. I sighed with pleasure.

"Thanks," I repeated, in an almost normal voice.

He smiled in the darkness.

I brought my hand up towards my cheek, from which a particularly sharp pain was radiating all over my face. I shivered as the memory of that devastating impact, the contact of the metal against my skin, ran through my mind. My fingers hesitated before brushing against my flesh. They finally made up their minds and encountered a soft, swollen mass. In the middle of it, a long gash ridged with small, hard obstacles, where the skin was pulling at me the worst.

"You were pissing blood. I did what I could to stitch you up. Sorry."

I pulled my hand away and huffed some air out of my nose in a kind of laugh.

"I was never much of an Adonis anyway."

The boy let out a laugh, frank and sincere, before thinking better of it.

"I'm Chris, by the way."

"Patrick," I replied as my head started to spin.

"Yes, Emma told me. Is she your daughter?"

I looked into his eyes with my misty ones and smiled:

"Sort of..."

"I understand. She seems to care about you."

"Maybe," I replied, still having a hard time accepting that Emma might really be attached to me, too.

A shooting pain suddenly hit me in the stomach, and I doubled over, gasping for breath. The young man stared at me, not knowing what to do; then, it stopped.

"I think I'll rest," I told him, grimacing, since the pills were far from taking effect.

"Good night, Patrick," he replied simply.

Good night? He was very funny, that one.

***

I woke up to the light of day. The sunshine entering through the narrow windows rushed into my half-open eye, forcing me to close it again amid a perpetual onslaught of pain.

The period of rest hadn't changed much: my muscles were still uncooperative, my breathing reduced to painful movements, and I was still just as hot. The fever had not come down.

I sat up, leaned against the wall, and looked around the room. Emma was still dozing where I had seen her several hours earlier, in the dark. A luminous line was sketched a few inches from her face, giving a golden sheen to the strands of straw that were mixed in with the packed dirt. I felt like my eye could follow the thread of light's movement across the ground as the sun rose in the sky.

At this rate, it would not take long for the star to lay its rays on the girl's cheeks. I was watching her, in the hope that the sun's delicate caress would wake her gently, when she opened her eyes slightly, gazing into mine at the same time.

She jumped up and rushed over. I thought she was going to throw herself against me, but she braked abruptly, coming to a stop within one stride of me, as if the memory of the many blows I had received had just hit her and she wanted to avoid inflicting any new pain upon me. But that wasn't it. She had frozen, a look of utter horror on her face. I would have preferred for her to jump on me, so I could hug her and not see her sadness, but looming before me was this portrait of terror. Her expression was transparent; I could sense from her eyes how serious my condition was. Sure, I was badly beaten up. But that wasn't what scared me the most: an icy coldness had filled her eyes. The light, that heat that used to burn behind her pupils, had gone out.

She seemed horrified to see me like this, but she also seemed to accept it, like something that was inevitable.

"You're going to die, too, then," she finally said, still staring at me, her eyes going back and forth between my good eye and the ravaged half of my face.

I swallowed uncomfortably and motioned for her to come closer.

"Everyone does," I responded, refusing to think about what the little one was promulgating as evidence.

"Yes, I know. I'm going to die, too. But you…"

"I'm going to die soon?" I interrupted her as my head lurched to the side from the fever.

"Yes…"

"Not if I can go get some meds," Chris interjected, having approached without my seeing him. "I don't have anything left, and you need some. I'm sure I can find something to bring down the fever and some antibiotics for the infection, too."

Surprised, I bravely lifted my head towards him.

He indicated my face with a wave of his hand.

"I did what I could for… for your cheek, but the wound is infected."

I brought my fingers to the injured area. My flesh was still swollen, and a foul-smelling liquid – or maybe it was me who smelled that way – ran between my middle and ring fingers. I let out a sigh. I didn't regret what had happened and would have let myself be roughed up again to protect the little one if I had to, but my inability to do anything was eating away at me almost as much as the pain that was consuming my body. Everything depended on Chris. A young man I only knew by his first name. I had no other choice but to place my trust in him.

"Emma, you better stay here and take care of Patrick while I'm gone. I'll be back very soon," he said, smiling at the girl.

I looked him straight in the eye and thanked him with a nod of my head.

"We're going to get you back on your feet," he added with much less conviction.

"Is Mr. Patrick going to be okay?" Emma asked, a new glimmer in her eyes.

"Of course," answered the young man, not batting an eye and stating with disconcerting ease the odious lie that I refused to dish up to the little one.

Emma turned towards me, convinced. I was glad Chris had said those words, and seeing the girl regain her childish optimism was heartwarming; I almost started to believe the dubious promise myself. Even if the young man managed to dig up the necessary medication and I pulled through, without professional care, my injuries would most certainly make me suffer for several weeks, an amount of time that would leave me at the mercy of any zombie. But Chris was right; there was still a chance. I had to rest and recover as soon as possible.

For myself.

For Emma.

Seeing me getting lost in my thoughts, the boy cleared his throat to attract my attention:

"I probably won't need to go very far. I'll be as fast as I can," he said, heading over to his bag, which he'd put near the door, which was locked from the inside.

"I don't think those two guys will come back, but Emma, don't open the door for anyone. Except me. Will you recognize my voice?"

"Yes, of course," she responded, nodding vigorously.

"I'll get going, then. Take good care of Patrick. Hang in there, Patrick."

He positioned himself in front of the entrance, turned the lock, and walked outside, letting a bright light flood into the room.

"Lock up behind me, Emma. See you later," he said, smiling.

The door slammed shut, and the interior became dimly lit again. Emma did not waste a second, locking us in as Chris had asked her to.

We were alone again. I wanted to ask her a whole bunch of questions about what she and Chris had talked about while I was unconscious, but I needed some rest. It wouldn't get rid of the fever, but it would help my muscles to recover bit by bit. They needed it. I closed my eyes to give in to sleep, which had been trying to pull me back in ever since I'd woken up, but Emma's voice, very close, forced me to open them again:

"We're going to stay with Chris, right?" she asked me.

She had approached silently and was sitting right next to me. I turned my face to her, and she snuggled up against me.

"I don't know, do you think we should?"

"Yes!" she exclaimed. "He's a nice guy, too. He saved us!"

"You're right. The three of us will make a great team."

"He told me he's from Marseille. I've been there a couple times before. We went shopping with Mama. But it was such a long car ride to get there, which sucked. Did you used to go there, too?"

"Sometimes, yes."

I hadn't thought about what might have happened elsewhere since the start of the outbreak, and the images that crossed my mind were terrifying. The metropolis on fire, its millions of inhabitants suddenly transformed into bloodthirsty creatures chasing after the few survivors. How could Chris have gotten himself out of such a hellscape? I imagined him mounting his bicycle at the first sign of contamination and fleeing as far as possible from the nightmare that was Marseille. His journey here must have been fraught with peril. And now here he was, saddled with treating me and risking his life in the backwoods of Provence.

"He hadn't spoken to anyone since..."

The little one searched for her words.

"Since the zombies arrived. I was the first!" she exclaimed, proud to be sort of the young man's confidante.

"He didn't cross paths with anyone?"

"He told me he saw people, but he didn't talk to them, because of the zombies."

I tried to register all this information, but I was having a harder and harder time combatting the fatigue and the fever. My body, hungry for rest, was trying to put my brain on hold, but I held on, eager to learn more about this young man on whose shoulders my survival rested.

"Mr. Patrick, are you okay?" the girl asked, worried about my silence.

"Sorry, Emma. I'm still tired."

She smiled at me and kissed my cheek as she stood up.

"Rest, then, and when you wake up, Chris will be here, and everything will get better," she said with infinite gentleness. "I'll be on the lookout for those nasty zombies, so don't worry, Mr. Patrick."

I loved her more than ever at that moment. As I watched her climb onto a large log that was leaning against the front wall, which allowed her to reach the bottom of one of the narrow windows, I finally let myself fall asleep.

***

"Mr. Patrick, Mr. Patrick, wake up," Emma whispered, shaking me lightly.

It took me several seconds to come around and understand what was going on.

"There's a car outside," she insisted, gripping my arm tightly.

I started to rub my eyes and moaned as my left hand brushed my injured cheek. The pain that suddenly erupted brought me back to reality.

"A car?" I asked, shocked and worried.

"A 4x4, black," confirmed the little one.

"Maybe it's Chris," I said, trying to reassure her.

"I didn't see anyone. I came to tell you right away."

"Can you go look?"

She ran immediately to her makeshift stepstool, climbed up on it, and peeked outside. The hum of an engine could indeed be heard. The unknown vehicle must have been stopped, the motor still running, just in front of the small building.

"I can't see, Mr. Patrick," whined the girl in a soft voice, aware that we needed to be discreet.

"You're sure it's not Chris," I insisted.

In my condition, I had no idea what to do if it wasn't the young man. What the hell was a car doing here? If these were other survivors, they were probably going to want to search our shelter. What would we do if they tried to steal our reserves?

"Come here, Emma. We need to hide," I said, trying to mask the concern in my voice.

"Wait."

I heard the creaking of a car door outside. Emma flinched and scrambled down to me in panic. Faced with her fear, one certainty took hold of me: the two youngsters from the day before had found a vehicle and god only knew what else, and they had come back to finish what they had started. But the voice that called out was one I had thought I would never hear again.

"Patrick! I know you're in there!"

A shiver ran down my back, and the weight of the fever seemed to dissipate for a moment, leaving plenty of room for apprehension. Refusing to believe it, I gritted my teeth, got to my feet, and approached the window.

The truth hit me right in the face: Gerald was standing on the passenger side running board of a huge 4x4, his face turned towards the building.

The narrowness of the window and the dim light prevented him from seeing me from the outside, but he was looking in my direction with a serious expression on his face, as if he had spotted me. I was paralyzed. How had he found us?

I swallowed and let him out of my sight for a moment. The little one had pulled out her knife and was holding it firmly, her fist clenched around the short handle of the weapon. She knew it as well as I did: Gerald was an enemy.

As I turned back to the window, praying that Chris would come back right away and not get surprised by Gerald, the latter stuck his head into the passenger compartment. The 4x4 had tinted windows, and I couldn't see whom he was speaking with, but the vehicle advanced a few more yards and then stopped. Gerald's head reappeared:

"Come on, Patrick! Get out here!"

I stepped away from the window, pressing my back against the wall and breathing fast.

"The bad guys found us again," Emma said sadly. "I liked being with you..."

I knelt down next to her and took her knife-armed hand in mine. My fingers caressed hers tenderly.

"It's going to be fine, don't you worry. I'll take care of him," I said, gently removing her weapon.

She grabbed my neck and buried her face in it. She wasn't crying, but she was terrified. Her grip was hurting me, but I could have stayed right there for hours, enjoying the love this little girl had for me. Another call from Gerald forced me to gently move her aside.

"Don't worry," I lied to her one last time, straightening back up.

I dragged myself to the door as Gerald threatened to come inside and get us himself. I unlocked it slowly, trying to control my breathing.

When I opened the door, sunlight blinded me for a brief moment, and then my eyes landed on Gerald, who was staring at me with an indecipherable smile. Roland, the burly guy who accompanied him everywhere, was obviously with him. The driver's side door was open, and he was walking determinedly towards a zombie who had been drawn by Gerald's yelling.

"Son of a bitch, those two brats weren't lying," Gerald said before bursting out laughing. "They really messed you up. You are not a pretty sight, Patrick..."

I took a step forward, leaving the entryway and letting the door close behind me.

"What do you want?" I asked him coldly.

He smiled and gestured with his hand.

"You know, I really didn't think I would find you again. We were lucky enough to come across those two little shits from the mini-market. I had a good laugh when they told me about your encounter."

"What did you do to them?"

"To the little shits? Are you concerned about them? You should be glad someone took care of them."

"You're nothing but a murderer, you sick fuck."

"A murderer!" he yelled, suddenly losing his temper. "You killed Karim and let the zombies into the school, you dirty son of a bitch, and you call me a murderer!" he continued, even louder.

"What!" I shouted, as surprised at his accusation as I was worried about his change of mood.

He glared at me and grabbed the rifle that still hung at his back. He pointed the weapon at me, resting the barrel on the edge of the door he was sheltered behind.

"I saved this fucking cartridge for you."

"Wait!" I said, feeling the situation slipping away.

"I had succeeded in uniting those people. They were listening to me. Things were going well at the school. Damn it, we could have done it. And you fucked it all up... taking off with that kid."

"Emma has nothing to do with any of this, and I don't..."

"Shut up!"

"You don't have to do this," I insisted.

A rear door of the vehicle suddenly opened, and a third person stepped out.

"Kill that old bastard!" Giselle cried in a gravelly voice.

"Stay inside the car, Giselle," Gerald said curtly.

The old woman hesitated a few seconds, then got back in, slamming the door behind her.

"Yup, we're the last three survivors. I can't believe it's because of a big shit like you."

I had nothing more to say. I knew I had to buy time, but calming him down seemed impossible, let alone convincing him that it wasn't my fault. Yet again, I was reduced to one thing: trying to protect Emma.

"Do what you want to me, but leave Emma alone. I'm begging you. She has nothing to do with this."

"So, you really love that kid."

"Leave her alone."

"You wouldn't want to see her suffer?"

"Stop, I'm begging you," I repeated, my eyes filled with tears.

It was getting increasingly difficult for me to remain standing, with the fever feeding off my fear.

"Roland, go get the kid. She must be inside."

The colossus wiped off the machete he had just plunged into another zombie's skull and started walking towards me.

"Stay where you are," I threatened him.

"Shut up, Patrick! If you take one step, I'll blow your brains out!" Gerald bellowed. "Come on, let's go, Roland."

The man crossed the distance between the vehicle and me in a couple of strides and slipped behind my back.

"Don't do this, please," I whispered to him. "She's just a child."

"Sorry, friend," he replied.

He put his hand on the door, ready to open it. The muscles in his arms contracted to push, but they suddenly stiffened as a gunshot rang out. The top of his head shattered, disappearing in a brownish cloud of flesh and brains that carpeted the wooden doorposts.

Gerald screamed like a demon. He did what he came to do and pulled the trigger on his rifle before hurling himself back inside the vehicle.

I had no time to react. The buckshot flew into my chest, tearing out part of my rib cage. I fell to my knees and, my head even heavier now, watched the 4x4 back up at full speed and then take off.

My mind refused to accept what had just occurred. I stared blankly into space, thinking about everything that had happened since the early days of the epidemic, as my blood bubbled out of my wounds. I did not see my whole life flash before my eyes. Only those recent weeks. Those days of madness and nightmares. But I didn't regret any of it.

"Patrick, hold on," a familiar voice suddenly broke in.

Chris's lower body appeared in my gradually narrowing field of vision. I could see the pistol he still had in his hand.

"We need to stop the bleeding," he said, panicked.

Unable to lift my head, I whispered, as if I were talking to the ground:

"Too late…"

I coughed and spat blood.

"Her," I added with difficulty, my pale, taut lips refusing to move.

As if to grant my last wish, she was there in a flash. Her frail body pressed against me, my last quarts of blood soaking into the clothes she had already worn too much.

"Mr. Patrick," she cried, hugging me tighter than ever.

I wanted to thank her for everything she had done for me, but my mouth remained definitively shut. Still, my stuck-together lips wore one last smile, that of a happy man. That of a bitter old man who'd had to wait for the apocalypse to rediscover love.

I love you, Emma.

EPILOGUE

Imperceptible in the dark, the creature moved in perfect silence. He threw his arms forward, stuck his dry, emaciated fingers into the ground, then yanked. Pull after pull, he gained yards, getting closer and closer to his target. An inexplicable energy dwelled in him, and a single idea occupied his mind, the last spark in his dead brain: to devour.

Because he was hungry. This wasn't a biological appetite; it was a true obsession, a powerful urge to grind flesh between his teeth.

Obsessed with this insatiable desire, he crawled, moving forward as fast as his condition allowed. He was oblivious to what was going on around him and didn't give a damn about the many pieces of glass that were stuck under the skin on his fingers. No, he kept going.

The dark, geometrically perfect shape of a building was silhouetted in front of him. He dragged himself in a straight line towards it, not taking any unnecessary detours, attracted by what was emanating from it.

It was an odor. A delicious fragrance that, each time it passed through his rotted nasal cavities, excited that unique glimmer that made impelled him forward. The scent of metal, the taste of life. The smell of blood, which was getting stronger as he got closer. He moaned with pleasure and went faster. His legs, reduced to long, useless bones, scraped against the concrete, slowing his progress. But it didn't matter to him; his prey was already there, within reach of his claws.

He threw himself on it and sank his teeth into the flesh. His spirits rose as his victim's blood, hot and succulent, flooded his mouth. His tongue, stiff from *rigor mortis*, gradually regained its agility and eagerly began to sweep inside. He devoured without restraint, tearing off ever larger pieces of flesh. He was gorging, oblivious to the long shreds of fabric he was swallowing during this orgy.

Then he noticed them, those soft, sinister things coming towards him. There were so many of them, a real flood. He again tore the skin from the man who lay dead in the doorway. This one was his.

But they had reached him and, being stronger, trampled him and pushed him aside to indulge in this divine meal in turn. The creature did not want to abandon it, but the man's corpse, almost completely cleansed of its flesh and reduced to a mere skeleton, had disappeared under a swarming mass of monsters.

He then picked up on another scent. More discreet. His arms shot out again, and he crawled towards the source of that aroma. Behind him, others had crossed the threshold by the dozens and invaded the courtyard that extended beyond. And for no reason, they began to follow him. Their steps were slow and clumsy, but they easily caught up to him. Some crushed him beneath them, not caring about his presence, and continued on their way.

A door, which had been left open, greeted the mass of the dead, and they entered the building in a sepulchral silence, like so many predators lurking in the shadows.

The creature, determined to have his share of the massacre that was about to happen, continued to drag his carcass along the ground as some stragglers arrived. Screams rang out, and he froze, captivated by the unusual sounds. The melody of these songs monopolized all his attention, and he let himself be lulled by the howls of suffering, so sweet to his ear.

Suddenly, an unfamiliar noise was added to this sad symphony. A little further away, a dark shape had burst out of the building with a loud crash and, after a few rolls, had come to rest in the courtyard. Throwing himself with all his weight against one of the windows, a man had carried the frame with him in a shower of glass and wood, creating an opening for the two shadows that rushed out after him.

The creature's mind raced as his glassy eyes landed on one of the two newcomers. He groaned with all his might and crawled in his direction, driven by a murderous and carnivorous impulse. The three figures, swift and powerful, rushed towards the exit, where the influx of monsters had ceased. Seeing him slip away, he cried out again in a hoarse, terrifying moan. He dragged his grotesque body vigorously, but his target vanished outside, evaporating into the night.

Enraged, he grabbed onto one of the stragglers, who had also set off in pursuit of the three survivors. The monster slowed down but didn't stop. With all the strength in his emaciated arms, he hoisted himself onto the dead man's back and wrapped them around his neck. His skeletal legs hung in the air like a ridiculous tail that had sprouted from his steed. He was one of the Horsemen of the Apocalypse, and he wouldn't stop. Not before that man, with a gun swinging at his back, had given him the last drop of his blood.

YOU LIKED THIS BOOK?

Please rate it and write a review on Amazon.

If you enjoyed spending time with Patrick and Emma, please don't forget that without word of mouth, there are no indie authors.

ACKNOWLEDGMENTS

Province of the Dead would have remained lost in the depths of my computer and my imagination without the support of my family and loved ones.

Thank you to my mother for the hours spent proofreading, for making suggestions, and above all, for agreeing to dive into my universe of horror and love.

Thank you to the woman who has shared my life for so long now, for reading the first few drafts of almost all my chapters, and for letting me get lost in my zombie world for long hours every night.

Thank you to the rest of my family, my father, my sister, and (even) my brother, and also to my grandparents, who dared to read through the end of the book, even though this genre is not exactly their cup of tea.

Finally, thank you to my first readers: my friends from the **My Zombie Culture** editorial staff – Juliette, Mathieu, Benjamin, Alexandre, Jérôme, and Yoan, who also furnished me with a superb cover; to Victor, Benoît, and Elody; and to Sébastien, who sent me a review that I will always remember.

ABOUT THE AUTHOR

In 2015, just after graduating from a famous French business school as well as from a university in Brisbane, Australia, where he specialized in "strategic advertising," Paul decided to dedicate himself to his passion for storytelling. In December 2015, he self-published *Les Décharnés* (*Province of the Dead*), his first novel. It was followed by *Creuse la Mort*, a horror thriller, in September 2016. Both books won several awards. In September 2018, Paul released the conclusion to his epic saga *Les Orphelins de Windrasor*. His most recent novel, *Elle est la Nuit* – a violent, suspenseful, and gut-wrenching tale of terror – is his long-awaited comeback to the horror genre.

Learn more about his future projects at:
www.paul-clement.com

Contact him at: contact@paul-clement.com

BY THE SAME AUTHOR

Available exclusively in French

Creuse la Mort
Horror / Supernatural Thriller – 2016

Les Orphelins de Windrasor
Adventure / Young Adult – 2017/2018

Elle est la Nuit
Horror / Supernatural Thriller – 2020